JACK O' LANTERN

Novels by
GEORGE GOODCHILD

JACK O' LANTERN

BY
GEORGE GOODCHILD

THE MYSTERY LEAGUE, INC.

PUBLISHERS 1930 NEW YORK

JACK O' LANTERN

CHAPTER ONE

THEY had opened the road along Bircher's Dock, and the customary untidiness of the place was made even worse by unsightly piles of dripping earth, mud-bespattered lengths of drain-pipe, and a miscellaneous assemblage of engineering gear, including a crane and hideous donkey-engine. To add to the impression of Inferno, a dank mist was invading the foreshore from the river, saturating everything with moisture. The night-watchman, in his timber cubby-hole, smoked a pipe of foul tobacco and watched with an anxious eye an array of crackling chestnuts reposing in the pan of a capacious shovel which lay across a coke fire.

He was a philosophic individual, which in the circumstances was fortunate, for Bircher's Dock at close upon midnight was as uninviting a spot as the human mind could conceive. All around were ghostly shapes, and diffused lights. The crane, but dimly visible in the encompassing mist, looked like some nameless creature from a nether world, and at intervals came eerie hoots from the river, where ships were endeavoring to make a safe passage to sea. The guardian of the coke fire and the roasting chestnuts took the shovel in both hands and gave it a vigorous shake.

"Help! He——!"

The shovel and its contents fell into the mud, and

7

the night-watchman felt his hair rising vertically, as the cry was followed by a splash. He gasped with horror, dived round the hut and caught a glimpse of a shadowy form making away from the water's edge. He possessed a police whistle, and he blew it with all the force of his healthy lungs. Then he ran across piles of litter to the spot whence the cry had come. He stared into the muddy water, but saw nothing but garbage. A few minutes later a light approached him through the mist.

"Hal-lo!"

Behind the light was the welcome glistening cape of a constable, and a dripping helmet.

"Did you whistle?"

"Yus. There was a yell and a splash—near here. Someone went into the river. It's murder——"

"Eh?"

"I saw him—him wot did it—running away—jest vanished into the fog. . . . Look! There's something—yonder!"

The mist had opened suddenly and disclosed a body —drifting slowly down stream. A little hiss left the constable's lips. He blew his whistle and then looked about him.

"Is there a boat near?"

"Aye. I'll show you. Mind that trench!"

Gasping, they reached a flight of stone steps, below which a small boat was moored. They entered it, and the night-watchman took the oars while the constable directed the ray of his electric lamp on the surface of the stream.

"It was that way—that way!"

A few minutes of anxious searching followed, and then the ray of the lamp fell on a human form, almost completely submerged.

"Pull your left! A-h!"

"Got—him?"

"Aye—lend a hand. He's a pretty good lump."

The victim was got aboard. It was a man of about fifty, well-dressed and of good physique. The constable put his hand to the heart, and when he removed it it was stained crimson. The night-watchman's eyes bulged.

"O-oh!" he gasped. "Stabbed!"

"Aye, murder it is. He's dead all right. Get ashore quickly."

By the time they reached the quay a second policeman was on the spot. They took the murdered man to the night-watchman's hut and laid him on a tarpaulin sheet. Another attempt was made to revive him, but it was proved beyond all doubt that he was beyond human aid. The second constable shook the wet off his helmet.

"He's a goner," he said. "Nasty bit o' work."

"Gentleman, too! Face seems a bit familiar. Better phone the office, Jim. Tell 'em to send along the ambulance."

The night-watchman, shocked by his first experience of brutal crime, kept nodding his head. He watched the remaining constable go through the dead man's pockets, but was too horrified to take much interest in that proceeding.

"Phew!" said the constable. "There's going to be a hell of a noise over this. He's Sir Randolph Cantler!"

"Eh?"

"Famous K.C. I thought I knew his face. My word, there will be a song. . . . Now, then, this man that you saw—what was he like?"

"I only just got a glimpse of him afore he disappeared into the fog. Seemed to be fairly tall, longish coat, soft hat—big brim. He went off like a cat. Blimey, my inside feels upside down!"

The constable made some notes in his pocketbook, took the night-watchman's name and address, and then left the hut with a view to finding footprints, but where the tragedy had presumably taken place there was a stretch of asphalt, and his mission was vain. Beyond the quay were many side-streets. Pursuit was out of the question—on such a night. He went back to the corpse, and waited for his comrade to return.

"Say," said the night-watchman, "do you think it was that fellow they're after—Jack o' Lantern?"

"It can be anyone. It might be you."

"Eh! What! 'Ere, you be careful——!"

Later came the ambulance, and the remains of the reputable and highly-respected Sir Randolph Cantler were removed. The night-watchman sat and shivered, and let his chestnuts lie in the mud at his feet.

On the following morning there was a brief—but start-ling—announcement in the morning Press, and the pub-lic waited with all its habitual eagerness for a big thrill. Ultimately fuller details were published, and London's latest murder was discussed by its teeming millions.

At Scotland Yard the police were more than usually worried. Murder of any kind was bad enough, but when the victim was an eminent King's Counsel, a man whose name was in common parlance "a household word," something had to be done to justify the existence of the C.I.D. But nothing was done, for the simple reason that no clue to the assassin was forthcoming. The puzzling element in the business was Sir Randolph's presence at Bircher's Dock at midnight. His secretary had asserted that Sir Randolph had left home at seven o'clock that evening with the object of dining with a fellow K.C. But the K.C. in question knew nothing of the alleged appointment. The whole thing was a complete mystery.

All the police had to go upon was the night-watch-man's very brief description of the man he saw running away—a description which did not carry them very far. That the motive was not robbery was proved by the fact that the dead man had in his possession a considerable sum of money and a valuable gold watch.

A strongly-worded leader article in *The Times* on the urgent need for some new system of criminal detection exasperated the Commissioner and the "Big Four." The Press expected miracles when the days of miracles were over. There was a wholesale round-up of suspicious characters, both in London and in the provinces, and several persons were detained pending further investigation.

About one month after the Cantler murder, Detective-Inspector John Wrench, of the C.I.D., made a brilliant capture of a notorious cat-burglar and safe-cracker, known as the "Slasher." Wrench had spent many weary days and nights on the trail of this ingenious scoundrel, but at last patience was rewarded, and Wrench had gone up still higher in the estimation of the authorities. Out of this capture had emerged an interesting fact, and it was in reference to this that Wrench presented himself at the office of the Assistant Commissioner. The latter was out, but Sweeting was present.

Sweeting was a superintendent, and not greatly enamoured of Wrench. He was an exceedingly difficult man to work under, and the friction that existed between himself and Wrench was due entirely to jealousy. The recent capture of the "Slasher" only served to exacerbate feeling, for Sweeting himself had failed utterly to produce any results.

"Hallo, Wrench!" he said. "Qualifying for the Commissioner's job?"

"No, the Home Secretary's," replied Wrench calmly.

"Well, hang on, dear boy. One never knows."

Wrench smiled as he sat down, and Sweeting turned over some papers noisily. It had taken him thirty years to reach his present position, and Wrench had gone three parts of that distance in less than ten. It was a stupendous achievement, and in Sweeting's eyes intolerable.

"How's our old friend—the 'Slasher'?" he inquired.

"Slightly mopy. He asked me to give you his love."

"The swine! Well, we have got things weighed up for him." He resumed his cynical banter. "You have only to march in Jack o' Lantern, and Scotland Yard is yours. Naturally you are quite optimistic?"

"I'm always optimistic, and a trifle more than usual at this particular moment."

Sweeting raised his eyebrows, but made no response. A few minutes later the Assistant Commissioner entered the room. He nodded at Wrench.

"You want to see me?"

"I have made a discovery, sir, which is a little interesting. This note was found on the 'Slasher.'"

The Chief took the proffered letter, and read it. His eyes lighted up, and he read it aloud:

> *Usual place. Better leave Kate out of it.*
> *Jack o' Lantern.*

Sweeting started, and the Assistant Commissioner raised his head and looked at Wrench keenly.

"That name again! Curious how it crops up, yet we never seem to get any closer to him. Have you interrogated the 'Slasher' about this?"

"Not yet."

"Where is he now?"

"Outside. I took the liberty of bringing him along."

"Good! Send him in!"

The prisoner was brought in by a sergeant. He was a cadaverous type of man, with projecting teeth and a slight cast in one eye. At the moment he was sullen and morose. He scowled at Wrench and bowed mockingly to Sweeting. The Assistant Commissioner walked up to him and held the letter before his eyes.

"Who sent you that?" he asked.

"Wot?" said the "Slasher" impudently.

"This note. Come, it may be in your interest to give us certain information. What do you know about this man who calls himself Jack o' Lantern?"

The "Slasher's" eyes moved nervously, as if he expected the writer of the note suddenly to appear before him. He hesitated, and then shook his head.

"Nothin'."

"You have seen him?"

"Maybe—maybe, I have."

"How long is it since you saw him last?"

"I can't remember."

"Where does he live?"

"I don't know."

"Don't lie. Tell me something about him—and this woman, Kate. Be sensible, and it is possible we may feel inclined to overlook certain charges."

The "Slasher" hesitated again, and for a moment it looked as if he were about to "squeal," but the old fear returned and he shook his head stubbornly. Every possible method of persuasion was resorted to, but all to no purpose. Evidently the "Slasher's" fear of Jack o' Lantern was greater than that of a long imprisonment. Ultimately the Assistant Commissioner waved his hand disgustedly, and the prisoner was led away.

"If that brute would only speak, it would save us a whole lot of trouble and worry," he mused. "You don't know the woman referred to—Kate?"

"There's Kate Spalding," said Wrench. "But to the best of my knowledge she has never been associated with the 'Slasher.' And since she last came out she has been doing honest work—strange as it may sound."

"Well, find this woman somehow. It is possible the 'Slasher' may change his mind when he hears what kind of a sentence he is going to get. But we need another string to pull." He hit the table with his fist. "We've got to get this mysterious Jack o' Lantern, who appears to be responsible for at least three murders."

"Do you include Sir Randolph Cantler?" asked Sweeting.

"It is highly probable. He died from a precisely similar wound to that found on the body of Richard Summers, over three years ago, and Summers lived long enough to breathe the name—or sobriquet—of his murderer. There is a link somewhere. Move heaven and earth, Wrench. We have to justify our existence."

CHAPTER TWO

A FORTNIGHT later the celebrated Judge Wallington sat in his comfortable and well-stocked library at his house near Regent's Park, perusing a work on criminology by Lombroso. He was a homely type of man, and divided his spare time between reading works of an abstruse and scientific nature and the collecting of art treasures. Despite his professional association with murderers, thieves and swindlers, he was inclined to take an optimistic view of life and humanity in general. Yet with all his impartiality he had gained the reputation of being harsh—some said the harshest judge in Europe. But this reputation was not merited, for Wallington in his wide experience of human nature knew when justice

could, with prudence, be tempered with mercy, and when
it could not.

He was yet young for one holding his eminent position
—a little over fifty years of age, and his appearance
belied his calling. One would have been more inclined
to take him for a simple-minded dreamer than a criminal
court judge who had sent to the gallows more than a
score of homicides. At this moment he was completely
at ease—his slippered feet resting on a large satin-
covered *pouffe,* and his fine head supported by two soft
cushions. His gold-rimmed pince-nez were pushed far
down his long straight nose, and he held a very fragrant
Havana cigar between his fingers.

Sitting immediately opposite him was his guest and
friend of long standing—Hugo Michels, a retired judge
from the Berlin Central Criminal Court. Michels displayed none of Wallington's comfort-loving propensities.
He had chosen deliberately a straight-backed Chippen-
dale chair, and was examining a fine collection of Baxter
prints. He was fifteen years older than his confrère—
a much heavier type of man, with a square head poised
on enormously broad shoulders; big hands and stubby
fingers. Wallington put down his book with a sigh.

"You know, my dear Michels," he said, "Lombroso
is inclined to become prosy—and rather out of date."

"Quite. This is a splendid collection—almost complete."

"Not bad. I have received many tempting offers for
them, but so far I have not succumbed, and——"

There came a light tap on the door, and a girl of about
twenty entered. Her light gown, fair hair, and rose complexion gave a relieving note of colour to the somewhat
austere room. She came to the Judge with the grace-
ful movements of one in perfect physical health, and
laid her white slim fingers on Wallington's arm.

"Sorry to interrupt you, Daddy," she said. "But John has just phoned up to say he might be a trifle late, and he hopes you will excuse him. Nali is out, so I took the message myself."

"Thank you, Sonia."

She smiled, and then hesitated for a moment.

"He was awfully mysterious."

"Eh!"

"Well, you see, I didn't know he was coming to-night."

"I didn't know myself until this afternoon. It is just a little matter of business, my dear. John, not to mention everyone else at the 'Yard,' is devoting his young life to the tracking down of a certain person."

"Oh, you mean Jack o' Lantern?"

"So you know that?"

"Everybody knows that."

"Well, I rather fancy I may be able to shed a little light on the matter. Nothing very brilliant—just a few facts. Why has Nali gone out?"

"I don't know. He just—disappeared."

"He oughtn't to go out without asking. Well, never mind. When Wrench comes, remember that his appointment is with *me*."

She smiled as she divined his meaning, and then reprimanded him for spilling cigar ash over the beautiful Persian carpet. He pulled her pink ear playfully as she adjusted the cushions under his head. Michels gave her an interested glance as she went out.

"So she calls you 'daddy'?"

"She loves to call me "Bunty' or 'Nunks' when no one is near to hear her."

"She is beautiful and charming."

Wallington nodded.

"Alas, I am to lose her soon!" he mused. "The in-

evitable interloper and smasher of homes—Cupid. It
seems but a year since I brought her from India—a mere
slip of a girl, and yet it is more than seven. I had to
complete the education which poor Pelling so shockingly
neglected. But I think I can understand that sin of
omission. He was lonely after the death of his wife,
and hungered for his little daughter. She went out to
him. Horrible job—District Commissioner, stuck away
in the Punjab. He went to pieces after his bereavement
—survived his wife by four years. Of course I had to
take the girl—that had always been his wish in the event
of such a catastrophe. Well, I've never had cause to
regret it. She brought something into this house that
was never here before she came. I'm afraid it has been
a little quiet for her."

"But the Hindu—Nali?"

"He was Pelling's servant and devoted slave. It was
Sonia's wish that I bring him along. The poor devil apparently convinced her that he would cut his throat after
she had gone. I succumbed to her blandishments, and it
hasn't turned out so badly. He is a kind of butler-cum-
valet, and perfect in both vocations."

"And whom is your ward to marry?"

"Wrench—the man who is coming here to see me.
Wrench is a good fellow, but he has rather turned the
tables on me—the scoundrel. He is the son of a country solicitor—an old Oxford associate. He went into
his father's office, but hated it so much he was on the
verge of running off to Canada, when I advised him to
join the police. More and more we need the educated
type of policeman, for the hare has changed since the
old days of Bill Sikes. Well, Wrench took my advice,
and in ten years has worked his way up from constable
to detective-inspector in the C.I.D. Not bad progress,

eh? It was inevitable he should meet Sonia—and the result, I fancy, was equally inevitable."

"You take it philosophically."

"It would break her heart if I didn't. But Wrench is all right. He is shrewd, clever, alert, courageous—and modest. At the present moment he is a little worried because Scotland Yard's *bêtenoire* consistently eludes him."

"The man you call Jack o' Lantern?"

"Yes."

"Lantern—Lantern! The name seems strangely familiar. There was a case—years ago——" Michels exerted his prodigious memory. "Yes, Tobias Lantern —that was the name. A murderer of extraordinary cunning."

"He was. I had the pleasure of sending him to his doom. Half a dozen crimes were proved, and I have no doubt there were as many more of which we knew nothing. Yet, strangely enough, two juries failed to agree, when the evidence was as conclusive as evidence could be——"

"Then why——?"

"He was an extraordinary personage. I sincerely believe he succeeded in hypnotising those juries. Even the third jury—on the occasion when he came before me—deliberated for six solid hours before they could make up their minds. Mass hypnotism! Is such a thing possible?"

"Why not? It is the only theory that will account for some of the tricks performed by fakirs in the East."

"Well, it may be. I certainly experienced strange sensations myself. I hated to go to court and face him. He wore me down as no other man ever did. I admit I had been ill, and was not in the best condition, but—I can see him: a loose-limbed horror of a creature, with pallid face and small, piercing eyes that seemed to bore into one's brain. That man might have been anything —a king among men, and yet he did nothing better with his amazing mental equipment than play upon the affections of women and dispose of them brutally when he was tired of them. Thank God, the earth is rid of him."

"Wasn't there a plea of insanity?"

"Yes, but the doctors wouldn't certify. It was, however, proved that there was insanity in the family. Tobias's grandfather was known as 'The Inkslinger of Putney.' But there was nothing to substantiate such a plea in Tobias's case."

Despite the Judge's emphatic assertion there was something in his face which led Michels to suspect there was just a shadow of doubt in his mind, and he knew from his own experience the questioning conscience of a judge when a capital sentence has been pronounced, and the line between insanity and sanity is reduced to the fineness of a silken thread.

"Curious—the similarity of the name," mused Michels.

"Not so curious. There is a link between the case of Tobias Lantern and the recent murders that have been attributed to Jack o' Lantern. That is why I have sent for Wrench. I should like you to be present, Michels, for the whole question rests on a matter of handwriting, on which you are an authority."

CHAPTER THREE

WRENCH arrived a quarter of an hour later, and was shown into the library. Wallington introduced him to Michels, whom he already knew well by sight, and then waved him into a chair.

"You have brought the note which was found on the 'Slasher'?" asked the Judge.

"Yes."

"Good! It may interest you to know that I received a communication from Jack o' Lantern this morning."

"What!"

"Oh, yes. Here it is. I have little doubt that the handwriting corresponds with that in the note found on the 'Slasher.' It will be interesting to compare them."

Wrench read the writing on the rough piece of paper which Wallington produced. It ran:

Be merciful to-day if you value your life.—Jack o' Lantern.

"That has reference to the trial of the 'Slasher'?"

"Obviously. Well, the 'Slasher' will do no more harm for ten years. The writing is the same, Wrench?"

"Exactly."

Michels examined the two notes and concurred.

"And now to the point," resumed the Judge. "Immediately after the Tobias Lantern trial I received an anonymous letter. It asserted that I had shown a prejudice in my summing-up, and contained a threat that so far has never been carried out. I have looked up that letter, and have it here now. I think you will agree that the three letters were written by one and the same hand."

He produced the anonymous letter, and Michels was quick to endorse his conclusion. Wrench also agreed.

"What do you infer from that, Wrench?" asked the Judge.

"It certainly looks as if Jack o' Lantern is connected in some way with the Lantern trial. But at the 'Yard' they are inclined to take the view that the name is a sobriquet to cover a desperate criminal—a name which designates one who flits by night—the elusive one."

"They see no real link between Jack o' Lantern and Tobias Lantern?"

"So far, no."

"Then they are less intelligent than I imagined. There is a link—and a strong one. Are you aware that Sir Randolph Cantler was acting for the prosecution in the Lantern case?"

Wrench gave a noticeable start, for there was no missing the significance of this. But the Judge had another card up his sleeve. He referred to some documents.

"I have here a list of the jurymen who served on the occasion of Lantern's conviction. It is only necessary to mention three names—Richard Summers, Albert Gale, James Henling——"

"By Jove!" gasped Wrench. "This is astounding! All murdered within the last seven years!"

"Precisely—and with no apparent motive. Then poor Cantler, and this threat to myself. I should say that 'coincidence' is not the correct word."

"I believe you are right, Judge. I can't imagine how these facts were overlooked."

"Jurymen come and go. It is not remarkable that their deaths were not connected with a case which occurred years before, and I appear to be the only one who had been honoured by a written threat. I presume I am regarded as the most important, and am being saved up. Well, I am not exactly terrified, and my only object in acquainting you of these facts is to enable you to run our friend to earth."

"Thank you, sir, but you must have police protection. This man is no idle——"

"No, my dear John. I have a great regard for your excellent force, but I don't want them parading outside my house, or walking over my flower-beds. I see quite enough of the guardians of the law, as it is. Your policemen will be better employed elsewhere."

"Very well, sir, if you insist."

"I do, and I am particularly anxious that Sonia shall know nothing about these foolish threats. You understand?"

"Quite! By what means was the last note delivered to you?"

"It was put into the letter-box—merely folded up and my name written on the outside. Nali brought it to me with the morning mail."

Wrench asked a few more questions, and made copious notes. The new light which had been shed on the Jack o' Lantern crimes aroused his keenest interest. It was evident he wanted to get on to the new trail, and when he left he was in a great hurry.

"A regular sleuth-hound," mused Wallington. "I should like to see him get this Jack o' Lantern fellow. But I feel it is not going to be a simple matter. His effrontery is amazing. Well, we shall see."

Michels took a much more serious view of the threat, for he knew the handwriting of a homicidal maniac, and that was what he saw behind those pencilled notes.

"You must take care of yourself, Wallington," he said. "I wish you had accepted Wrench's offer of police protection."

The Judge laughed lightly. He was in love with life, but at the same time he was remote from fear of threats. The reception of the first note had aroused in him a desire to see if any attempt would be made against his life, and when nothing happened he was almost disappointed. His one anxiety was on Sonia's account.

CHAPTER FOUR

A FEW days later Sonia went to a theatre with Wrench. She had looked forward with some eagerness to the event, for of late she had seen less of him than she considered was her right. The love affair dated back to the preceding summer, but had been kept very secret until recently, for she had feared that the Judge might not give it his approval. Ultimately the truth came out, and her heart bounded when "dear old Bunty" came up to the scratch, and told them they were very foolish, but not more foolish than a great number of other people.

Her life with Wallington had been pleasant enough, though somewhat devoid of social distractions, for the Judge was a retiring personage, and hated visiting and receiving visitors, except the very few that really interested him—such as Michels. But Sonia had adapted herself to the quiet existence, and derived pleasure from books, music, and the fine old-world garden that surrounded the house. The Judge was very susceptible to music, and encouraged her to practise assiduously. Occasionally he sang, but he much preferred to sit and listen to the new Bechstein piano which he had bought for her.

Unfortunately Wrench was not very musical, but he was, notwithstanding, an admirable companion. She liked his blunt ways, his sense of humour and the general atmosphere of jollity which he radiated. Also she admired his mental equipment, though it was on a different plane to that of the Judge and Michels. Those two could always talk above the heads of normal persons. But she thought they were inclined to be too self-centred, for they could sit for hours together and never utter a word. Wrench was not like that. He had to be either working or playing, and she loved him best when he was playing.

"You've got work on the brain, John," she chided, as they drove towards the West End. "Drop it! It isn't like you."

"Sorry, old girl! This Jack o' Lantern fellow has got us all guessing. Anyway, I will bid him adieu for to-night. You look wonderful enough to drive him completely into the limbo of dark and noisome things. Where shall we dine?"

"Anywhere."

"I'll take you to a new place where they serve courses strange and weird."

"Not *too* weird."

"We'll have a competition to solve their ingredients. I hope the show we are going to is not a mystery play. I simply can't stand those things."

"I should have thought that would have been quite in your line."

"Not to-night. I want something soft and romantic —roses and a warm summer night."

"In other words—slush."

"Well—perhaps."

While they sat and watched love's entanglements in process of being straightened out, the Judge and Michels were matching their brains in a game of chess. At length Wallington chuckled as he moved up his knight.

"I think the end is now in sight."

"So. I give you best. You are much too good for me. And now I am going to bed."

The Judge sat on a little longer, roasting his toes in front of the still active fire. In the dead silence he could hear faint strains of music—a curious reedy air that came in pulses from a distant part of the house. He had heard that strange air before, and knew that

Nali was the musician. Upon his pushing the bell by the fire-place the music ceased, and soon Nali entered the room as noiselessly as a cat. He was a tall Hindu of striking appearance. The eyes were large and jet black, set wide in a handsome but pallid face, above which was a silken immaculate turban. Other than the picturesque headgear his garb was modern. His deportment was majestic—perfect.

"My nightcap, Nali," said the Judge.

"It is ready, *sahib.*"

He vanished and came back quickly with a tray on which was a steaming glass of whisky-and-water. This he placed on the small low table in front of the Judge.

"What was the air you were playing just now, Nali?"

"It is called 'The Hymn of the Soul,' *sahib.*"

"It is familiar."

"Miss Sonia sometimes plays it on the piano, *sahib.* But it is not suited to a Western instrument. Only the pipe of my people can do it justice."

"Bring your pipe and play it to me."

Nali bowed, and brought in his instrument. It was akin to a small clarinet, but was fashioned out of white wood, and had a number of gilt keys. The Judge bade him seat himself on the *pouffe.* The Hindu commenced to play in a smooth *pianissimo,* his long fingers moving silkily on the keys, and his shoulders swaying slightly. The air developed from a chromatic whine, rose and fell in strange intervals, grew wilder and wilder. . . . It brought to Wallington's mind vivid scenes of India— temples, minarets, yellow-robed Buddhists, lotus flowers . . . lotus flowers. . . .

* * * * *

It was just past midnight when Sonia returned home, after an evening of unmarred delight. She rang the bell, but there was no response.

"Locked out!" teased Wrench. "I shall have to take you to the police station."

"Oh, I remember telling Nali that he could go to bed if he felt tired. I have a key in my bag. Here it is."

She unlocked the door and bade Wrench a long farewell on the doorstep.

"Wednesday, John, and don't forget."

"I am scarcely likely to. Cheerio!"

She stood there for a few minutes watching him stride down the drive. At the gate he turned and waved his hand, and she kissed her fingers. Then she entered the house and bolted the door after her. Late as it was, she determined to have her customary evening read, and went into the library to find a book which she had left there earlier in the day. To her horror the fire was burning brightly. The Judge was inclined to be careless in such matters, but Sonia had once witnessed a dreadful fire in the Punjab and was never likely to forget it. She removed some of the burning coals and waited for them to cool before retiring to her room.

Her book was not in the place where she had left it, so she searched in some unfilled shelves of the bookcase, in the belief that the too tidy Nali had been at work. She was still searching when she heard a slight noise in the direction of the window. Turning her head she saw a sight that caused her blood to run cold. Pressed hard against a pane of glass in the left-hand casement window was a hideous face, white as a sheet of paper, with all the features distorted. The eyes glared glassily and the mouth was twisted and awful. She stood there, petrified with horror.

While the flattened, awful face still stared at her, Sonia's voice functioned, and she gave vent to a piercing shriek. Then she ran through the doorway and into the hall. She heard a door close upstairs, and a few sec-

onds later Michels appeared, clad in a dressing-gown.
"So it was you, Miss Pelling? What is the matter?"
She pointed to the open door of the library.

"In there—someone was trying to get in. I saw a face
—a terrible face at the window and——"

Michels looked round for a weapon, and his glance
rested on an old sword that served as an ornament. He
took it from its rest and entered the library. Sonia
choked down her fear and followed him. Immediately
her eyes went to the window, but the face had gone.

"It was—there," she said. "I was standing by the
bookcase when I heard a slight noise and turned round."

Michels went to the window and unbolted it. Outside
was a veranda, with steps leading down to the garden.
But no living soul was in sight. He came back to Sonia,
after bolting the window behind him.

"You are—quite sure you saw something?"

"Yes, yes. A man's face—a hideous face."

"Nothing else?"

"A hat, I think, and the collar of an overcoat."

"What sort of face was it—old or young?"

"I—I don't know. It was misshapen by being pressed
close against the glass. It stayed there perfectly still—
looking at me—staring horribly. What—what does it
mean?"

"A housebreaker obviously."

She had regained her composure, and his reply did not
satisfy her, taken in conjunction with his grim countenance.

"I don't believe—— Mr. Michels, why did the Judge
send for Wrench? Isn't it possible——"

She stopped as she saw Nali descending the stairs.
Michels turned his head and saw the object of her glance.
The Hindu approached them and looked at Sonia inter-
rogatively.

"You heard?" snapped Michels.

"Yes, Nali hear loud cry. He come——"

"You have been a long time."

"Nali sleep at the far end of the corridor. Lady is very pale and distressed. Why did lady cry out?"

"Someone was trying to get in, Nali."

"You and I had better go into the garden, Nali—in case anyone may be lurking there," said Michels.

Nali nodded.

"Better take a stick—or something."

"Nali take mistress to her room first. Come back then."

Sonia was quite agreeable, for the shock to her nerves had been considerable. Michels waited while Nali escorted his beloved mistress upstairs. At the top Sonia hesitated.

"Go, see if the Judge is all right," she begged.

He left her and entered Wallington's room, but returned to her in a few seconds.

"He sleeps deeply," he said. "It is as well."

"Good! I am all right now," she said. "I am sorry I lost my nerve."

"Mistress must not worry. She kept the thief away. He will not come again."

He bowed as she left him, and then went to join Michels. Together they went over the garden, but found nothing. Ultimately they returned to the house and sought their respective rooms. Sonia sat up for some time pondering the incident. An attempted burglary was quite a natural event, but she had an intuition that that was not the motive. Since Wrench had had that interview with the Judge he had been peculiarly secretive, and had given very vague answers to several questions which she had put to him. And the attitude of both Nali and Michels was strange. They seemed a little more constrained than would have been the case had a common attempt at housebreaking been frustrated. It gave her furiously to think, and spoilt an evening which otherwise would have been completely successful.

The Judge was up and about at his usual early hour, and was opening his mail in the library when Michels came downstairs. He welcomed his friend with a jest, and begged to be excused.

"I like to get this tiresome business over, Michels," he said. "Did you ever see such a plethora of begging letters? One would have to be a Crœsus to comply with all of them. Missionary work in India! Well, I don't exactly approve of missionary work in India. That, like charity, should begin at home. There are plenty of people needing conversion in this tight little island. Splendid bout of chess that was. I was thinking about it in bed. If you had moved your bishop and sacrificed the pawn the result might have been different."

"Perhaps. Did you sleep well?"

"Solidly. I thank God for never being troubled with insomnia. The secret, my dear Michels, is early to bed. There, that's the last! Three letters of real importance. The remainder are appeals for subscriptions, offers to lend me money up to any amount, and a delightful epistle from a lady who seems to imagine that the best corrective for a murderer is to put him in a nice comfortable home, with free drinks and all the social amenities for the rest of his natural existence. Was that the gong?"

"I think not. Wallington, I have something to say to you."

"Say on."

"Something happened last night."

The Judge deposited a pile of paper in the basket and looked at Michels interrogatively.

"Well?"

"An attempt was made to break into this house."

"You don't mean that?"

"I do. I was awakened by a scream—about midnight —and ran from my room to find your ward in a state of terror. She had just returned from the theatre, and had come into this room to find a book. She saw a face at that window."

"A face!"

"A hideous face pressed close to the glass. Naturally she was very distressed and ran into the hall. I subsequently examined the window, and Nali and I went into the garden. We found no trace of the man."

The Judge tapped his finger on the side of his chair and looked troubled.

"I had no idea. Too bad—too bad! Somebody after my silver or prints . . ."

"No."

The emphatic negative caused the Judge to raise his eyebrows. Michels was looking uncommonly grim.

"It was not the silver that was in jeopardy," he said. "It was your life."

"My dear Michels!"

"Wait! I have good grounds for making that assertion, quite apart from the fact that you yourself received a warning. When I examined the window I saw something written on the glass—some letters scratched by a diamond. They were—J. O. L."

"What!"

"Come and see for yourself."

Wallington went to the window and Michels indicated the inscription. It was clearly engraved on an upper pane, in small capitals. Wallington looked over the top of his glasses at Michels.

"This is rather—disturbing."

"Very."

"Does Sonia know—about this?"

"No. I made no comment and I am sure she never saw it."

"Confound! He must be an impudent sort of scoundrel to come here and leave his mark."

"In my opinion he is a deadly menace. You were inclined to take his threat too lightly. You had better get Wrench up here without delay."

"That will mean that Sonia will learn the truth. I don't want her happiness marred by thoughts of dangerous criminals and threats against my existence."

"Why not send her away—on a holiday?"

"That would most certainly arouse her suspicions. No, it would be useless to try. She wouldn't go. But I will get Wrench up here, and we must convince her that the motive was burglary. After all, it is the obvious motive, and it may yet prove to be the correct one."

"I might have believed that but for those marks."

"You may be right." Wallington's mouth grew tighter. "Of course you are right. But if Mr. Jack o' Lantern's work on the window pane was done to scare me into a state of nervous prostration I am afraid he will fail. But for the presence of Sonia I think I should rather enjoy the adventure. It adds a spice to life. Anyway, I will communicate with the police."

During breakfast the incident was discussed. Wallington treated it quite casually, and Michels emulated his example.

"One of my old victims," said the Judge. "That is what I call a mean sort of revenge. But for your timely arrival, Sonia, I might have lost the Georgian tea-set. Well, did you enjoy yourself?"

"Oh yes. The play was not too brilliant, but there were other diversions."

"I can quite believe you," replied the Judge with his eyes twinkling. "I have just telephoned the Yard about the attempted burglary. The police may possibly discover some clue that may put them on the trail of this midnight marauder."

"Then John may come?"

"Quite possibly."

But in place of Wrench the superintendent himself turned up, and the Judge rather regretted his telephone call, for Sweeting had a habit of being a little too thorough. Sonia frowned when she saw him, for she was well aware that he was on none too friendly terms with his subordinate.

"Ah, Superintendent," said the Judge. "I scarcely expected you. But come inside."

Sweeting strolled into the library and looked about him interestedly. The Judge waved him into a chair and offered him a cigar.

"No, thank you, Judge. I never smoke on duty. Wrench has gone off on another tack, so I thought I would come along myself. If I am not mistaken it is something more than attempted robbery?"

"What makes you think that?"

"The information that is already in our possession. But I should like full details if you please."

The Judge recapitulated, with the assistance of Michels, and Sweeting examined the lettering on the pane of glass. He made no comment for a while, but wrote a great deal in his notebook, possibly with the object of impressing the Judge. Afterwards he went on to the veranda and into the garden, leaving the Judge and Michels together.

"Uncommunicative," mused Michels. "I believe he is Wrench's superior officer?"

"Yes, and a trifle jealous of Wrench. It's a pity we

can't eradicate that feeling in public services, but it seems impossible. Nevertheless I think he is very capable."

Sweeting was still prowling in the garden when the Judge had occasion to leave. But he came to the house later and presented himself to Sonia, who knew him slightly.

"Ah, Miss Pelling," he said, "I should be glad of a little further information—at first hand. Will you describe to me as well as you are able exactly what you saw?"

"Merely a face, pressed hard against the window. I can't describe it in any detail. The nose was flattened, and the mouth was misshapen. Almost any face would look the same in the circumstances."

"Can you recall exactly where you saw the face? Indicate the exact spot to me. It may give me some idea of his height."

"I am not sure."

"Well, try."

She went into the library with him, and did her best to recall the exact place where she had seen the face. Then she noticed the inscription on the glass.

"Why, this—this was not here before!" she gasped.

"No. It was left by the burglar."

"But why——? J. O. L.—is that——?"

He looked at her curiously and then inclined his head.

"You—you have some idea who—who——?" she asked.

"Why should I?"

"You look—so strange."

"I am merely trying to piece a few stray ends together. This—burglar——"

"You—you don't believe it was a burglar. You have

cause to believe it—it was someone who—who hates the Judge? Isn't that so?"

"Would that idea startle you?"

"It would be horrible."

He communicated no more, but became very officious. The servants were called one at a time—the cook, the housemaid, and Nali. It seemed a positive waste of time to Sonia, but Sweeting held a different opinion. The major part of his time was devoted to Nali, until he dismissed him summarily.

"Is that all?" asked Sonia, rather chillily.

"All for the moment. I have a certain theory, Miss Pelling—a certain interesting theory. Well, we shall see."

CHAPTER FIVE

In the sitting-room of an old and somewhat dilapidated house in the neighbourhood of Mayfair three people sat and played cards. Two of them were men and the other a woman. The elder man was an imposing personality—a big-boned, gaunt individual with the head of a philosopher, and unkempt hair. He dealt the cards with the dexterity of one who had served a long apprenticeship at the game, and handled them like the born gambler. The younger man was totally different. He looked what he was—a cunning thief, of the non-intelligent class, with no principles worth mentioning. Unlike Banting—the elder man—he paid some regard to his dress, and at this moment was attired in a pepper-and-salt suit, patent boots with cloth uppers, and a very high starched collar adorned with a large purple tie.

The woman was Banting's daughter—Kate. She had her father's intelligent head, his straight nose, and firm mouth, but in place of his grey-black hair her own was of a deep shade of auburn, bobbed very short and displaying a shapely milk-white neck. She played her cards listlessly, as if she had no great interest in the game, and she smoked a gold-tipped cigarette held in a short tortoiseshell holder, for she had a fine regard for her long and slender fingers.

"Full House!" chortled the younger man, as he displayed his hand. "Got you by the short hairs, Banting."

Banting held up his finger, and quietly exposed four Kings, while he scooped up the money in the pool. Kate stifled a yawn and flicked the ash of her cigarette on to the floor.

"It's no use, Sam," she said. "You can't beat the 'old 'un.' Your face is not your fortune. It gives you away."

"My luck's rotten. Your deal, Kate."

But Kate shook her fine head.

"I'm fed up," she said. "Can't we go somewhere—do something? This musty old house gets on my nerves."

"It's raining cats and dogs," asserted Sam. He stole a look at Kate's reflected countenance. "What's wrong with you, anyway? You bin as mopy as a dog with distemper these last few days, and whenever I talk to you you jump on me."

"Don't be ridiculous."

" 'Strue. Ever since you met Lefroy——"

"Lefroy!" Kate turned on him fiercely, and Banting raised his head at the name and looked tense.

"Yus—Lefroy," went on Sam determinedly. "You bin in a kind o' dream. Dam' 'im, I say—dam' 'im!"

"Shut up, you fool!" snapped Banting. "What do you know about Lefroy?"

"I know that he's got Kate sentimentalising. I wouldn't trust the blighter—I wouldn't."

"Oh, shut up!" said Kate, reddening.

"I'm not going to shut up. Didn't he let us down last Wednesday? Why wasn't he where he said he'd be? The whole thing went wrong through 'im. And we ain't seen a sign of 'im since—not a blinkin' smell of 'im."

"We may have misunderstood his instructions," argued Banting.

"Instructions! That's 'im—Lord High Admiral of the Fleet. Seems to have a pretty good hold on you two."

Banting shot him a scornful glance, and Kate bestowed on him a withering look. It was like Sam Knudge to cast stones at Lefroy when he was absent, but it was a very different Sam when Lefroy was in the offing, with his burning eyes and mighty personality. Sam was a mere kitten then. Kate threw off her resentment and touched her devoted slave on the arm.

"Try to be sensible, Sam, and I'll play the piano to you," she said. "What would you like—Chopin, or 'Ain't She Sweet'?"

"Garn, you can't kid me," retorted Sam. "You're 'ead over 'eels in love with Lefroy. I'm not so big a fool I can't see that. And you're moping to-night because you ain't seen 'im for nearly a week. What do you know about 'im, anyway? He comes like a blooming ghost and goes like one. He makes appointments and don't keep 'em. I'm fed——"

Kate put her fingers to her ears and went to the piano. Sam resumed his castigations, but a volume of music drowned his words. He picked up his bowler hat and stuck it on the side of his head.

"I'm going to play a game of billiards," he said.

"Leave me not—oh, leave me not!" sang Kate.

"Let him go," growled Banting. "It will cool his head."

Sam walked out in high dudgeon, and Kate went on playing. She was a good pianist and possessed an excellent memory. The piano, like the house, was full of damp, but she managed to create an effect, and Banting watched her through half-closed eyes as she went from the classics to music-hall songs.

"Poor old Sam!" she said, without turning her head. "Doesn't he look ridiculous in that appalling suit?"

"He can be a damned fool when he likes."

"He can be that without liking," she replied. "I suppose he will now go and get drunk."

Banting was watching her closely—and curiously. What Sam had alleged was true. He had seen his daughter coming more and more under the influence of Lefroy, and that fact caused him considerable apprehension. But exactly how far that affair had gone he did not know.

"Kate!" he said suddenly.

She swung round on the piano stool.

"Come here!"

"What's the matter now?"

She walked across to him and sat on the couch by his side, with her white teeth gleaming and a querulous look in her blue eyes.

"Is there any truth in what Sam said?"

"What did Sam say?"

"You know—about you and Lefroy?"

Kate's lip quivered. Her glance went into space, and then came back to her father's stern face.

"Sam is furiously jealous without reason," she said.

"Are you sure?"

"Well——"

"Go on."

"It's nonsense—just nonsense. But if I were—isn't that entirely my own business? Sam means nothing to me. He thinks he does, and if he gets any sort of joy

out of it there is no reason why he should not go on—
dreaming. But Lefroy——"

"I am asking you about Lefroy."

"He's different—like no one else I have ever met. If
I'm interested, is that very strange? The only men I
have ever met are of Sam's type. Could he hope to
interest any woman? Billiards, beer, and biliousness—
that's Sam."

"Are you in love with Lefroy?" he demanded.

"No."

"A-h."

It was a long sigh of relief, and Kate narrowed her
eyes at the sound of it.

"Why this stupendous relief?" she asked. "Isn't
Lefroy good enough for you? I always thought you
admired him."

"Admiration—yes, but——"

"Ah, you are like Sam—mistrust——"

Banting caught her by the shoulder and gazed into
her eyes steadfastly. She read in his expression the
deep affection which he had always had for her, mingled
with lurking fear.

"Lefroy is a dangerous man," he said. "Cut him clean
out of your mind. With Sam you know where you are,
but Lefroy—he's deep and dark."

"And I thought you two were friends," she said a
little bitterly.

"Friends, yes—in business, but——"

"You are as bad as Sam," she interrupted. "You
fear Lefroy because he has brains—genius. I know you
are clever, father, but Lefroy—he's different. . . . This
life of ours, it puts us outside the pale. It kills every
hope of decent society. Oh, I know what you are going
to say, but it makes no difference. Even if we got away

with a big thing we'd still have to associate with crooks, swindlers, thieves—like ourselves——"

"Kate!"

"I'm not squealing—not exactly. But there are times when I feel I'd like to mix with decent people—hear good and intelligent conversation. Well, Lefroy can give me the latter. He—he knows everything. And if I display a desire to hear something about a world which is closed to me, can't you give me the credit for keeping my head?"

"It's playing with fire."

"So is life—our life, anyway. And what do we get from it? Little more than bread and butter, a dance, a song, a few feathers. And for them we pay in hard coin—the coin of anxiety, creeping fear, visions of—of stone walls and——"

"For the love of Mike, shut up!" said Banting. "What's the matter with you? Your nerves are all to pieces."

"Not my nerves—my soul. I'll wager you never knew I had a soul."

Banting turned his eyes away, and stared across the room. For some years Kate had been a disturbing influence—ever since she had grown to womanhood and was able to look with open eyes at the world in which she lived. It could not be hidden from her that her parent was a professional thief, and an associate of other thieves, rogues, blackmailers; and the facts had come to her so slowly that there had been no shock worth recalling. She herself had never actually engaged in crime, but she had partaken so freely of stolen fruit that she had come to accept the philosophy of thieves—*"Get what you can, how you can, and when you can."*

Notwithstanding, there were many good traits in her character. She hated lies, was modest of her good looks, detested brutality in any form, and had a fund of sympathy for the submerged tenth. And at times there came to her the desire to cut adrift from her father, Sam Knudge, and the rest, and seek to redeem herself in her own eyes. The only obstacle was the will to put this good resolution into practice. It was much easier to drift with the tide—down, down to the sea of lost hopes.

Both were suddenly startled by the ring of a bell from without—a staccato, triple ring. Then, after a few seconds' dead silence, the door opened slowly and a figure entered the room. It was tall and erect, and the white face of it seemed all the more deathly in contrast with the black overcoat and dinted black hat that was pulled well over the broad forehead. The mouth was curled in a curious smile, and the eyes were piercing in their intensity. "Lefroy!"

Banting rose from the couch, but Kate still remained seated, her breast heaving visibly. Lefroy turned his back on the pair of them and removed the coat and hat. Then he sat down at the piano and commenced to play softly, as if no one but himself were present. He stopped suddenly and slammed down the lid of the instrument.

"Awful! Why don't you get the thing tuned, Banting?"

Banting waved his hands.

"What's it matter? We don't live on music."

Lefroy laughed—a curious, cackling laugh that was eerie to listen to.

"What does the prophet say—'man does not live by bread alone'? There is an atmosphere of intense boredom here. We must banish it forthwith. A bottle of something, Banting. Let us drive dull care away. Hurry —hurry!"

He waved his long arms impatiently, and Banting nodded and left the room. Kate, with the expression of a hypnotised rabbit, strove to find her habitual calm, for this strange man stirred her to unimaginable depths. He walked across to her and sat down beside her.

"You are quiet and reflective."

"I was bored."

"Then you shall be bored no longer." He took one of her hands. "Shapely and soft—and warm as a bird. See, I have brought you a little present—a bauble, a thing that men slave for, and women—some women— sin for. That is no reflection upon your sex in general. I hold it in great esteem."

It was a diamond bracelet in the form of a snake, and he slipped it over her hand and kissed it when it lay across the white skin of her arm.

"Where—where did you get it?"

"I forget—but that is a matter of no consequence whatsoever. Ask not whence cometh and whither go- eth——. Ah, now we shall commence to live."

This, as Banting reappeared with a decanter of whisky, water and glasses. His cat-like lassitude vanished as he drank heavily. He became alert, vivacious and more garrulous than ever. He had forgotten the appointment of the previous week, but made no apology for the over- sight. Then, for no apparent reason, he stood up, drained his glass and flung it into the fire-place, where it was shattered into fragments.

"Lefroy!"

"To the piano!" he ordered. "Time is passing. Every hour—every minute—is a step nearer the grave. Kate and I will show you the latest dance. . . ."

"I want to talk business——"

"Business—business! This is the business of life— to cheat the festering sore of melancholia. Play— play——!"

Banting retreated before the blazing eyes that he never

could withstand. He sat down at the piano and commenced to play—appallingly badly. Lefroy seized Kate, and swung her round in a wild Jazz. Banting grew tired, but not so Lefroy. His steps grew wilder and wilder, and he laughed from time to time as Kate grew breathless and exhausted. Then the door opened and Sam Knudge entered. He had been drinking, and his face became contorted as he realised what was happening.

"Hel-lo, Kate!" he growled as she passed him.

"Get out!" snapped Lefroy. "You're in the way."

"Yus—I'm in the way," snarled Sam. "And you're in the way—in my way, and don't you forget it."

Kate was sent hurtling across the room towards the couch. She almost fell on it, and Lefroy strode up to the bemuddled and infuriated Sam.

"Does it occur to you that you are completely spoiling the festivities?" he asked.

"So I am—blast you!" shouted Sam. "You leave her alone, or I'll tell her something. I'll tell her that you——"

Banting rose from his seat and ran at Sam. In a second he had him outside the door. Sam expostulated and spluttered.

"Take your 'ands off me. You know who he is, and so do I, and it's time——"

"You fool!" said Banting. "If you ever breathed the name of Jack o' Lantern to a living soul, your life wouldn't be worth twopence. Go home and get sober."

"He's got Kate——"

"It's only his mood. It means nothing."

"You're a fool!"

Banting's brow came down.

"Not quite such a fool as you imagine, Sam. But I know on what side my bread is buttered. See nothing—

know nothing. That's best. It's not wise to infuriate him. As for Kate—I'm watching after her—you understand?"

He succeeded in placating Sam, and sighed when that worthy left the house and slammed the door behind him. When he entered the room again Jack o' Lantern was making shadowgraphs on the wall with his dexterous, supple hands, and laughing weirdly.

CHAPTER SIX

WRENCH heard of Sonia's nocturnal experience with surprise and misgivings, and he frowned when he learned that Sweeting had been investigating in the neighbourhood. He saw the Judge again and tried to make him see the existence of real danger, but Wallington was as obdurate as ever.

"We shall hear no more of him, John," he opined. "I should very much like to make the brute pay for giving Sonia a shock. I want her to continue to think it was nothing but an attempt at burglary. You understand?"

"I fear that is impossible. She knows already."

"How can she——?"

"Sweeting let the cat out of the bag. She questioned me this morning and it was useless to attempt to mislead her. Apparently she saw the marks on the window pane before the glass was replaced, and in the meantime has connected it with the real culprit. She asked me point blank if the initials stood for Jack-o'-Lantern?"

"And you told her they did?"

"I demurred—but she knows the truth."

Wallington looked very perturbed, and expressed his regret that the superintendent was interesting himself so deeply in the affair.

"He's such an interfering person, and is likely to worry the life out of me. He has been interrogating the servants, for what reason I cannot imagine. I suppose he is keen to steal your thunder, John?"

"He seems to have a bee in his bonnet," agreed Wrench. "It's difficult to work with him with any satisfaction."

"Hm! You looked up the Lantern trial?"

"Yes, and I went down to Salisbury to look up Elizabeth Lantern—the mother of Tobias. She moved there soon after the trial and has been running a small provision shop. There is a daughter—a woman of about forty, and another son—Luke, who follows the trade of a carpenter. They seem to be a very respectable family. I represented myself as a journalist who was keen to write up a number of celebrated murders. Of course they were not keen to revive the past—were obviously deeply ashamed. The mother was a little bit bitter. She averred that Tobias had always been a mental case, and that the capital sentence was cruel and unjust."

The Judge frowned and looked over the top of his glasses.

"Does any mother ever admit that her son had a fair trial after he is found guilty?"

"I quite understand, sir. Well, I made a few inquiries about Luke, and the result was the same everywhere. He is highly respected, the secretary of a local club, a church sidesman and altogether an admirable citizen. Ultimately I saw him personally. He was quite a cheery individual, and took quite a different view to that expressed by Mrs. Lantern. He ascribed Tobias's awful crimes to drug-taking, and admitted that in his opinion justice had been done."

Wallington nodded and looked a little pleased, for he

had scarcely expected this compliment from any member of the Lantern family.

"Of course it may be a pose," he mused. "Luke may be as cunning as Tobias."

"Quite. I am taking steps to get a specimen of his handwriting. It may help."

"It may. What do you think, Michels?"

Michels was still burrowing among old prints, but he had heard everything, and his eyes revealed his interest.

"There are some strange elements in the affair," he replied. "This murderer is clever enough to entice Sir Randolph to a dirty and deserted part of London, and succeeds in murdering him. Yet in seven years all he had done in regard to you is to send you two written threats, and presumably make a futile attempt to enter the house. Yes, it is very strange!"

"It is very annoying," said the Judge. "I had rather he attempted to carry out his threat anywhere but here."

Later Wrench found Sonia. She was a little paler than usual, and obviously troubled in her mind. They walked in the garden, admiring the Judge's fine display of winter flowers, but even those gay blossoms failed to bring sunshine to the girl's heart.

"I'm worried, John," she confessed.

"I know that, but it isn't a bit of good, and I doubt if there are any real grounds for it."

"Are you speaking the truth?"

"What makes you suspect that I am not? Admitting that someone bears him a grudge, do you think it likely that they would risk any attempt at molestation?"

"But an attempt was made!"

"Not a serious attempt. A futile threat. There is a vast difference between that and assault and battery."

"But what about Sir Randolph Cantler?"

"What has that affair to do with the Judge?" he asked guardedly.

"I don't know, but I feel it has some connection. It's no use—I can't explain, but I have a kind of intuition that this danger which threatens 'Bunty' is real. He makes too light of it. He has tried to pretend that the man I saw was a mere burglar, and in his regard for my happiness he laughs as if it were a comical business. But I have seen him when he wears a different expression. He is no coward—but he is perfectly aware of the fact that this—this Jack o' Lantern is a menace to his life. And you know it too."

Wrench protested, but it was quite useless. She knew him too well to be hoodwinked by him.

"Why does Sweeting come here so often?" she asked. "It seems such a waste of time."

"Has he been here recently—I mean, since Wednesday?"

"Yes. He came yesterday afternoon, and asked if he might look over the house and garden again."

"Was the Judge here?"

"No."

"Curious! For the life of me I can't imagine what he expects to gain by it. Did you accompany him?"

"Oh, no. He made it fairly clear that he wished to be alone. Before he left he came and asked me a lot of questions about Nali, and my life in India. I don't think he meant to be rude, but he certainly was."

Wrench frowned. During the past week he had had a surfeit of the superintendent's arrogance and thinly veiled sneers. It looked as if Sweeting were doing all he could to goad him into losing control of himself. But it was highly regrettable that these petty jealousies should exist at all, at a time when they should be collaborating in a common cause.

It transpired that Sweeting's visits to the house were not entirely unproductive, and a bombshell was burst on Wrench that same evening. The Assistant Commissioner was indisposed and Sweeting was in charge—and completely in his element.

"Ah, Wrench," he said. "Any news of the woman—Kate?"

"None."

"Hm! I had another look over Acacia House yesterday."

"Really!"

"You seem surprised."

"Naturally."

"Why—naturally?"

"I can't see the connection."

"Then you are a little obtuse. Hasn't it occurred to you that it is a queer *ménage?*"

"In what way?"

"Well, you have the Judge—a very eminent personage, who lives alone with a ward and a Hindu."

"What is there strange in that?"

"We might accept the adoption business as more or less ordinary, but the Hindu——"

"The Hindu came at Miss Pelling's request. He was devoted to her father and to herself, and was in addition a most excellent servant. But what is the drift of all this?"

Sweeting smiled exasperatingly. That he was concealing something was perfectly obvious.

"Have you ever considered the possibility of a scapegoat?" asked Sweeting.

"A what?"

"A kind of red herring drawn across the trail. Seven years ago Judge Wallington's life was threatened. Well, nothing happened. Now we have a second threat—

following the conviction of a quite ordinary burglar. I submit that does not ring true—after a dead silence of seven years."

"But you saw the note!"

"I did. In fact I have it here—now."

"Well?"

"Suppose the threat to the Judge is not from Jack o' Lantern, but from someone who saw an excellent opportunity to use that old bogy—in case something tragic should suddenly happen to the Judge?"

Wrench shrugged his shoulders impatiently.

"You are getting out of your depth," he said.

"Am I? Am I, indeed?"

"I don't follow you. Do you mean that you suspect someone—someone in the Judge's house—of plotting his death, and using that man as a blind——? It is unreasonable—incredible."

"Not so incredible as you imagine. Here is the note that was delivered to him on the morning of the 'Slasher's' trial. It is a piece of brownish paper, torn roughly from a parent sheet. Do you agree?"

"Well—yes."

Sweeting's eyes gleamed as he opened a drawer and produced some folded paper of the same texture and colour.

"While you have been chasing phantoms I have had the good luck to find the sheet of paper—from which that ragged bit was torn. Look!"

He unfolded the sheet which he had taken from the drawer, and Wrench saw that it was a stout paper bag, of the type used by West End milliners for small feminine articles. While he stared at it, Sweeting placed the small severed portion in position. It filled the gap perfectly.

"What about that—eh?"

"Where did you find it?"

"At Acacia House—in a wardrobe in—Miss Pelling's bedroom. There were some articles inside it and——"

Wrench's face grew crimson with resentment.

"You—you went into her bedroom——"

"I did. It is my business to go anywhere that promises to produce a clue—and yours, too. This is no time for sentiment. Where does Jack o' Lantern come in now?"

"Where he always did. You forget that the writing was the same as that we found on the 'Slasher'——"

"I forget nothing. It is you who forget that in that house there existed a specimen of that same handwriting. It could be copied and——"

"Wait! At the time when that note was sent the first note was unidentified. Miss—Miss Pelling did not know of its existence, and even if she had she could not possibly have known it came from Jack o' Lantern. It is all wrong—muddled. An outrageous theory based on——"

"Based on this paper bag, eh?" Sweeting thrust his head forward. "I have yet to be convinced that she did not know, at that juncture, who sent that anonymous letter to the Judge. Did you ever show the 'Slasher' note to Wallington?"

"Yes."

"And you are sure Miss Pelling did not see it?"

"I am almost sure she did not."

"There I beg to differ. In what other way can you explain this paper bag? Do you suggest that Jack o' Lantern gained access to Miss Pelling's bedroom and tore this piece from the bag, then wrote his message, and calmly walked out?"

Wrench, shocked and bewildered, strode up and down. trying vainly to see through the fog.

"It's all theory," he said. "Wild, impossible theory. There is nothing to support it. She is devoted to the Judge—just as much as if she were really his daughter. He is ready to indulge her every whim. With what motive would she——"

"There, my dear Wrench, you are on unsafe ground. Wallington is reputed to be rich. He has a house full of valuable antiques, and no relations for whom he cares two pins. To whom do you think his estate would go in the event of any—misadventure?"

Wrench winced. His whole soul revolted at the theory that the superintendent was propounding. It was the maddest thing he had ever listened to, and yet to explain the note and its connection with the bag was very difficult. He left the office ultimately, with his heart heavy and his mind baffled. His sense of honour forbade him ever to mention Sweeting's suspicions to Sonia, or to any other living soul. It was a horrible situation.

CHAPTER SEVEN

SONIA was finding life a curiously mixed thing—with shadows and high-lights violently contrasted. Until comparatively recently her existence had been singularly free from any kind of depression or disappointment. Relieved from domestic cares by the capable and reliable Nali, who seemed to anticipate every requirement, she had plenty of time on her hands to indulge her tastes, and sufficient pocket-money to satisfy her quite modest needs. But now there was a rift in the lute. She imagined that John Wrench was lacking in his customary solicitude. His visits were less frequent, and even when they were made he displayed a noticeable air of constraint. She tried to ascribe his changed attitude to the friction which existed at the office, and to the fact that he seemed to have matched himself against a phantom.

And there was Superintendent Sweeting, prowling around like a sick dog, getting on everyone's nerves, and bringing on his own head the castigations of the Judge, who hated to have his home thus invaded.

"He seems to have taken matters clean out of John's hands," he remarked. "For what reason I cannot understand. John is on the right tack, and will succeed if Sweeting will only leave him to his own devices. What on earth does Sweeting expect to find in this house?"

"He is finding a good deal of animosity," said Sonia.

"Of course. I think I shall give him a gentle hint that I resent being disturbed—as he disturbs me. If he persists, I shall speak to the Commissioner."

"He may have his own reasons," put in Michels quietly.

"Indubitably, but it does not alter the fact that he is an unmitigated nuisance. What time do you make it, Michels?"

"Nearly half-past ten."

"Then I must hurry, as I have to be in court at eleven o'clock. Sonia, will you tell Nali to phone for the car?"

She nodded and went out.

"Have you never considered running a car of your own?" asked Michels.

"No. In that respect I am hopelessly old-fashioned. I prefer to walk when the weather is suitable, or take a bus. When I need a car there is always one available at the excellent garage close by. Our modern life is being made a hell by machinery. I loathe the noise and smell of it. When I retire I shall move into the country—keep pigs and ride each morning before breakfast. In fact I am incurably Victorian—and proud of it."

Michels laughed, and looked out at the drenching rain. When the Judge had left, Sonia came into the room.

"Oh, I thought you had gone to the court with the Judge," she said.

"No, I am going to roam over the British Museum later—that marvellous store-house so shockingly neglected by you Londoners."

"Not guilty," she replied. "I am not a Londoner. I never saw London until the Judge brought me home from India. Before my father sent for me to join him I was at a school in the west of England." She switched off suddenly. "Mr. Michels, you have said very little about—about the events that are baffling the police, and in which the Judge seems to be mixed up. Is there something—something unusual in it?"

"What do you mean by that?"

"Wrench is so strange—he tells me nothing. Of course I don't expect him to divulge professional secrets, but somehow I feel that he is tremendously worried. And the superintendent—why does he come here so often?"

"I do not know. Perhaps he still hopes to find some clue that will lead to the identity of the man you saw that night."

"I don't think so. I believe—I believe he doubts my story. The last time he came he harked back to that, and there was a supercilious sneer on his lips. It was not fancy on my part. He made it too obvious."

Michels stirred uneasily. Then he suddenly put a question that startled her.

"Does Nali go out much—at nights?"

"Scarcely ever," she replied. "Of course he is free to take some evenings off, but he seldom does. He prefers to squat in his room and practise on his curious musical instrument. He has a means of muting it, and seldom creates any disturbance. But why do you ask that?"

"I was just wondering. He has a key to the door?"

"Y-yes. But you are keeping something from me."

"No—no. It was just a casual question. Won't you play the piano to enliven a particularly vile morning?"

His remark troubled her, but it was evident that he was not inclined to be more communicative, and she agreed to play for him. She selected a piece by Schumann from the "Phantastuke," and Michels literally drank it in, for he had all the German's love for his national classics.

"Exquisite!"

"I prefer Chopin," she said iconoclastically. "Though you may not forgive me. Perhaps it is because I am temperamentally romantic."

"Yes, it is all a matter of temperament."

"Here is a compromise," she said. "Something Eastern —and unique, arranged for the piano by yours very truly."

She commenced to play Nali's queer pipe-tune, with her own improvised accompaniment. Michels listened attentively, but shook his head slowly when she had finished.

"It is not for me," he admitted. "But I grant it is unique—and—what is the word?—haunting. Where did you find that?"

"In the Punjab. Nali sometimes plays it. He calls it 'The Hymn of the Soul.' It is a little bit sugary on the piano. One cannot get the same effect as Nali creates. I think he hates me for treating it so. At any rate he always sniffs in superior fashion when he finds me murdering it."

Michels left the house a little later and Sonia spent the rest of the morning attending to some overdue correspondence. But again and again her mind reverted to Michels' strange remark in reference to Nali. She

saw everywhere mystery and the brooding atmosphere
of impending evil.

*   *   *   *   *

Brooking's was termed by its proprietor a "dance
club," but most of its habitués knew it as something else.
It was situated over a hairdresser's shop off the Gray's
Inn Road, and usually started business when most other
places of entertainment were closed for the night. The
entrance was at the back, in a narrow alley that twisted
snakily through a maze of buildings, and comparatively
few people knew of its existence. Many of those who
did kept the knowledge to themselves, for Brooking's
had not been raided by the police.

On this particular night Brooking's was unusually gay,
for Sam Knudge was giving a party. A particularly
fortunate piece of "light-fingering" had resulted in considerable personal gain for Sam, and with rather remarkable perspicacity he had hit upon the idea of entertaining
a few friends, with the ulterior motive of patching up
things with the adorable Kate. Their little party com-
prised eight persons. There was himself, Kate and her
father, a literary hack fast on the road to ruin, and the
Denton crowd. The Dentons were two brothers and two
sisters, who had until quite recently run a roulette-wheel
farther West, but had managed to burn the table before
the police broke in and found a kind of prayer meeting
in progress.

The special table for eight was now littered with
glasses, bottles, and the remains of lobsters and what-
not, and was pushed into the corner to make room for
the dancers. A piano and a fiddle provided the necessary music. Kate's fit of the "blues" had vanished under
the influence of lots of "bubbly," and Sam was in the
fifth heaven of delight.

"Hey, Banting!" he cried. "Shake a leg! Make 'im dance, Gwen."

Gwen Denton, of the tousled hair, seized Banting and forced him into a jog-trot. Ned Denton had found a carmined-lipped beauty at the other end of the room, and was performing marvellous terpsichorean feats. Kate's eyes glowed as she went round with Sam, but not from the causes attributed by that worthy. She loved gaiety, music and champagne in moderation, but she was as far from loving Sam as he was from taking an interest in Greek. But she teased him, with all the artlessness of a worthy daughter of Eve, and Sam preened himself and dreamed wild dreams.

"Give us a kiss, Kate," he murmured.

"Don't be absurd."

"Why not? You're fond o' me, ain't you?"

"You can be very nice at times, but that's no reason why I should slobber over you in this place."

"Aw—who cares?"

"I do. Behave yourself!"

"Come and have a drop more fizz. Lumme, ain't it 'ot!"

"I've had enough."

"Just a little 'un—a weeny-teeny drop—big as a bee's knee."

She concurred to please him, and another bottle was opened. While they toasted him a waiter came to Banting to tell him that he was wanted on the telephone. He went out, and when he returned his face was grim.

"Who was it?" asked Kate.

"Lefroy."

Sam nearly choked, and Kate's eyes gleamed.

"What the 'ell did——?"

"He's been looking for us."

"Is 'e comin' 'ere?"

"Yes."

"Then he can't come in," snarled Sam. "I never invited 'im. I won't 'ave——"

"Don't be a fool," said Banting. "He's been here before. You can't stop him."

"Who is this joint—Lefroy?" asked Denton.

"He's——"

"Old Nick—that's wot I call 'im," interrupted Sam. "Gives me the willies." He sidled up to Kate. "Let's go to my lodgings and 'ave a quiet talk?" he whispered.

But Kate shook her head. She was thrilled against all her powers of resistance. This fatal love of hers— it *was* love, although she had not yet quite admitted it— was like a scorching wind. Her eyes were eloquent of her emotions, and Sam felt like murder when he witnessed the effect upon her.

When Jack o' Lantern arrived he was in his most vivacious mood. He jested with Sam, without any show of ill-feeling, took the Dentons by storm, drank what was left of the champagne, and flung money at the musicians. Dancing recommenced, and Sam was left to practise steps with one of the Denton sisters. Banting danced, too, but he kept his eyes on his daughter, and his mouth grew hard when he realised certain facts.

Again Kate was under the spell. When the music ceased her strange partner led her to a corner and began to talk to her with all his damnable eloquence. What did she think of life, of love, of adventure? He could tell her of wonderful places, where the sun always shone, and one grew drunk from the odour of flowers. And in the midst of rhapsodising on this earthly paradise he would break forth into bitter condemnation of certain people. The law was wrong—corrupted. There were judges, barristers, police officials rotten with bias. Injustice everywhere. There was Judge Wallington—his eye blazed at the mention of the name—the hanging judge, the cruel monster who extended no mercy. Well, one day—one day—— Then back again to idealism, his mind swinging like a pendulum.

Again they danced and came back to the corner seat, and all the time Sam was getting madder and madder. At last he could contain himself no longer. He went across to Kate and caught her by the arm.

"I'm engaged, Sam," she said angrily.

"I want a dance. You—you leave 'er alone," he snarled, shaking his fist at Jack o' Lantern. "Or, by Gawd, I'll——"

Jack o' Lantern stood up and approached the trembling form of Sam. The irate lover backed before that threatening form. With all his rage he lacked the courage to stand his ground. He retreated like a hypnotised rabbit—right down the room. The spectators gasped as Jack o' Lantern made a lightning movement and Sam ran clean through the open door. Jack o' Lantern went back to Kate.

"The louse has gone," he said.

"Why—why did you do that?"

"He opposes me—because of you. Is it possible you can lose your heart to trash like that?"

"No—no, but he is my friend."

"Not your—lover?"

"I have—no lover."

"Are you sure?"

She moved uneasily, and when he found her hand and held it she made no attempt to repulse him. But the observant Banting was alive to the situation. He came across and joined the pair, and instantly love-making was taboo.

"Better go off and find Sam," he said to Kate. "The drink has got into his head."

It was more of an order than a suggestion, and Kate obeyed. Banting turned to Jack o' Lantern with a serious face.

"Is it wise to chivvy Sam?" he asked. "It doesn't need much to send him clean crazy."

Jack o' Lantern laughed easily, but immediately his face changed and he looked vicious.

"A brainless rat!" he said.

"A useful rat, Lefroy."

"To you?"

"To all of us. Humour him—if you can. Now about that other business—at Sloane Square. Are we ever going to get on the job? We've wasted weeks. It must be done on a Thursday. Can we fix it for next Thursday?"

"Sloane Square! Sloane Square!" Jack o' Lantern pressed his hands to his forehead. "Yes, of course—we had planned that. But they got the 'Slasher' before—— The fool didn't take my advice——"

"You didn't turn up. You left it vague. We couldn't wait on that occasion. I had the narrowest squeak myself. Anyway, we've got to manage this time without the 'Slasher.' That's why it isn't policy to upset Sam. He's reliable at that sort of job. Will you make it Thursday next?"

"What a craving you have for money," mused his auditor. "Is hard cash all you care about, Banting?"

"Yes. It's necessary. There's Kate—I've got to think about her. I've got to lay up a nest-egg before that damned Wrench gets his claws into me, too. What's going to become of Kate if that should happen to me?"

"Kate! Ah, she's your problem, eh? Why not leave that to solve itself? Kate may find her happiness—in her own way."

Banting gritted his teeth and looked Jack o' Lantern straight in the eyes.

"No—not that way, Lefroy," he said tensely. "Flirt a little if you will, but, by God, I won't let it go any further. I won't have her hands stained——"

Jack o' Lantern leaned forward until his face was within a foot of Banting's. The eyes were full of fierce resentment at the innuendo, and the mouth was like a slit.

"Stained! What are you saying?"

"I know," replied Banting bravely. "And what I know I keep to myself—— Sh! Here's Kate. Will you make it Thursday—ten o'clock at my place?"

Jack o' Lantern nodded as Kate came forward, and informed them that she could not find Sam. Dancing was resumed, but there was no more love-making. Jack o' Lantern seemed to have closed up like an oyster. Kate found herself shut out by a kind of icy barrier.

"You're strange," she complained. "So strange!"

He acted as if she did not exist, and shortly afterwards put on his long coat and hat and left the place without a word.

*   *   *   *   *

In the meantime Sam Knudge had been living in a miniature hell, born out of his soul-eating jealousy. Hatless he had wandered up and down the street, cursing the man who was fast robbing him of the woman he loved. He did not stop to reflect that Kate had given him little or no encouragement. All he saw was Jack o' Lantern— that tall, cadaverous, frightful figure standing across his path. He fingered an automatic pistol in his pocket and wished he had the courage to use it.

But at last he grew a little more composed, and realised that he was acting against his own interests in leaving

Kate with the other man. He thereupon wended his
way back to Brooking's. On entering the alley he was
almost knocked over by a person coming in the opposite
direction. Sam gasped as he recognised the form of his
inveterate enemy, but Jack o' Lantern never even turned
his head.

A bold idea entered Sam's mind, and it grew to a
flaming resolution in a few seconds. He followed the
tall form—at a safe distance, through unfrequented
streets that were ill-lighted and silent. At last he trailed
the sinister form to a passage that ended in a cul-de-sac.
Sam halted at the entrance and peered round the brick-
work. In the dim light of a gas-lamp he saw Jack o'
Lantern enter the second house on the left-hand side of
the court. He waited and then saw a light appear in
the window on the third floor. The name of the place
was painted on the wall—Watling Court.

He chuckled to himself. Not even Banting was possessed of this information. Hitherto Jack o' Lantern's
abode had been a complete mystery. He just came and
went like a spectre. Sam thought of Kate—Kate, who
was getting deeper and deeper into the toils. Then he
cudgelled his brains to remember where the nearest telephone was.

In a quarter of an hour he was calling Scotland Yard!

CHAPTER EIGHT

IT was John Wrench's turn for night duty, which he
always regarded as the bugbear of his profession. As
a uniformed constable he had nurtured the same dislike
for duty during those long, and sometimes torturesome
hours, when other folk slept. His was not a very
philosophic mind, and any long stretch of inactivity came

hard to him. There had been times, indeed, when his mind revolted at the irksome and thankless business of patrolling a "beat" upon which nothing unusual ever happened, and he had seriously considered taking up some other kind of career which offered a man freedom after night had fallen.

But he had survived the ordeal fairly well, and the worst he had to say about it was that it was an infernal nuisance. Night duty at the "Yard" had not the same soul-eating loneliness as a "beat" in a country town. The telephone was always busy, and on occasion important events took place.

On this evening he was more reflective than usual, for Sweeting's recent discovery troubled him greatly. For the superintendent's theory he had nothing but contempt, and his feelings would have been the same had he never met Judge Wallington's fascinating ward. That the threat to Wallington came from outside he was positive. The connecting links were too obvious to be overlooked. But his investigations at Salisbury carried him no farther. He had managed to get possession of a number of letters written by Luke Lantern, the brother of the notorious Tobias, and the handwriting bore no resemblance to that of the various notes. It looked as if further time spent in that direction would be wasted.

In the meantime Sweeting was concentrating upon the Wallington *ménage*, dismissing the Lantern connection as a mere subterfuge, and leaving his subordinate to pursue that elusive phantom. To Wrench it was mortifying to realise that Sonia was under suspicion—and it would have been amusing had he not had so deep an interest in her welfare. But the idea of Sonia plotting the death of the Judge, who literally worshipped her, and for whom he knew she had nothing but the deepest devotion, was so amazing that even now he had doubts whether Sweeting was in earnest.

Yet the incident of the paper bag still wanted explaining. True, there were the other occupants of the house, but in no single case could he find any reasonable motive. Sweeting had also hinted at Nali, but he placed Nali with Sonia—completely outside the ring of suspicion. It looked as if Sweeting had seized an opportunity to indulge his ridiculous jealousy by striking at the woman he (Wrench) loved.

At about half-past two in the morning a sergeant entered the office, and aroused Wrench from a brown study. He was wet and covered with mud, and there was a long scratch down his left cheek, which he dabbed with a pocket handkerchief. Wrench grinned at him.

"Domestic trouble, Mitchell?"

"Not much. We've got that Grove Lane woman. She'd got the stuff hidden under some steps in Penn Street. Hopkins found it this afternoon, and we've been watching it for eight solid hours from the pickle factory opposite. Well, she came for it after midnight, and we nobbled her. It's a good job there were two of us. She's thirteen stone, and has a punch like a prize-fighter, what's more, she was drunk. . . . Had a kind of reaction just now and is blubbering. . . . Appears her old man has run off with another woman, and she wants to make a statement about him, but she wouldn't give it to me."

"H'm! If we can rope in Charlie, so much the better. I'll go and see her."

His visit to the wild woman of Grove Lane was not altogether unfruitful. She was full of venomous hate for her unfaithful spouse, and under the influence of drink, and the quelling effects of the cell, she said a lot that she would doubtless regret when she became sober.

"And I bin his faithful wife for fifteen years, Inspector," she concluded. "But I'll learn him to run off with that ginger-haired——"

When Wrench reached the office he found Mitchell in a state of suppressed excitement. He was hanging up the telephone receiver, and had a message written on a piece of paper beside him.

"For you, Inspector," he said. "Is it a fake?"

Wrench took up the message and read it aloud.

If you want Jack o' Lantern you will find him in the second house on the left-hand side of Watling Court—second floor.

He turned to Mitchell. "Wouldn't he give a name?"

"No—nothing more than that."

"Where is Watling Court?"

"Back of Bloomsbury. I asked him if that was the place, and he said it was."

"Good! I am going down there. Who is there available—two men?"

"Russell and Grainger."

"Warn them. We'll need a conveyance. It may be a fake, but on the other hand there may be something in it."

In a very short time Wrench and his assistants were at Watling Court. Russell was posted at the entrance to the house, and the remaining officer and Wrench went upstairs. They halted outside the door on the second floor, and Wrench searched for a name-plate or card. But he found nothing. He gave two resounding knocks with the heavy brass knocker and waited. There was no response of any kind. He put his weight against the door, and found it a very solid obstacle.

"H'm! We had better make a few inquiries," he said.

"Stand by while I try the occupant of the downstairs apartment."

Here he had better luck. The door was at length opened and a sleepy-eyed man blinked at him like an owl from inside an enormous dressing-gown. The blinking stopped when Wrench announced that he was a police officer and a look of astonishment passed over the Semetic face.

"Vot you vant?"

"I want some information about the apartment upstairs. Do you know the occupier?"

Isaac Garstein scratched his head. A Mr. Cartwright had lived there until six months ago, but he believed Cartwright had gone abroad and had let the place furnished to someone.

"You don't know the name?"

"No."

"Have you ever seen anyone enter the place—recently?"

He had not, but he had heard sounds from up above—not very loud noises—and only on rare occasions.

"Did you hear any noise to-night—a little while ago?"

"No. I have been asleep since eleven o'clock."

Wrench questioned him on a number of points, but got no nearer to the solution of the mystery. Ultimately he went to the top floor and rang up the occupant there. It was an elderly woman, living with her daughter, and she corroborated Garstein's information. She had known Mr. Cartwright quite well, and he had told her that he had sub-let his apartment for twelve months, but had mentioned no name. Cartwright had had to go to New Zealand on business and hoped to return in July. Once she had met a man coming up the stairs, and suspected that he was the new tenant of No. 2—but it was dark and she was quite unable to describe him.

It was evident that the mysterious tenant had done his business direct with Cartwright, and as that gentleman was some twelve thousand miles distant the chance of securing any further particulars seemed somewhat remote. He went down to the second floor again.

"Not much luck," he confessed. "It's quite difficult to form any opinion. There is a tenant and he certainly seems to be a queer sort of customer."

"Are we going to enter, sir?"

Wrench hesitated, and then resolved to take the risk. Russell was brought up from below, and after some little delay the door was forced. Inside was an electric-light switch, and the illumination it supplied revealed a short passage leading to a fairly large sitting-room. To the right of the sitting-room was a bedroom, but the bed had not been slept in for some time, for the blankets were piled upon it, and were both dusty and damp. There was a wardrobe facing the window, and inside it were sundry articles of male attire. They seemed to belong to a man of fairly tall stature, but they were of no value as clues, for there was no mark of any kind upon them.

The sitting-room was more interesting. It contained a lot of old furniture and knick-knacks—a book-case half-filled with books, and a writing-table. There was an open fire, and the grate contained some burnt wood and ashes. On the top of these was a mass of burnt paper. Wrench felt this.

"Warm!" he muttered. "So someone *has* been here within the last half-hour. It would be interesting to know what these burnt papers contained."

"Here's a drinking glass," said Grainger.

"Don't touch it!"

Wrench examined the glass and sighed with disappointment when it failed to reveal a finger-print, for such a discovery might have been of the highest importance.

In the drawer under the writing-table there were pens and pencils, a paper-weight and a number of other small articles; but nowhere did there appear to be a scrap of handwriting. Wrench was mildly disappointed.

"It doesn't get us much farther," he admitted. "There is absolutely nothing here to prove that the man we want frequents this place. Move that settee!"

Grainger pushed back the heavy piece of furniture, and a cry of delight came from Wrench. The gilt handle of a knife was protruding from under the bottom of the loose cretonne cover of the settee. He picked it up. It was an Oriental dagger—about eight inches long, with a crinkly blade on which was engraved some curious characters.

"Chinese?"

"No—Indian. This is Hindustani."

"Things are looking up."

"They certainly are. I happened to see some old potatoes in a basket under the sink in the kitchen. Bring me the largest of them."

Grainger seemed a little mystified at this curious request, but he did as he was bid, and brought a huge potato to Wrench. Wrench thrust the point of the dagger into it, and pushed home the blade. When he withdrew it the potato bore a puncture in the form of an S. Then Grainger understood.

"Sir Randolph Cantler!"

"And the others too. Their wounds were exactly similar. This is a lucky find."

"There may be something else." Grainger lifted the end of the cover and searched beneath the settee, but it concealed no other article.

Wrench gazed at the dagger reflectively. Was it merely a coincidence that it was Indian? Sweeting had mentioned the possibility of Nali being implicated in the business, as well as Sonia, but even he with all his hasty theorising had never gone so far as to connect Nali with the Jack o' Lantern crimes. No, it was a mere coincidence. An Indian dagger was no unique weapon in London. Such a deduction was decidedly premature. But what was significant was the fact that this dagger was undoubtedly of similar design to the weapon used by Jack o' Lantern on several occasions, and that it had been found on premises reputed by an unknown informant to be frequented by the murderer in question.

"It makes our action justified," he said. "I want this place watched. You had better take duty to-night, and Russell can relieve you to-morrow. Get acquainted with the occupants of the other apartments, and arrest any person who comes to this flat. The postman may be helpful."

Sweeting displayed great interest in the discovery. To a certain extent it backed up his theory—in his opinion. But Wrench remained sceptical.

"If your suspicions were proved," he argued, "it would make the Hindu the murderer of Cantler and the rest of them—or, at least it would give us good grounds for postulating that. It won't work."

"And why not?"

"The complete absence of motive. You may argue that Miss Pelling would benefit by the Judge's death, but that does not apply to the Hindu."

"How do you know? We assume that Miss Pelling is heiress to Wallington's estate, isn't it feasible that the Hindu is remembered in the will? Those two came to England together—and the Hindu came at the girl's request. Why should they not be acting in concert? I will hedge a little—assume that the Hindu exercises an influence over the girl. He is a queer character—with a hypnotic eye and——"

"God! How you ramp on!" ejaculated Wrench. "Don't you see that you are not only shifting your ground, but confusing the issue? Your first theory was that Nali, or Miss Pelling, used Jack o' Lantern as a blind—a scapegoat. Now you calmly suggest that Nali is actually Jack o' Lantern—that he murdered Cantler and several other persons——"

"Someone murdered Cantler, didn't they?"

"Yes—someone with a motive—someone who had cause to hate him. You are suggesting that Nali is plotting the death of his master for personal gain, and yet he leaves one victim with a wallet full of money and other articles of value on his person. That is a little inconsistent."

"We must explore every likely avenue."

"That is not exploration. It is the last word in premature conclusion. I am convinced that there *is* a Jack o' Lantern, and that his crimes are closely connected with the trial and conviction of Tobias Lantern; that the Hindu is a devoted servant of the Judge and knows no more about these crimes, or about the threat to the Judge, than I do. As for Miss Pelling, if you knew her as well——"

"As you do," added Sweeting. "That is just the trouble, my dear Wrench. Love is apt to blind one to facts. I think it is rather regrettable that you were selected to deal with this business, and it might be advisable and discreet to switch you——"

Wrench's gorge rose, and it required all his will-power to prevent him from telling Sweeting that he was an idiot. At the same time he suspected that Sweeting was not the fool he appeared to be, and that he was merely having a dig at the man of whose meteoric career he was incurably jealous. He walked out of the office amazed that any man could be so intractable, and so hopelessly prejudiced.

CHAPTER NINE

WRENCH'S watch on the house in Watling Court produced no immediate result. The days slipped by and there was no visitor to the apartment on the second floor. Neither the postman nor the tradespeople who called knew anything of the present occupant. Each day the detectives' reports were the same, and it certainly looked as if the bird had flown. Wrench was obliged to relax his efforts to some extent. In the meantime the Chief had returned to duty, and Sweeting was free to meddle again. He came to see the Judge one afternoon, and was received with anything but cordiality, for Wallington was not feeling well, and wished to see no one.

"It is a matter of some importance," said Sweeting. "You are aware that we received a mysterious communication some days ago, alleging that the man we want was at a certain house?"

"I did not know."

"Wrench did not tell——"

"Wrench does not gossip with the freedom you evidently imagine," replied Wallington. "But why do you tell me this?"

"It has some bearing. The place was found empty, and it looks as if, by some means, the fellow was warned. But an important discovery was made. A weapon was found which bears a remarkable resemblance to the instrument habitually used by Jack o' Lantern. I have brought it with me."

He thereupon produced the Indian dagger and handed

it to the Judge. Wallington adjusted his pince-nez and examined the thing closely. His brow became wrinkled as he fingered the ornate handle.

"Curious!" he said. "Am I to understand this was found in a house in Watling Court?"

"Yes."

"It is a strange coincidence that we have an absolute replica in this house. Will you push the bell—there?"

In response to the summons Nali came. Sweeting watched him like a lynx, and thought he saw a flash of the black eyes towards the dagger long before he was close to it. But when he stopped before the Judge and bowed his face was as immobile as ever.

"We have a dagger like this, Nali—have we not?"

The Hindu glanced at the thing and then shook his head slowly.

"Nali does not remember such, *sahib*."

"Tch! I have seen it many times. It used to be at the end of the hall—on the wall under the big picture."

"Surely the *sahib* is mistaken. There is an old pistol——"

"Go and look!"

Nali went out and the Judge pursed his lips.

"I could not be mistaken," he mused. "I have a good memory for knick-knacks—it is my hobby. I think it was my ward who brought it back with a lot of other souvenirs. As a matter of fact the dagger had a history. It helped to hang a man who made too liberal use of it. Miss Pelling's father was the District Commissioner and——"

Nali reappeared with empty hands.

"Well?"

"There is nothing but an ancient pistol under the big picture, *sahib*."

The Judge frowned, for he hated to have it thought

that his memory was at fault. He told the Hindu to find Sonia.

"If I am wrong I will consult my doctor," he said to Sweeting with a smile. "A judge with a defective memory is no good to the country."

"You are not looking too well, if you will pardon me saying so," said Sweeting solicitously.

"Tired, that's all. I have had a very full week. Ah, Sonia! My memory has been challenged, and you shall be referee. Did we or did we not possess a dagger exactly like this?"

Sonia gave but a glance at the weapon.

"Why, it *is* ours," she said. "Where did you get it?"

"You are sure?"

"Positive. But it has been missing for years."

"How many years?" put in Sweeting eagerly.

"Practically since I came to England—seven years ago. It used to hang in the hall, and I suddenly missed it."

"You did not tell me," said the Judge.

"Didn't I? Well, I remember asking Nali if he had removed it for any reason."

"And of course he had not?" said Sweeting.

"No. Why should he? Where did it spring from?"

"It was found in rather curious circumstances," said Sweeting. "At any rate the Judge's reputation is saved, as I ought to have known it would be."

His laugh did not disabuse Sonia's mind. She saw from the Judge's face that some matter of importance was involved.

"That is all, Sonia, thank you," he said. "I was right and the superintendent was wrong."

It was an unspoken request for her to leave them together, and she went out in deep reflection. The Judge turned to Sweeting.

"This is very strange. What was this dagger doing in that house?"

"There is something more vital in it than that, Judge. We have grounds for believing that Sir Randolph Cantler was stabbed to death with this very weapon—also others. If we can discover who took it from this house we shall be very close to the murderer—to Jack o' Lantern."

The Judge looked very grim. This revelation had taken him completely by surprise. He could not see the connection.

"Have you any theory?" he asked.

"Will you forgive me if I introduce an entirely personal matter?"

"Go on!"

"I presume you have made a will?"

"Naturally."

"Are there any servants in this house who would become beneficiaries under that will?"

"All of them who happen to be in my service at the time of my death. But none of them are aware of it, and the obvious inference does not hold. Even so I fail utterly to see what it has to do with the removal of this dagger. You are not going to suggest that I am actually harbouring this mysterious person known as Jack o' Lantern?"

"I am going to suggest that someone in this house is closely connected with that assassin. Wait! The evidence establishes that fact. It does not rest entirely on the question of the dagger. There is an equally strong link. I have the means of proving that the note which threatened you—the last one—was written on paper found in this house."

"What!"

"It is true—beyond doubting."

"But it is incredible—fantastic! The maid is a raw

country lass, and the cook has been with me for twenty years. As for Nali—he is beyond——"

"Are you sure?"

"Tut! It is all wrong. There is a serious flaw somewhere."

"I admit there are several inconsistencies, but take the salient points. How can we explain the removal of the dagger and the sending of the note from this house except on the assumption that some member of the household is working with Jack o' Lantern? Why did the Hindu profess ignorance of the existence of the dagger, when your ward assures us that she mentioned the loss to him? Someone is certainly guilty of prevarication."

The Judge concurred and was evidently at his wits' end to explain these strange occurrences, but, as with Wrench, his mind revolted at Sweeting's theory. Like a wise man he deferred judgment on the matter. When Wrench called on the following day he was told that Wallington wished to see him, and went into the library where the Judge was closeted with Michels.

"Ah, John! I had a visit from your esteemed senior officer yesterday. I suppose you know his mind?"

"I am not sure that he knows it himself," replied Wrench. "I presume he told you about our latest discovery?"

"Yes. What do you make of it?"

"Frankly, I don't know what to think. He was positively gloating last night when he had substantiated the fact that the dagger was once in this house. I take it you have never suffered a burglary?"

"No."

"Then the matter remains a complete mystery."

"He suspects Nali."

"Only Nali?"

"The maid and the cook as well in smaller degree. Of course it is possible that one of them has got entangled with the real murderer, but highly improbable. The cook is a respectable widow and the maid has a sweetheart in Devon."

"Have they both been with you since Sonia came to England?"

"Yes."

Wrench stroked his chin reflectively, and then shook his head.

"Nothing fits in."

"Exactly. But it is all very disturbing. You have learnt nothing fresh from that house which you are watching?"

"Nothing."

"A blank wall, eh?"

"Yes—at the moment. But I am going on a new tack. Sweeting is welcome to his theories, but I am convinced the solution of this mystery lies elsewhere."

Michels displayed no desire to take part in the conversation, but he was very alert and missed nothing. Before he left the premises Wrench took the opportunity to have a word with Sonia, whom he had not seen for several days. She seemed rather pale and agitated, and her welcome was a little colder than usual.

"I thought you had entirely deserted me," she said.

"What nonsense! I have had a gruelling time with no compensating reward."

"I know you have changed a great deal, John."

"That is not true—only apparent. I have never been so worried as of late."

"Sweeting again?"

"He contributes his quota. But it isn't only he. I am up against a whole forest of obstacles, and clues which promise to shed light only lead deeper into the wood."

"That dagger, for instance?"

"That—and other things. Yet I am optimistic enough to believe that before long everything will be explained."

"I wish it could. I—I feel that I, too, am caught up in a web of intrigue from which there is no escape. The house seems sombre and full of evil."

"You must not let your imagination run riot."

"But it is true. There is something going on here—something sinister—horrible."

"You are getting unnerved. It is my fault—I have left you too much alone. Sonia, give me a day or two to carry out certain investigations and then we will seek a little gaiety. In the meantime don't pay too much attention to anything you may hear. Sweeting is quite capable of raising all kinds of bogies."

"I wish I could think they were merely bogies."

"What do you mean?"

"I—I can't explain—quite."

He laughed to dispel her obvious gloom, and kissed her ere he left. It was then she realised he had not shaved for a couple of days at least, which was rather remarkable for a man usually so careful of his toilet—and appearance.

CHAPTER TEN

DURING the next few days Wrench visited various clubs and rendezvous of ill-repute, mingling with crooks, ticket-of-leave men, suspects and what not, in the hope of overhearing something that would shed some light on the Jack o' Lantern mystery. He was an artist at make-up, and few of his intimate acquaintances would have recognised him had they met him in the haunts of the damned. He shunned disguises of the spectacular type, and was

content to pose as a common type of racing man, with a
cocksure attitude and blatant apparel. Well acquainted
with men of this type, it would have taxed the wits of
a super Sherlock Holmes to have labelled him as anything else.

He smoked and drank with women whose ways of life
were certainly open to suspicion—even made love to
them in a mild way. On several occasions he accepted
bets and did quite well out of them. But never a word
did he hear about Jack o' Lantern. It was evident that
that name was not bandied about. In this underworld
of crime the notorious murderer kept his secrets well.
But one night luck served him better. He was in a
night club known as "The Pigeon" when he saw two
familiar faces. One was that of Phil Denton, and the
other his sister—Gwen. Wrench knew them as the late
proprietors of a roulette club, but he doubted very much
if either of them would recognise him even had he taken
no pains to obliterate his natural characteristics. He
drifted across to the table occupied by the Dentons.

"Hallo, Denton!"

Philip Denton looked up.

"You don't remember me, eh?"

"Can't say I do."

"Then your memory is rotten. You had enough of
my dough at that place in Paul Street. How's the old
wheel going? I haven't had a flutter for three months."

"It doesn't go," growled Denton. "Some damned fool
gave us away. But I'm hanged if I can place you."

"Oh, I came in with Langley. And that reminds me,
I want to see Langley—about a matter of business. I
went to his old digs but the place was closed up. Has
he moved?"

"Moved? Oh yes, he's moved all right. He's taking
a little rest cure at Princetown."

Wrench whistled and pushed his billycock hat on the side of his head.

"You don't mean they got Langley?"

"They did. But you ought to know that."

Wrench grimaced.

"I had to clear out—for a bit. If I hadn't I might be where Langley is. Gosh, but he was a smart lad. Here, let's have a drink! What is it?"

Denton was quite agreeable, for he was on the rocks. Wrench extended the invitation to Gwen, who accepted with avidity.

"I remember you," she said, with a desire to please. "Phil's memory has got holes in it."

In a few minutes any doubts which Denton might have had were completely dispelled, for Wrench knew the history of many queer cases, in some of which associates of the Dentons had figured. It was obvious to him that the Dentons were on the rocks, and he played up to this.

"Would you like a sure thing for to-morrow?" he said. "I'm laying off a bit on Black Badger. It's the only thing I'm afraid of. You ought to get fives. It's a cert."

Denton hadn't the hard cash.

"Leave it," suggested Wrench. "I'm not hard up for a pound or two. In any case you won't have to pay. Shall I shove on a quid for you?"

"Well, if it's like that——"

Wrench nodded and took out his book.

"Come here to-morrow," he said. "Same time, and if I don't hand you a fiver call me a jinny."

Black Badger did not win, so Wrench promptly shifted the bet in his imagination to the winner of the race, and went along to "The Pigeon" in the hope that Denton would turn up, despite his apparent loss. He was duly rewarded at shortly after eleven o'clock.

"Some tipster you are!" said Denton.

Wrench laughed and sat down by the disconsolate man.

"I'm not so green as I look," he said. "I got a wire from the course half an hour before the race and shifted the bet to Son o' Mine. What about that?"

"Son o' Mine! Why, it won!"

"You bet it did—at seven to two. That makes three pounds ten shillings. Better than a kick in the neck, what?"

Denton was overjoyed. He collected his "winnings" and promptly ordered drinks—doubles.

"Why didn't you let me in?" complained Gwen. "What have I done to be left out in the cold?"

They pacified her by giving her a very large port, and very soon they were all pals together.

"So you're making a book?" asked Denton.

"Aye. But how are things with you?"

"Rotten! The damned tecs have got us taped. Can't move for the blighters. This is a fine sort of country, where a fellow can't run a game without the police barging in. Anyway we were a bit too fly for them."

"Pity!" mused Wrench. "I enjoyed those little punts. There was a woman used to come—girl called Kate— Kate something. She knew Langley——"

Denton reflected and shook his head.

"Can't remember any Kate at that place."

"Well, Langley used to call her that," persisted Wrench.

"Banting's girl—perhaps," put in Gwen.

"No. Kate Banting never came to those do's."

"Banting!" mused Wrench. "I believe the name was Banting—or something like it."

"I don't ever remember Kate coming to Paul Street," insisted Denton. "It's a bit of a job to drag old Banting into the open. Queer sort of bird."

"Crazy on his daughter," said Gwen to Wrench. "Maybe you met her somewhere else. Was she fairly tall, blue eyes, and red hair—auburn, I ought to say?"

"Yes," lied Wrench.

"Good-looking kid," said Denton. "But temperamental—takes after the old man. Wonder if she'll ever fall to Sam Knudge?"

"Sam Knudge!" scoffed Gwen. "Why, he hasn't had a look in since Lefroy came on the scene. There'll be murder done one of these days if Lefroy doesn't look out for himself."

"Who is Lefroy?" asked Wrench.

"God knows," said Denton. "I've only set eyes on him twice. Gosh, that man can freeze the marrow in your bones. He's the brain behind the Banting outfit, if I'm any judge. You can't tell what he is going to do next. At one minute he's drinking and dancing and playing the fool—then some little thing will upset him and he goes right off the deep end. Got a kink, I'm thinking. Not the sort of man to get too friendly with."

"And Kate is in love with him—you think?"

"Well, she hob-nobs with him, with Banting prowling round to prevent any mischief."

"Doesn't he approve?"

"Not much. I'm thinking he'd rather have Knudge for a son-in-law, with all his chuckle-headedness. But it's doubtful whether Kate sees it in that light. She's fascinated, and gets the blues when Lefroy is not about."

Wrench missed not a word, and he considered his money well spent. Immediately he had set eyes on Denton he was of the opinion that Denton might be able to help him, for the ex-gaming-room keeper was the trusted associate of scoundrels of all types, and had figured in many shady transactions. So far he had successfully wriggled through the police net, though on several occasions he had been fined heavily for keeping a disorderly establishment.

The triangular love affair mentioned by Denton gave Wrench a gleam of hope. That would account for the telephone message with reference to the abode of Jack o' Lantern—if Jack o' Lantern was Lefroy. What better motive for squealing than jealousy? The next step was to locate Knudge or Kate Banting—Knudge for preference, since he had cause to desire the removal of Jack o' Lantern from the field of romance. So drink flowed freely, and Denton became very confidential—also slightly incoherent. Wrench was discreet enough to avoid putting direct questions. It was to a large extent a waiting game.

He danced with Gwen later in the evening, and encouraged her to flirt with him, at which game she was a past-mistress. The port had gone to her head, and gave birth to amorous impulses, which Wrench had some difficulty in playing up to, but his zest to get on the trail of Jack o' Lantern was so keen he would seriously have considered marrying her had the necessity arisen.

"You can dance like a pro," she said. "It isn't often I get a chance. Phil hates it. Why don't you come to Brooking's on Tuesday next?"

Wrench had heard of the place, although he had never had occasion to go inside it.

"What's on?" he asked.

"Special night—tripe supper and music. Five bob—all in. Phil can't come—but I can."

"Who'll be there?"

"A whole crowd of people I know. Philton, Rogers and probably Banting—the man we were mentioning."

She gave him a sly glance. "Maybe he'll bring Kate—the girl you fancy."

"Who said——?"

"Aw—I know. You can't kid me. Anyway she's safe from you, what with Sam Knudge and Lefroy. Lord! I hope those two don't turn up together."

"I might fix it," he demurred.

"Do. There's a sport. Meet me at the Russell Hotel at nine o'clock. Will you?"

"Yes."

She kissed him on the cheek, and he winced as he thought of Sonia. But it was all in a day's work, and duty came even before personal interests.

"By the way—what's your name?" she asked.

He handed her a card (one of many spurious ones).

"Henry Simmons, Commission Agent," she read. "Good! Hen, we are going to have a dam' good time together."

He left soon after midnight, quite pleased with his progress. His plan was to identify the Bantings, Knudge, and, if possible, Lefroy, raid Brooking's and arrest them. It might all end in smoke, but there was always a chance that something of value might emerge. And he was intensely interested in Lefroy!

At the top of Kingsway a gigantic surprise was in store for him. He was about to enter the Tube station when he saw a miserable creature selling the last edition of an evening newspaper. He turned with a view to buying a copy, and saw a taxi pull up behind an omnibus. The bright light from the portico of the station clearly illuminated the interior of the taxi. He saw—as clearly as in daylight—the unmistakable features of Sonia, leaning slightly forward and peering through the window. While he stared in speechless amazement the taxi moved on!

CHAPTER ELEVEN

On the following evening Wrench carried out his promise to Sonia, and they spent a few hours together. He noticed at once that she was not her usual self, and it was difficult to arouse in her any enthusiasm for anything. He had hoped she would volunteer some information concerning her strange movements of the preceding night, but she made no reference to it. It was bewildering—mystifying. For the first time since their engagement he was finding himself locked out, and the thought was by no means pleasant. He even went as far as to put a leading question.

"You look a little tired, Sonia. Late nights?"

"No. I'm—quite all right. But what have you been doing with yourself?"

"Attempting to solve the ever present problem."

"Does that mean you have got no further?"

"I am not sure. It may transpire that I have succeeded in getting a little closer to Jack o' Lantern, but it is yet too soon to draw such an optimistic conclusion. So Michels is still staying with you?"

"Yes. He was going to leave, but the Judge begged him to stay a little longer. He is the one man who does not bore 'Bunty' to death."

"Common interests, I suppose?"

"Yes. The Judge will miss his bout of chess when Michels goes."

"He's rather queer—isn't he?"

"Michels?"

"Yes—secretive. One never knows what he is thinking. He is obviously interested in the Jack o' Lantern mystery, but he seldom expresses any opinion."

"It is not lack of enthusiasm. With German thoroughness he hates to jump to premature conclusions."

"I wish Sweeting would take a few lessons from him. Sweeting is full of idiotic theories."

"What is the latest?"

"He has an idea that—that the threat to the Judge does not come from Jack o' Lantern, but from someone who is using that villain as a scapegoat."

She seemed to tremble slightly.

"You don't believe that, John?"

"No. Do you?"

"Oh, it is impossible. But one thing is certain—this strange business is upsetting the Judge. He was not able to go to the court to-day."

"I didn't know that."

"He will not be pleased at my telling you. There is nothing he hates so much as sickness—in himself, and inability to carry out his duties."

"But he is not really ill?"

"He says he is merely—tired, but I am worried about him. He has tremendous will-power, and would not have kept his bed had he not been unusually weak. Despite his protests I rang up Sir Henry Fuller just before you came. At any rate it will do no harm, and—and I don't like the look of him."

Sir Henry, who was Wallington's medical adviser, called half an hour later. He was a cheery individual and a man of the highest reputation professionally. Sonia knew him quite well, but to Wrench he was but a familiar name.

"And what has the Judge been doing to himself now?" he inquired of Sonia.

"He seems listless—exhausted even. But he'll be very annoyed when he sees you."

"So you have disobeyed instructions?"

"I had to. He has eaten nothing all day, and I am sure he has a temperature, but he will not let me take it."

"The stubborn man! Well, we will soon attend to that."

He went upstairs, and Nali escorted him to Wallington's room. The Judge stared hard at him as he entered.

"What now?" said Sir Henry. "How dare you forbid me to earn an honest fee?"

The Judge smiled wanly, but he was not in a state to protest. Sir Henry examined him, and pursed his lips.

"What have you been doing to yourself?"

"Overworking—worrying a bit. I've had a whole series of complex cases. I'm knocked out—that's all."

"You are indeed!"

Sir Henry stayed with the patient for some time, and while he was there Sweeting called. Wrench bit his lip when Nali came to announce the fact.

"Ask him into the library Nali," said Sonia.

"What the devil does *he* want?" mused Wrench impatiently. "Why does he take a delight in haunting this house?"

"I wish I knew. I suppose I had better go to him."

"No—leave him there," begged Wrench. "Michels is there, and can talk to him. I suppose his real object was to disturb me. He knew I was coming here."

"Isn't it a pity that you two hate each other?"

"You are wrong. The hate is all on the one side. But he simply won't work with me peacefully. We clash consistently—at every point. I feel that nothing would annoy him more than for me to lay hands on Jack o' Lantern—but that is what I mean to do, and before very long too."

"I wish it could be to-morrow," she said. "That monster seems to rule our lives. He—he has even come between you and me."

"Sonia!"

"Yes, he has. I can't explain—it is just feeling—and sometimes feeling is nearer the truth than logic. Here we are—together, but isn't there something between us —something like a cold breath that——?"

He caught her and held her close.

"No. Banish that thought. There is much to be explained, but time will let in the light. Sonia, this is a queer business, and I want you to trust me. Can I be assured of that?"

"What do you mean?"

"Only that—that I want your absolute confidence."

"You—you have that," she said huskily.

But he knew he had not. Again she had failed to take the opening he offered. Why? Why? Was it usual for her to be out alone in a taxi after midnight? The thing was trivial enough in itself, and there might have been a half dozen good reasons, but the fact that she gave none, when she must have been conscious of his hints, troubled him greatly.

Michels had been interrupted by Sweeting's call, but he did not appear to be displeased. Sweeting grinned at him, and sat down near the fire.

"Don't mind me," he begged. "I presume my delightful and ingenious confrère is engaged in strictly private business in the other room?"

"Why not? Life is not all work."

"True. I understand that the Judge is indisposed?"

"That is so."

"H'm. And the doctor is here?"

"Well—yes."

"I should like to have a word with him before he leaves. The servant will tell him."

"You suspect that the Judge's indisposition may not be the trivial thing it appears to be on the surface?"

"I should like to believe it was."

"You would like to believe it was *not*. I do not blame you. We cherish our theories."

"Well, up to a point you are right. Wrench and I are on different tracks. We converge now and again, but not for long. There is overlapping of a kind. He is after Jack o' Lantern—I am after the person who threatens the Judge's life."

"You think they are not identical?"

"I have grave doubts."

A few minutes later Sir Henry was shown into the library. He had already been introduced to Michels by the Judge, and now Michels made him acquainted with the superintendent.

"I think you wished to see me, Superintendent?" he said.

"Yes."

"If you would prefer—" commenced Michels.

"No. Please stay. You have a great interest in this business, and are the Judge's best friend. Doctor, what is the matter with your patient?"

"I don't know."

"You mean that?"

"Well—I have doubts."

"That is more to the point. His condition, I take it, is rather peculiar?"

"Unusual—for him."

"Would you agree that the symptoms are such as might indicate poisoning?"

"Well—yes."

Sweeting's eyes gleamed. He had been wanting to hear that. The theory held.

"Naturally you are in a dilemma?"

"It is difficult to account for. But of course I may

be mistaken. The same symptoms might arise from other causes."

"But they do not," said Sweeting emphatically. "I cannot express the same surprise as yourself, Sir Henry, for I have been expecting something like this for some time."

"Am I to infer that you suspect——?"

"I have every reason to believe that a person—or certain persons—have designs upon the life of the Judge."

Sir Henry tapped his hand with the end of his forefinger, while Michels sat with furrowed brows.

"This is a very serious matter," said Sir Henry.

"It is. I will admit that I did not anticipate the means apparently adopted. The plan has been changed."

"Might there not be another solution?" asked Michels.

Sweeting swung round as if he did not welcome any theory that clashed with his own.

"What?" he asked.

"Drugs. The Judge has been overworking himself. His nerves have not been too good of late. He might, in order to induce sleep, have recourse to drugs."

"I asked him that," said Sir Henry. "But he assures me that it is not so, and knowing him as I do, it is the last thing that I should expect."

"Quite," put in Sweeting. "There are certain facts connected with this business that it is impossible to overlook. Personally I am convinced there has been an attempt at poisoning." He addressed himself to Michels. "Was he well yesterday?"

"No. I remarked upon his tired appearance, and refused to play my usual game of chess with him. He did not look up to it. He retired early."

"Did he see anyone between leaving you and going to bed?"

"Only the valet—Nali. It is Wallington's custom to take what he calls a 'nightcap' before sleeping—a glass of hot whisky. I heard him tell Nali to bring it to his room."

"That is a regular habit?"

"Oh, yes. He usually has it here."

"H'm!"

Sir Henry suggested sending a nurse, but Sweeting hoped this would not be necessary. The presence of a nurse, he pointed out, might prevent a repetition of the poisoning. He had a plan in his head, and wished to put it into operation.

Ultimately the worried doctor left the room, but he ran into Sonia in the hall. He put on his habitual cheery smile as he met her questioning eyes.

"Nervous breakdown," he said. "A few days will see him right again. I have given the valet a prescription—for a tonic. The Judge should have a dose to-night."

"I will see that he does. You are sure it is nothing serious?"

"Nothing to worry about."

"I'm so—glad."

CHAPTER TWELVE

At ten o'clock Nali returned with a bottle of medicine and a box of pills. He gave them to Sonia and she read the instructions carefully.

"I will attend to it, Nali," she said.

The Hindu bowed and left her. John had been gone half an hour, and Sweeting appeared to have left also, but he had not apprised her of his departure. She wondered why Sir Henry had been called into the library, and why he had stayed there for so long. Also she wondered if he had told her the truth about the Judge, for she had a fine intuitive sense.

On entering the Judge's bedroom she found him wide awake, and looking no worse if no better. She sat on the edge of the bed and smiled down at him.

"Behold your nurse! I am going to dose you."

"Has Sir Henry sent up a lot of filth?"

"It may not be half so bad as it looks. Which will you have first—the pill or the medicine?"

"Neither. Fling them away."

"Now—now!"

"Well, if you insist——"

"I certainly do. I am going to be strict with you."

"Heavens! what an awful-looking thing, I shall never succeed in swallowing that."

"Try."

Wallington raised himself on his elbow, and managed to deal with both the pill and the medicine. He pulled a wry face as he gave her the empty glass.

"Horrible!"

"Have a glass of water?"

"Yes—no. Tell Nali to bring me a little whisky— as usual."

"Do you think you ought to have that?"

"Most certainly I do. I have done your bidding— now you do mine. I am too wide awake, my dear."

"But the pill——!"

"That is just the point—I need something potent to put the pill under."

"You're a stubborn old man."

"I am."

"All right," she said. "I suppose you must be humoured. You are looking better than you did this afternoon."

"I'm perfectly all right. Just—nervy. I went to sleep

just now, but something woke me up. I think it is the
window that makes a noise when it is open. Close it,
my dear. There is plenty of fresh air in the room
now."

She tucked the bedclothes about him, closed the window, and then came back and kissed him on the forehead.

"Good night, Nunks dear—and get better quickly!"

A few minutes later Nali entered the room with a
steaming glass of whisky and water on a tray. He
looked at his master rather curiously as he laid the tray
on the small table beside the bed.

"The *sahib* want—nothing else?"

"That is all, Nali."

The Hindu bowed and then shuffled to the door. There
he lingered for a brief moment before going out. The
Judge raised himself slightly and stirred the whisky with
a spoon, for the sugar in it had not yet dissolved. A
slight noise caused his glance to go towards the door
of the dressing-room—to the right of, and in line with,
the bed. It opened and Sweeting came to view. The
Judge's brow became wrinkled with astonishment.

"You must forgive this intrusion, Judge," said Sweeting. "It was rather necessary."

"Really, I——"

Sweeting picked up the glass and sniffed the contents.

"Here is the motive," he said. "I came to prevent
your drinking this."

"And why?"

"Because—because I have grave doubts that it is precisely what you believe it to be."

The Judge stared hard.

"What exactly do you mean, Superintendent?"

"I mean to suggest that the nature of your disposition is such as to cause me—and, I may add, Sir Henry

—grave alarm. It may be possible that we shall ascertain the exact cause."

"You suspect—you suspect——"

"The worst sir. It is as well you should know."

"You believe that someone—someone in this house is attempting to poison me?"

"I do."

"Pshaw! It is ridiculous—fantastic! The innuendo is plain—you suspect Nali—my valet—a man who is devoted to me. I never heard such nonsense. I have a vile taste in my mouth, and I will prove to you that your suspicions are utterly without foundation. Give me the glass."

But Sweeting shook his head pugnaciously.

"With your permission, Judge, I should like to retain this innocent-looking beverage. In the meantime I have been able to concoct a substitute, which I can vouch for. Excuse me!"

He took away the glass, and returned from the dressing-room with a substitute drink. The Judge took it and drank from it.

"No," he said. "I will not believe it. Moreover there is nothing the matter with me, but a common nervous breakdown."

"Sir Henry is of a different opinion."

"He told you—that?"

"Yes, and your whole appearance bears witness to it. When did your indisposition start?"

"This morning."

"You passed a good night?"

"Yes. I went to bed early—I felt very tired. I think I must have gone to sleep immediately."

"Immediately after your 'nightcap'?"

"Yes—yes. But you are wrong——"

"I wonder. In the circumstances it would be better

not to take any food or drink that is offered you, for a
day or two. I should like to have samples of anything
that is brought you. With that end in view I will leave
a few small bottles in the drawer of the table close to
your hand. Sir Henry will call in the morning and bring
some kind of nourishment."

The Judge nodded, but remained as sceptical as ever.
He suggested that Sonia might bring him refreshment in
place of Sir Henry's chemical concoctions, but Sweeting
shook his head emphatically.

"What a horrible web of suspicion," mused the Judge.
"I will humour you until to-morrow night, Sweeting,
after which I intend to get up and attend to my business. I had imagined that I was going to be murdered
and the blame put on Jack o' Lantern. Now it seems
I am to be poisoned, and Jack o' Lantern is not going to
be indicted. One cannot be oblivious to certain incon-
gruities. If I were you I should drink that whisky—
if that is not already your intention."

Sweeting laughed, but he did not share the Judge's
levity. He was anxious to get an analyst at work. When
he left, with his precious liquid safely bottled, it was
by the old secondary staircase at the back of the house.
But even then he was observed by the vigilant eyes of
Nali, who knew quite well that the human sleuth-hound
was still hanging around the place.

At the office the next morning Wrench found his confrère in a state of obvious excitement, as arrogant and
cocksure as ever, but happily less cynical. Sweeting believed he was on the right track, and could afford to
be more generous minded.

"Any developments in your quarter?" he asked.

"A few. I believe that in a day or two I shall meet
the woman mentioned in that note found on the
'Slasher.' "

"Kate?"

"Yes. It is too early to be sanguine, but things are shaping that way."

"What are you going to do about her?"

"Arrest her—and several other persons. With that end in view, I want authority to raid Brooking's on Tuesday."

"Brooking's! Well, it wouldn't do any harm. They've been skating on thin ice for a long time. I wish you luck—but you know my opinion?"

"Fairly well. You doubt this threat to the Judge from an outside source?"

"I do. I agree it does not dispose of Jack o' Lantern, but it dissociates him from that threatening letter. He may, too, be innocent as regards Cantler. The assumption of his being the murderer was made on a most unlikely hypothesis. If I prove that there is a conspiracy to murder the Judge—a conspiracy planned in his own house—and that the attempt is now being made, that rather spoils the other theory, doesn't it? And I have every hope of establishing that—immediately."

"What are you up to now?"

"The Judge is ill. Isn't that significant?"

"He is run down. That is natural."

"It might be if that were the true diagnosis. No, my dear Wrench, Wallington is suffering from poisoning——"

"What!"

"Ah, that wants some swallowing, doesn't it? My authority—none other than Sir Henry Fuller."

"Great Scott!"

"Last night I didn't leave when you—and others—thought I did. I wanted to observe a certain act. It happened, and I brought away with me some liquid in a bottle, which I prevented the Judge from swallowing.

That drink was administered—and concocted—by Nali. It is now being analysed, and I hope to have the analysis at any moment."

Wrench was for the moment nonplused. The pieces of this jig-saw puzzle did not fit anywhere, and it was because of this that he refused to accept Sweeting's theory. But, on the other hand, Sir Henry was not likely to be mistaken. Also there was that dagger to be accounted for, and the piece of paper torn from the bag which was found in Sonia's bedroom. To fit all these things into one frame made it necessary to postulate that Nali, or some other person actually in the Judge's house, was Jack o' Lantern himself. It didn't work—on the face of it it was impossible.

"I can't follow you, Sweeting," he said. "Our trails may converge somewhere, but at the moment I cannot see where."

"Nor can I. But the first thing is to protect the Judge."

"Finding Jack o' Lantern and protecting the Judge may be one and the same thing. I am hoping that Tuesday may throw some light on the matter, for I have hopes of meeting this Jack o' Lantern face to face."

"Eh!"

"Hopes—I said."

"Well, forge ahead. If——"

There was a rap on the door and the analyst entered. Sweeting's eyes gleamed expectantly as he waved the bald-headed, spectacled expert into a chair. The latter slowly produced a phial and pursed his lips.

"Well?"

"Whisky—water—and a little sugar."

"Nothing—nothing else?"

"Absolutely nothing."

Sweeting looked bitterly disappointed, and Wrench

smiled to himself. The analyst left, and the superintendent sat gnawing the end of a pencil.

"It disproves nothing," he said savagely. "The symptoms are clear. I'll get them yet—damn them!"

That evening the analyst produced results of further work on various fragments of food and drink. They were all perfectly innocuous. Sweeting nearly tore his hair.

CHAPTER THIRTEEN

THE Judge made a lightning recovery. In a few days he was attending court, looking little the worse for his recent indisposition. Sonia marvelled at his recuperative power, but warned him not to court a repetition of his illness. He laughed and patted her hand affectionately.

"I know what you will advise—breakfast in bed, a bath chair, a hot bath, and the miscellaneous stock-in-trade of the happy and contented invalid. My dear, has it never occurred to you that I am, as things go, a comparatively young man?"

"Not so young as you were twenty years ago."

"That is, of course, unanswerable." He glared at his newspaper. "I appear to be in the limelight again. Here is a long harangue from Lord Hinnindale which carries the innuendo that Pat Murray received an unduly harsh sentence. I should have guessed Hinnindale penned it, even if he had not signed it. If the noble Lord had his way Regent Street would not be safe to walk in—after dark. We are cursed with a sloppy sentimentalism these days. Too much psycho-analysis and too little corrective in the form of the 'cat' and hard labour. In an age of transcendent socialism a judge may be expected to show a leniency towards larceny, but I know of no kind of 'ism' to excuse brutal assault."

Michels agreed. He, too, was of the old school, and had no patience with some of the new-fangled ideas that were being disseminated and fostered by well-meaning idealists.

"But isn't it true that the more you punish a man the more embittered and vindictive he becomes?" asked Sonia.

"It is true that the less you punish a man the more inclined he will be to repeat his offence."

"Isn't crime chiefly ignorance—I mean, ignorance of one's better self? Isn't it possible that knowledge may be a better deterrent than physical punishment?"

The Judge smiled and shook his head.

"Most theories have something in their favour," he said. "But the degenerate is always the degenerate. Leniency in some cases is sheer foolishness, that the born criminal will be quick to take advantage of. No, the punishment must outweigh the gain. Crime must be made a bad business proposition."

Sonia was reflective. She was temperamentally incapable of being impartial in such matters. Her big fund of human sympathy found a too-ready outlet every time some poor devil stood in the prisoner's dock. She was too prone to judge people on her own standard and to imagine half a hundred extenuating circumstances. With her, heart came before mind. Nevertheless, she sided with the Judge on every occasion, for she had come to venerate him, almost to place him in the ranks of the infallible.

"I suppose you are right," she said ultimately. "But why do people do horrible things?"

"Why do cats catch mice?" asked Michels. "Because it is their nature to. Ah—the Channel crossing—'mod-

erate to rough!' I shall certainly have recourse to
Mothersill."

"Mental suggestion—self-hypnotism," laughed Wallington. "My dear Michels, I am surprised."

"You are really leaving this afternoon?" asked Sonia.
Michels nodded.

"I have business to do in Paris. In any case, I feel
that I have outstayed my welcome."

"Nonsense!" expostulated Wallington. "When you
are tired of Paris, come back, and we will resume our
old arguments."

Michels left later in the day, and the house seemed
very quiet afterwards. Sonia had not quite realised
what a difference the removal of that big personality
would make. And before he left Michels had made
a strange remark to her.

"If you should ever want me, telephone to Claridge's
Hotel, Paris," he said. "Remember I am your guardian's closest friend. One never knows——"

It left her wondering exactly what he meant to convey, and she felt that he would not have uttered so
cryptic and discomfiting an expression without good
reason. Then she remembered certain other facts equally
disturbing. Sighing, she pulled the curtains and commenced playing the piano.

In the meantime Wrench had made his plans for the
raid on Brooking's night-club. Before keeping his appointment with Gwen Denton he called on Sonia, who
welcomed him warmly, for she was feeling depressed in
the absence of the Judge, who had gone to a reception
in the Inner Temple.

"Take off your coat," she said.

"I can only stay a very short time. I've a big event
on to-night, and I have yet to change into other garb."

"Oh!"

"Sorry, old thing! But I have been waiting anxiously for this evening. A great deal may depend upon my success in a certain quarter."

"Is there—danger?"

"Nothing out of the usual. How is the Judge?"

"Completely recovered. He has resumed his duties with more zest than ever. But Michels has left us."

"Rather sudden, isn't it?"

"Yes. He left for Paris this afternoon. What a queer man he is. So wrapped up in himself. I have never seen him exhibit any kind of enthusiasm—no emotions. I don't wonder he never married."

"He lives in a world apart. Even the Judge has hobbies, but Michels' only form of relaxation is human analysis. What a book he could write if he chose, but he seems to be quite content to keep his vast knowledge to himself. Rather a pity, that."

"Are things any better at the office?"

"They were for a very short time. Sweeting was buoyed up by certain hopes—on top of the world; then his castles of sand collapsed and left him gasping in mortification. He held some impossible theories."

"About this house?"

"Yes. And I doubt if he is completely disillusioned even now."

"What—what did he suspect?"

"Everything and everybody. But we won't talk about him. To-night I may get a little nearer to my man."

"Jack o' Lantern?"

"Yes."

"You still believe in his—his close proximity?"

He nodded, and thought he saw her flinch. It was clear to him that she had a mild attack of "nerves," for she gave a start as a motor horn in the street bleated noisily, and then laughed mirthlessly.

"Sonia!"

"Yes."

"What is the matter with you?"

"The matter? Why—nothing. I—I am just a little lonely—that is all. This is a big house, and it grows dark so early. Michels has gone, and the Judge is out, also the maid and the cook. And I can't help think- ing——"

She hesitated and shook her head.

"Thinking what?"

"Horrid things."

"Then don't. This is London. A hundred yards away there is a busy thoroughfare, buses and taxis and bustle. The trouble is this sepulchral gloom in the house. Why are you so stingy in the matter of lighting? Bogies can't exist in bright illumination. Let's have some more light."

He went to the switch which controlled a fairly big light, but on pressing it nothing happened.

"I think the lamp has gone," said Sonia. "And we haven't a spare one."

Wrench made an attempt to take the lamp from its socket, in order to examine the filament, but it stuck fast. He exerted a little pressure and the thing broke in his hands. A minute piece of the glass penetrated his finger and the blood flowed.

"You've cut yourself!"

"Only a scratch."

He searched for his pocket handkerchief, and then re- membered it was in his overcoat. Sonia ran to her hand- bag and whipped out a small square of pink silk. Simultaneously something else came out and rolled along the floor, stopping at Wrench's feet. It was a small, circular, ivory box, and the lid fell off ere it came to rest. Some of the contents were spilled on the carpet

—fine white powder. Wrench picked up the box and the separate lid. The latter was inlaid with gold in the shape of a dragon.

"The secret is out," he said jestingly. "And I believed you never tried to improve upon Nature."

To his astonishment she did not budge an inch, but moved her hands nervously and uttered an inarticulate sound. Then he became aware of the fact that the greyish powder was not face-powder. It was not fine enough. It looked very much like something far more dangerous, and there was Sonia's eyes giving grounds for that suspicion. Purposely he spilt a little on his sleeve and then handed her the box with a smile.

She tied up his finger, but he felt her breast heaving as she did so. Then with an effort she regained her composure, and called Nali to pick up the pieces of glass that were strewn about the room. Wrench looked at his watch.

"I must go," he said. "Better send me the bill for the new lamp."

"Must you—really——?"

"Yes. Time presses."

She went with him into the hall.

"Well, au revoir, dear!"

She looked at the outstretched hand.

"Is that all, John? Don't you think we have got a little—a little beyond that?"

"Of course!"

He kissed her, and then made away, with his brain swimming. A taxi whirled him along to the "Yard." He changed his under coat carefully and then visited the analyst. The chemist was at work on an important job. Wrench handed him the coat with a grim face.

"There is a little powder on the sleeve—there," he said. "Is there sufficient to analyse?"

"Ample."

"Let me have a report, will you? I shall be in the office for some little time. You might phone me."

"I'll go right ahead."

"Good!"

Wrench changed into the semblance of Henry Simmons, Commission Agent, and then assured himself that his assistants were fully prepared for the pending raid. But his mind was not so deeply centred on that now. He was uncommonly agitated—anxious. . . . Suddenly the telephone bell rang.

"Inspector Wrench—wanted!"

He went to the instrument.

"Hallo!"

"Is that you, Wrench? Gluck speaking. The stuff is cocaine—yes, cocaine—C-O-C-A-I-N-E."

"Thanks!" said Wrench huskily.

The inspector in charge looked at his confrère as he left the telephone. He saw a grim face—a twitching mouth.

"Anything wrong?" he inquired.

Wrench shook his head and walked out. He had laughed at Sweeting's theories, but here was something that could only be explained that way. And the Judge's recent illness— All the joy that the thought of the impending raid had given him was dissipated. Incredible things were happening. Theories—theories! He was sick of them. He seemed to be like a man in a torturous maze, blundering into dead-ends, and hurting himself in the process.

CHAPTER FOURTEEN

WRENCH met Gwen Denton as arranged. She had got herself up well for the occasion and welcomed her new "friend" warmly. It was clear that she anticipated a quite hectic evening, and Wrench wondered what her feelings would be if she knew of the dramatic climax that had been planned. He played his part exceedingly well, putting on a rich Cockney accent, and lapsing into slang and vulgarisms at times. She wanted to know how the "gees" were going, and he had to admit that things were rather dull in the bookmaking world.

"Phil is going to come along presently," she said. "He's a bit blue these days. Down on his luck."

At Brooking's there was no hitch. Gwen was well known there, and they passed through the passage into the dance and refreshment room. Wrench had an excellent memory for physiognomies, and observed several familiar faces among the crowd—faces that had on more than one occasion peeped over the prisoner's dock.

"Good crowd!" said Gwen. "Lord, they've actually got a saxophone in the orchestra! Do you know Reggie Philton? Some boy that!"

Wrench knew the man in question quite well, but pleaded ignorance. Philton had served time for indulging in the remunerative occupation of making two five pound notes from one, exhibiting such consummate skill in his art that even bank managers had been deceived. What he was engaged in now Wrench had no idea, but that it was anything but honest toil went without saying.

Gwen introduced her "friend" with some gusto, for she was getting somewhat *passé* and was not everybody's "money." Men and women were present in approximately equal numbers, and as a result "wallflowers" were few. Wrench danced with half a dozen different women from out-of-work chorus girls to less respectable characters. Some he had been introduced to and some he had not. In a very short time drink began to flow and spirits rose higher.

"Is Banting here?" he asked Gwen.

"Not yet, but I'm sure he's coming. There's Sam Knudge! My, ain't he spruce!"

This was no exaggeration. Sam had got himself up to kill. His black hair was smothered in oil and plastered over his forehead, the ends "quiffed" as if by curling tongs. He wore his best pepper-and-salt suit, and his highest collar.

"Out to hypnotise Kate," opined Gwen. "He's not a bad sort, but horribly conceited. Hallo, Sam!"

Sam turned his head and grinned at her.

"What cheer, Gwen!"

"Come and be introduced to Mr. Simmons. This is Sam Knudge of the boneyard," said Gwen facetiously. "Worst dancer on earth—bar none."

"'Ere, you come orf it," grumbled Sam. "I had three lessons larst week. Howdydo, Mr. Simmons!"

Wrench shook the fishy hand that was offered him.

"Where's Banting?" asked Gwen.

"Coming along presently."

"And Kate?"

"She's coming too—at least she promised."

"Is Lefroy——?"

Sam's mouth tightened, and something very much like fear came to his small bird-like eyes.

"Don't want him 'ere," he muttered.

"Of course not," teased Gwen. "But he's got a habit of turning up when he's least expected."

Sam mopped his perspiring brow with a silk handkerchief and mumbled something unintelligible.

"Going to give me a trial?" he asked. "I'm great on the Yale Blues. Come on!"

"Must I?"

Wrench let her go and wandered across to a table. Already the place was foul with smoke and scent, and what it would be like by midnight he could not imagine. And all the time his mind was besieged by disturbing thoughts that had been aroused by his remarkable discovery earlier in the evening. But he knew that to dwell on that incident now was not desirable. Other business was on hand. While he sat there a stoutly-built man and a woman entered the room. Both were impressive individuals, but the woman the more so. His eyes were held by her pure complexion, the amazing blueness of her eyes, and the mass of auburn hair that glinted in the light. She carried herself rather proudly—as if she counted herself superior to most of the people present. Then he heard the name "Banting" and knew this was Kate, and probably the woman he was anxious to meet.

By the time the tripe was served he and Kate were on speaking terms. He and she, and Banting and Gwen shared a table in the corner. Wrench hated tripe like the devil, but he managed to eat a small portion, and created a good effect by ordering a bottle of champagne and also a decanter of port wine. Gwen helped herself liberally, but he noticed that Kate took very little. Later Sam inflicted himself upon them, and tried to take Kate by storm. She smiled at him occasionally, but it was obvious that he bored her, and that her thoughts were elsewhere.

"You don't come here often, Mr. Simmons?" she asked.

"No. This is my first visit. Gay little place, isn't it?"

"Gay enough when one is bored."

"You shouldn't get bored."

"Don't you listen to Kate," put in Banting. "She's got the philosophic mind. She's never really happy unless she is miserable. That's the type."

"Garn!" said Sam. "It's that dingy old 'ouse you live in—all creaks and rats and smells. Gives me the willies whenever I come there."

"Then the obvious remedy is to stay away," retorted Banting.

"You're a joker, you are."

"Pass along the red stuff—woman's ruin," said Gwen, who was fast becoming intoxicated. "Oh my, wouldn't it be a joke if Lefroy popped in?"

"Shut up!" snarled Sam. "You got him on the brain."

Kate stirred uneasily and Banting motioned to Gwen to hold her tongue. Later Wrench sat out a dance with Kate, who pleaded she was tired.

"Why does Knudge get so enraged whenever Lefroy's name is mentioned?" he asked. "Are they enemies?"

"They don't love each other."

"Lefroy! Seems familiar somehow. Now where have I heard that name?"

Kate gave him no encouragement.

"It must have been the 'Slasher,'" he mused. "I'm sure he mentioned——"

"You—you knew the 'Slasher'?"

"Well—I met him once or twice—not under that name though. It was only when I saw his photograph in the paper that I knew he was the same man. He got a pretty long stretch, didn't he?"

She nodded.

"I am sure that was how I heard the name of Lefroy. Does a bit of backing, doesn't he?"

"No," she replied emphatically. "He is not that sort of man."

Try as he might he could get nothing from her respecting the strange personality whom he devoutly hoped would put in an appearance before the time fixed for the raid. But already she had tacitly admitted that Lefroy was acquainted with the "Slasher," and that was a decided step forward.

He took compassion on Sam and bought him a few

drinks. Sam was a little more communicative than Kate had been. He admitted he hated Lefroy, and that Lefroy was a "dark one," a man to avoid. The police wanted him, but they wouldn't get him. Cunning as a fox he was, and he seemed to know everything.

"Well, he sounds interesting," said Wrench. "What is he like to look at?"

"Pasty-faced, I call him. Might be thirty, forty, fifty—blowed if I can tell. At times he looks quite different—as if he was dazed—blotto. Then he sits and says nothing. But sometimes he's a raging lion, flinging things about and shouting blue murder. It's dope, I reckon, that gets him that way. I wish to Gawd he'd take an overdose."

"Kate is keen on him, eh?"

"She's gone crazy. I'll bet she only came here because she thought he might come. If he did you'd see her face light up—a different woman. But he ain't got her yet, and——"

Banting seemed to suspect that Sam was becoming too garrulous and interrupted the conversation. Wrench knew in a moment that it was useless to attempt to pump Banting. He was not the type of man to indulge in gossip. Banting had too much at stake to risk anything.

Phil Denton turned up a little later. He greeted Wrench, but not with any great warmth, and Wrench's observant eyes took in everything that followed. By some means or other Denton had become suspicious of the self-styled bookmaker. That was the deduction Wrench drew from the whispered conversation between Banting, Denton, and some others. But he went on with the frolicking, hoping that Lefroy would turn up before the time fixed for the raid.

*   *   *   *   *   *

Denton, Banting and Philton had repaired to an an-
nexe and were talking together in low but excited tones.

"I'm sure of it," said Denton. "He gave a fake visiting card to Gwen. I went to the address to put a bit
of money on a horse. He wasn't there. But there had
been a Mr. Simmons living there, and a man told me
he was sent to quod three months ago, and was still there.
What's more, he wasn't a bit like our friend outside. I'll
bet my boots he's a 'nark.' "

Banting was inclined to agree. He had observed
Wrench talking with Sam, Kate and others, and he
thought that those conversations were by no means
disinterested.

"What can we do, anyway?" asked Philton. "Brooking doesn't want any fuss made here."

"I'll fix him," said Denton.

Banting knew what he meant, for Denton was an
accomplished pugilist.

"Don't be a fool!" he snapped. "If you start any
quarrel it'll be our funeral. Better warn Brooking there's
a plain-clothes man here, and tell that damned idiot Sam
to guard his silly tongue a bit. I heard him mention
Lefroy's name——"

But their cogitations were too late. They heard an
uproar without. A woman's voice shouted "the police!"
and a general mêlée followed. Denton pushed a pistol
under the cushion of the couch and attempted to find a
passage through the scared crowd. But he found his
way barred.

"Get that man!" cried Wrench. "And the woman
—there!"

Kate was seized by a burly guardian of the law. She
shot a glance of hate at Wrench. But Wrench was busy
indicating his prospective prisoners. They were six in
all, including Banting and Sam Knudge. Gwen, who

was still in a fuddled state, blinked at her late "friend."

"A bloomin' 'tec!" she hiccoughed. "Ooh, you dirty dog!"

"Shall I take her, Inspector?" asked a sergeant.

"No. These are all I want."

Denton smiled at him scornfully.

"I had you taped," he said. "But you've got nothing against me."

"Get 'em down below!"

The prisoners were hurried off, and the evening closed so far as Brooking was concerned. He was trying to guess what sort of a fine would be inflicted on him, and he cursed Gwen Denton for being so blind as not to know a policeman from an ordinary individual.

CHAPTER FIFTEEN

"So you've found Kate?" said Sweeting. "You're damned smart at times, Wrench."

"Thank you!"

"And will it get you any further?"

"That remains to be seen."

"You think she is actually the woman referred to in the note which we found on the 'Slasher'?"

"There is no doubt about it."

"And if she is dumb?"

"She probably will be, unless we can bring pressure to bear upon her. The circumstances have changed a little. Until recently she was the only link—omitting the 'Slasher'—between us and Jack o' Lantern. But now we have a whole crowd of people who have seen him, although some know him only as Lefroy."

"Kate only knows him as that?"

"I am not sure."

"How do you propose to make her talk?"

"She might be brought to believe that we can put Banting away on a serious charge. At the moment we can't, but she is not to know that."

"Is she likely to squeal on her lover to save her father?"

"That is a very nice psychological problem. But conversely we might make the same threat to Banting in regard to his daughter. He has quite a strongly marked paternal instinct."

"You can't pull that stuff over Banting," said Sweeting. "He's as cute as they make 'em. No, I agree the girl is our best hope. But what about Knudge?"

"I think he has told us all he knows. There is no doubt he is the man who sent the telephone message. That didn't help us much, for the flat has not been visited by anyone since we broke into it. Still, I brought him in, in case he should have learned anything since."

An hour later the office was the centre of deepest interest. One by one the prisoners were brought in, and questioned by the Assistant Commissioner and Wrench in turn. Nothing was gleaned from the first four. Denton swore he had only seen Lefroy twice in his life, and then in public places. Banting averred he knew Lefroy casually. He hadn't the slightest idea where he lived, or how he gained a living.

"Do you know him also under another name?" asked the Assistant Commissioner.

"No."

"Have you ever heard of Jack o' Lantern?"

"Why, yes. Naturally I read the newspapers."

"Is not this Lefroy actually Jack o' Lantern?"

"Not to my knowledge. Why should he be, any more than—than you or I, sir?"

"A clever devil!" said Sweeting as Banting was led out.

"It would take the rack to make him squeal. Will you see the woman now, sir?"

"Yes. You had better cross-question her, Wrench."

Kate Banting was brought in. She was pale and a little flurried at first, but in a few moments she gained control of herself and met Wrench's eyes unflinchingly.

"Your name is Kate Banting?"

"Yes."

"Age?"

"Twenty-two."

"You are acquainted with a man named Lefroy?"

"Slightly."

"On how many occasions have you seen him?"

"I cannot remember."

"I suggest a dozen times."

"Well—perhaps."

"When did you first meet him?"

"Just over a year ago."

"Where?"

"At a friend's house."

"The house of a man known to the police as the 'Slasher.' "

Kate hesitated, and then nodded.

"Where have you met this man—Lefroy—on subsequent occasions?"

"At our own house—and in clubs."

"Never at his own home?"

"Never"—emphatically.

"How long is it since you last saw him?"

"Just over a week ago—at Brooking's."

"You know where he lives?"

"No."

"Come, you must have some idea. Do you mean to tell us that you have known this man for over a year, and yet have no notion where he lives?"

"It is true. I know nothing more than what I have already told you."

"But he writes to you."

"He does not. He has never written a single word to me."

Questions were put from every conceivable angle, but Kate maintained her ignorance of the whereabouts of the wanted man. She gave a vague description of him, but it did not help matters to any great extent. It became obvious that they were dealing with a very mysterious entity, who covered up his tracks wherever he went.

Knudge confessed it was he who telephoned the police, and his motive was made clear. He seemed as disappointed as the police were that Lefroy had not been taken. Yes, he knew Lefroy was Jack o' Lantern, but he swore that Kate was innocent of that fact. And then one item of interest emerged. It was the fact that Lefroy was left-handed. Knudge had seen him write and smoke left-handedly—also drink. Before he left he begged the Assistant Commissioner not to give him away in regard to the telephone message, and it was clear that his fear of Jack o' Lantern was as deep-rooted as his hate.

Later the prisoners were charged with being on licensed premises and obtaining intoxicating drink outside the licensing hours. Banting and Kate were detained for a day or two, but no further information was wrung from them, and ultimately they were discharged.

*   *   *   *   *

In the meantime Wrench had seen Sonia. He told her what had transpired on the night of the raid, and she listened attentively. But all the while she was fidgeting, and Wrench remembered the chief object of his call. But it was difficult to broach the subject—to this woman

that he loved with all his heart. At last he came to the
point.

"Sonia, there is a small matter that has been troubling
me. You can shed light on it. About a week ago I had
occasion to visit a certain night-club, and I arrived at
the top of Kingsway after midnight. To my amazement I saw—you."

Her face went crimson.

"I!"

"Yes—as plainly as I see you now. You were inside
a taxicab—alone."

"Well?"

"On the following day, when I called here, I threw
out a hint, but you ignored it. Was there any serious
reason for ignoring it—for giving me to believe that
nothing out of the common had happened?"

"Was that—out of the common?"

"Wasn't it? Are you in the habit of being out at half-
past twelve at night—alone?"

"John, this is——!"

"For God's sake, don't think this is an outburst of
stupid jealousy or Grundyism. I know that many young
women go out to places of amusement by themselves
at nights, but that is the last thing you would think of
doing. And, if you had, you would have told me. No,
there is much more in it than that. Are you in trouble—
about anything? If so, don't you think you might confide in me?"

Sonia gulped, and her resentment vanished when she
looked into his serious face.

"I am worried," she said. "It may be unnecessarily.
I suppose I ought to have told you. It is Nali. I have
not been sleeping well these past weeks, and about a
fortnight ago I heard a noise in the corridor—footsteps.
It was nearly eleven o'clock, and we had all retired early.

I was too nervous to go outside the door, but a little later I went to open my window, and I saw Nali going down the drive. It was brilliant moonlight, and his form was unmistakable. I did not hear him come back, but he was about the house early the next morning. A week elapsed and then the same thing happened again. On this occasion I had been busy in my bedroom and was fully dressed. He had said good night to me an hour earlier and gone to his room, so I was naturally amazed. I decided to follow him and quickly donned a coat and hat."

"Go on."

"He walked down the street for some distance, until he reached a taxi-rank. There he engaged a vehicle. I did the same and told the driver to follow the other taxi, but not to overtake it. We passed through the West End and made eastward. I do not know much of London east of the Bank, and it was too dark to see the names of the streets. Ultimately the leading taxi stopped in a very narrow and untidy street. I told my driver to pass it, and as we passed I saw Nali get out and enter a house farther up. I saw the number—118. I asked my driver to wait at the end of the street, from where I had the house under observation. Half an hour passed, but no one left the house. I returned home—in the same taxi-cab."

"I see. Did you find out the name of the street?"

"Yes. The taxi-driver said it was Little Orchard Street. When I reached home I sat up for a long time, but Nali never returned. Ultimately I fell asleep. The next morning I found him at his duties. But he looked tired —exhausted."

"Did you interrogate him?"

"Yes."

"What did he say?"

"He swore I was mistaken—that he had never left his room. He lied to me—and I am sure he knew I knew it was a lie, but he stuck to his story. I was worried. I did not know what to do. To have told the Judge might have brought about Nali's discharge. I—I decided to watch him carefully in future. Two days ago I came upon him suddenly. I was wearing soft slippers and he did not hear me. He had a little box in his hand —The small ivory box which fell from my hand-bag— you remember?"

Wrench nodded and uttered a sigh of great relief.

"Go on," he begged.

"He had taken a small portion of the white powder between his fingers and was, I am sure, on the point of snuffling it when he caught sight of me. He tried to conceal the box, but I took it from him. I taxed him with taking 'dope,' and he confessed abjectly. Of course I was horrified, and at once deduced that the possession of the drug had some connection with his nightly missions. He admitted that too, and begged me to have pity on him, and to keep it from the knowledge of the Judge. I—I was sorry for him, for he has been an excellent servant. I promised to say nothing to anyone, provided he would swear to drop that terrible practice. An hour later you called. I wanted to tell you, but I felt it would be like a betrayal of confidence. You—you do understand, don't you?"

Wrench did, but how much of the story to believe he did not know. That Sonia was telling the truth he had no doubt, and it banished from his mind a terrible spectre that had settled there against his reason and common sense. But it was a remarkable coincidence that this drug should be discovered immediately following the Judge's strange illness.

"Why so serious?" she asked. "Haven't I explained
—everything?"

"It is not your story that is open to doubt—but Nali's."

"I don't quite understand. It was a voluntary confes-
sion, and is——"

"It is plausible up to a point. But there is a factor
of which you are not aware. I think you should know—
now. When the Judge was ill you were given to understand it was merely a nervous breakdown?"

"Yes—of course. Sir Henry——"

"Sir Henry had his reasons for misleading you. But
his diagnosis pointed to poison——"

"Poison!" she gasped.

"That was why Sweeting came here, when he heard
that the Judge was indisposed. All along Sweeting has
been of the opinion that the threat to the Judge's life
came from inside this house. Don't you see——"

She stared at him with wide and horrified eyes. Such
a dreadful possibility had never entered her mind.

"But Nali——! You don't imagine that Nali——?
No—no. It is incredible. Nali is devoted to his master.
You have no idea how deeply attached he is to the
Judge."

"From my own observation I should deduce that, but
the coincidence is disturbing. That box contained cocaine, and such a poison introduced into drink or food
might produce exactly the symptoms which the Judge
displayed. It is all very perplexing."

"It is horrible. Sweeting is wrong. There is no person
in this house who does not admire and reverence the
Judge. It is all wrong—I know it is."

Wrench was recalling the discovery of the paper bag,
but he felt he was not justified in apprising her of this
fact, since Sweeting had brought that to light. There

was a vast difference between demanding explanations
of facts disclosed by his own efforts, and divulging information confided to him by a brother officer.

"I hope you are right," he said.

Then the Judge came in, as cheerful as if there was
no cloud of any kind in the offing. He laughed at their
concerned faces.

"Working out the cost of establishing a home, John?"
he inquired. "Well, I warn you that the notion that two
young people can live on love and kisses is a popular
fallacy. I haven't tried it myself, but I have witnessed
the dramatic results."

"We are a little more practical," retorted Sonia.

"Then you are notable exceptions—and I congratulate
you. And how is business, John?"

"Hopeful."

"That sounds encouraging. I suppose Sweeting is still
as full of nonsensical theories as ever?"

"Not quite. But he is not as chastened as he will be
when we have Jack o' Lantern under lock and key."

"Then go ahead, John. I should like to have the
pleasure of trying that worthy. Now let us have some
music, and cease to remember our personal problems.
You have not exercised your voice of late, John. Let
us have that little song of Gilbert's:

" 'A po-liceman's life is not a happy one.' "

Wrench did not feel like singing, but the Judge was
adamant, and Sonia was keen to dispel the gloom which
their recent conversation had created. She went to the
piano, but had scarcely played a bar when Nali entered.

"Excuse!" he lisped. "Someone ask if Inspector
Wrench is here. He say it is very important."

Wrench went out to the telephone. When he returned
he brought his coat with him.

"Extraordinary thing has happened," he said. "I have kept a watch on that house in Watling Court—from the office at Kemp Street. I left word at the 'Yard' that I was coming here. Kemp Street have arrested a man in the act of entering No. 2. I am going along at once." Sonia sighed as he kissed her and left hurriedly.

CHAPTER SIXTEEN

WRENCH lost no time in getting to Kemp Street. After so long a lapse of time he had almost given up hope of anything of evidential value emerging from the house in Watling Court. He had arrived at the conclusion that the recent tenant of No. 2 had received a warning of some kind, and vacated the place for good. In the meantime attempts were being made to get into touch with the tenant who had sub-let the flat, and who was believed to be in Australia. Having on many occasions been the victim of over-optimism, he refused to be prematurely jubilant over this new arrest. But, on the other hand, it might forge a new link in the very incomplete chain of evidence.

He was shown to the superintendent's office and greeted warmly by his confrère, with whom he was on the best of terms. The superintendent confirmed what Wrench had already learned from Scotland Yard. A detective-constable had observed a man loitering near the house in Watling Court. He had followed him inside and had caught him in the act of entering the apartment on the second floor. An arrest had followed.

"Did the constable interrogate him?"

"Yes. His story is that he found a key to which was attached a tag bearing the address of the house, and that he came to return the key to its owner. But our man swears that the prisoner was attempting to open the door when he saw the constable."

"Is his identity established?"

"Not yet. I took no steps to do that, as he requested particularly that you should be sent for. He gave his name as Hugo Michels, and he carried visiting cards and letters which——"

"Hugo Michels!" exclaimed Wrench. "That is extraordinary! Is he unusually broad of shoulder, bullet type of head, large limbs—intellectual?"

"All that. He would give no further information about himself, but assured me that you could vouch for his character."

"If it is the Hugo Michels that I have met, I certainly can. He is a retired Judge from the Berlin Criminal Court, a friend of Judge Wallington, and a highly respected personage. But it can't be—— Let us have a look at him."

The prisoner was ultimately shown into the office. Wrench started as he saw him. It was indeed Michels, not so bland as usual, for he seemed to be suffering from the sense of the indignity to which he had been subjected.

"Good day to you, Inspector," he said. "I am delighted to see you. There seems to have been a slight—misunderstanding."

"It would seem so," agreed Wrench. "But I should like to put a few questions in regard to this unexpected incident. What brought you to that particular house?"

"I found a key—in Great Russel Street. It carried a tag on which was written the address of its owner."

"And you went to return it?"

"Yes. My first impulse was to hand it in to a police station, but the address was so close to the place where

I found the key that it seemed a simpler matter to go straight to the owner."

"Were you not aware that that house was under observation?"

"Certainly not—or I should not have gone there."

"You did not attempt to enter the place?"

Michels shrugged his shoulders.

"Is it likely? I knocked and rang and received no response. The constable was probably mistaken through my having the key in my hand when I was about to knock a second time, for I was under the impression that the bell was not in order."

"I was informed you were in Paris."

"I was until yesterday. I crossed by the evening boat and am staying at the Russell Hotel. It is all a remarkable coincidence—and extremely embarrassing."

"It is indeed! I am sorry, Mr. Michels, for the inconvenience you have suffered. I will see you in a few minutes."

Wrench stroked his chin reflectively when Michels had left. In this strange case it seemed he could not move a step without being confronted with new complications.

"Then he is the man he purports to be?" asked the superintendent.

"Yes. You cannot possibly detain him. But what knocks me flat is the fact that he found the key to that place—he of all the millions of people in London."

"Well, someone would have found it."

"I don't think you quite appreciate what an amazing coincidence this is. Michels is a friend of Wallington, and Wallington has been threatened by Jack o' Lantern. We have reason to believe that Jack o' Lantern lived in that flat. Michels has been deeply interested in this matter, and here he is popping up—— I should like a word with the constable who made the arrest."

The superintendent nodded and used the telephone. A few seconds later a smart plain-clothes man entered.

"You made the arrest at Watling Court?" asked Wrench.

"Yes, sir."

"You have given it as your opinion that the prisoner was on the point of entering the place when he saw you?"

"I am positive of it, sir. The key was practically in the lock when a board creaked under my foot, and he turned and saw me on the lower landing."

"Did he appear to be embarrassed?"

"No, sir. He said he had been knocking and could get no response. Then he explained his business. I told him I was a police officer and would have to arrest him. He said there must be a mistake, but made no other comment."

The constable was dismissed, and the superintendent decided there was no alternative to releasing Michels with due apologies. But the incident rankled in Wrench's mind. He could not imagine a person of Michel's social position returning a lost key in person to a common tenement house in an insalubrious thoroughfare, unless from interested motives. Moreover, Michels had pretended that he was ignorant of the fact that that particular house was under suspicion, when Wrench was certain that that fact had emerged in conversation with the Judge when Michels was present. The fog seemed to be getting denser and denser.

He visited the house in Watling Court and found the rooms exactly as they had been when he last saw them. He had purposely placed certain articles in such a position that anyone entering the place would have disturbed them. So far as he could see such entry had not been made. The incident was duly reported to the Assistant Commissioner, who realised as Wrench did certain flaws in Michels' story, but on the other hand it seemed ludicrous to imagine that the celebrated ex-judge and criminologist had any connection with the Jack o' Lantern crimes.

"We must rule out such a hypothesis," he said. "But I agree with you, Wrench—he needs watching."

Michels himself narrated the incident to the Judge, in the light of an amusing adventure. The Judge laughed, but it was somewhat forced. He, too, fastened on the weak points, but he could do no other than accept the story.

"I had no idea you were going to cut your Paris trip so short," he said. "Was the alleged gay city so deadly dull that you fled so unceremoniously?"

"I prefer London in winter. Paris is a summer city. My business with the *Chef de la Sûreté* was soon completed, and I do not propose to return to Berlin until the spring. At the *Sûreté* they are very interested in the Jack o' Lantern business. They are working hand in glove with Scotland Yard, and it is astonishing that with so much intellectual machinery at work the fellow so constantly evades detection and arrest."

"What do they think?"

"I don't think they have any fixed theory. They have been following the movements of one or two notorious characters, but the links are missing."

"Paris will not help. It is on this side of the Channel that we shall find the miscreant. What is your own opinion, Michels?"

"I have not yet formed one."

"That is strange for you."

"Experience has taught me the folly of leaping at premature conclusions."

The Judge became very reflective, and then he suddenly put a bold question.

"Did you really find that key, Michels, in the circumstances narrated?"

Michels looked at him fixedly.

"No," he replied.

"Ah! I thought not."

"You have a penetrating mind, Wallington."

"I am not quite a fool—that is all."

"It was necessary for me to depart from the truth."

"To what end?"

"This case interests me. In many respects it is unusual —I might say unique. I found the key—by accident, but not where I said. It was in this house."

"That is incredible!"

"It is true, notwithstanding. I retained it for personal reasons—reasons that I am not at the moment ready to divulge. If that was an ungrateful and illegitimate act I beg you to forgive me."

"Must you create a fog?"

"Yes—at the moment. Wallington, you and I have lived cheek by jowl with crime and criminals. We have learned to be unmoved in the face of appalling details. But there comes a time when one is confronted with possibilities that make one quail as before Hell itself, when all our notions of what is natural and logical are knocked on the head. I have reached that pass, and I want time to breathe."

Wallington shrugged his shoulders. Never before had Michels displayed so much emotion, so much secrecy.

"You are tantalisingly enigmatical, my dear Michels," he said. "But if you prefer to keep your own counsel I cannot complain. I presume you went to Watling Court with the intention of entering the place?"

"I did."

"That was rather—daring."

"I know. I retained the key for some weeks because

I was fully aware that our excellent inspector had that house under observation. I imagined that by this time he would have ceased to keep a watch on it."

"You do not know John. He is like a leech. But if I may put a reasonable question—why not work openly with Scotland Yard? They would appreciate your assistance."

Michels shook his big head.

"I must go my own way—at the moment. But I'm worried, Wallington—worried."

"Not on my behalf?"

"Yes."

"You believe my life is really in danger?"

"Yes."

"Tch! Then you are more worried than I. My dear Michels—let us agree on that. Let us accept the fact that there is a homicidal maniac at large who, through the peculiar working of his mind, believes that he is justified in removing from this mortal coil certain persons who were instrumental in sending to the gallows his friend, relative or accomplice—whatever the exact relationship might have been. Well, he has had seven years in which to put that idea into practice, and he has not done so. Even assuming that his last threat had more behind it than his first, I am but one man among millions, and I have never regarded death in the nature of something from which one should shrink in mortal terror. Such an event, in the circumstances imagined, might be a desirable thing, since in order to bring about my demise he must take extraordinary risks. In any event the law goes on."

"That is not at all the point."

"I can see no other."

So the Judge continued to live a more or less placid existence, contemptuous of threats, and behind the scenes

at Scotland Yard intricate machinery was in motion.
More brains were brought to bear on the Jack o' Lantern case. A score of houses and public places were
under rigid observation. The movements of old offenders
were carefully recorded. All kinds of information
poured in from many quarters, sorted, analysed, filed.
And yet nothing of prime importance materialised. The
weeks went by and Jack o' Lantern remained as well hid
as a hibernating tortoise.

The Bantings too were lying low. Their associations
with Lefroy kept them under the vigilant eye of the
Scotland Yard men. Banting saw these "pests" everywhere. Brooking's had to toe the line in regard to closing
hours, and more obscure dens were not free from the
fear of a raid at any moment. But Sam Knudge was not
quite so "rattled," for he could always resort to his occupation of sneak-thief, at which he was expert. It was
only the bigger game that was barred.

Kate Banting had not yet quite recovered from the
indignity of being arrested, and her smouldering rage
against Wrench was mingled with anxiety on Lefroy's
behalf. Where was he? Why had all those weeks passed
without a sign from him?

Sam drifted into Banting's house late one evening.
He pushed his hat to the back of his head and winked
at Banting, who was reading a book.

"Old flat-foot outside," he said. "Prowling around
like a bloomin' spectre. Looking for Lefroy."

"Damn him!" muttered Banting. "He never gives us
a moment's respite. We'll have to clear out of here if
this goes on much longer."

"Fat lot of good that would be," said Sam. "Wrench
would hunt you down. It's Lefroy that is to blame. Why
the hell did we ever have anything to do with him?"

Kate shot him an angry glance and he gulped impotently.

"How is things?" he asked Banting, after a pause.

"Rotten! I wish I knew where Lefroy is."

"I wish he was where I wish he was," snorted Sam. "If you ask me, we had better cut him." He made an expressive gesture. "We don't want to be dragged into anything—bloody."

"S-sh!" said Banting.

Kate opened her eyes at this.

"Why do the police want Lefroy?" she asked. "What has he done to make them so keen?"

"What do you think?" blurted Sam.

"Hold your tongue!" snapped Banting, and Sam closed up like an oyster.

But Kate's curiosity was fully aroused. The unusual activity of the police was in itself proof that Lefroy was wanted on more serious charges than mere larceny, forgery, or uttering, and she could not fail to observe her father's constant intrusions whenever she and Lefroy were together, as if he feared any closer relationship between them. And here was Sam throwing out sinister hints.

"You two are hiding something," she said. "Why do you keep me in the dark? Is Lefroy a—a killer?"

Banting started and Sam made a wry face.

"It—it can't be!" she gasped. "He isn't that type— I know he isn't."

"What do you know about him?" demanded Sam. "He whirls you off your feet with a few pretty words, and you fall——"

"For God's sake don't rate me! I'm asking you a question. Is Lefroy—that?"

Banting shook his head, but Sam nodded, and let his

eyelids fall. Banting turned on him furiously, but Sam stuck his ground stubbornly.

"It's time she knew," he argued. "I'd have told her before if you hadn't stopped me." He wagged his finger at Kate. "That's the cause of all the fuss. That's why they're watching this house, and stopping our business. If we're not careful they'll lug us too for——"

"Stop!" she cried. "I don't believe you. You have some grudge against him. Father——!"

But Banting had nothing to say. The cat was out of the bag and it was no use trying to put it back. He had wanted to keep this from Kate, but now he was wondering whether it was not better that she should know. That she loved Lefroy was certain, but in his ignorance of the depth of the passion he believed she would stifle that affection.

"So you too believe—that!"

He looked up with a very grim face.

"It's true, Kate. But keep it to yourself. For God's sake never let him know that——"

The door was pushed violently open and a police officer entered. It was the detective-sergeant dubbed "flatfoot" by Sam, and he had an automatic pistol in his hand. Banting winced and Sam dodged behind the sofa.

"A man called here just now," said the sergeant.

"It was me," said Sam. "Lumme, I passed within two yards of you——"

"I'm speaking of another man—taller. He climbed over the fence at the back two minutes ago. I warn you that if you are sheltering anyone——"

"No one has been here," protested Banting. "And no one was expected. Why the hell can't you leave us alone?"

"You're playing a dangerous game, Jim Banting. The man I saw was wearing a long black overcoat and a soft hat. He might have entered by the window there. Open that cupboard!"

Sam obeyed with alacrity, but the tall piece of furniture was comparatively empty.

"What's in the next room?"

"See for yourself." Banting opened the door, and the sergeant moved back in order to get a full view of the room in question. It was a dining-room and contained no article of furniture in which a man could hide himself. "I tell you no one has entered this house since Knudge came in."

"I'll satisfy myself on that score. I'm going over the house. If he's here I'll lug you, too, Banting."

The sergeant left the room and they heard him mounting the stairs. Kate sat with ashen face, twisting her fingers nervously. Sam fanned himself with his bowler hat.

"Getting a bit warm," he said. "Old flat-foot don't usually have halloo—whatever you call 'em. Strikes me this ain't a safe place to visit."

"Then stay away," snapped Banting.

All of them suddenly started as a noise was heard at the window. Sam's cigarette rolled from his lips as he saw a piece of white paper adhering to the centre pane of glass.

"Look!" he cried.

"Get it quick!"

The window was opened and the note procured. It was the flap of an envelope and it bore a message.

"Blimey! It was 'im!" gasped Sam.

Banting snatched the note from him and read the message. It ordered him to go to "the arches" and wait there for Lefroy—also to bring Knudge with him. He rolled up the piece of paper and threw it into the fire.

"Are we going?" queried Sam.

"Yes—later."

"I don't want——"

"Better do as you're told."

"Damn 'im—ordering me about."

"What—what was it?" asked Kate.

"A little matter of business."

"A message from Lefroy?"

"S-sh!"

The sergeant returned, obviously disappointed. He gave a cursory glance round the room, and then went out. Some time later Banting and Sam made their departure. Kate sat on, staring into the fire. From time to time she moved restlessly. Common sense told her that this love of hers was madness, but because it was madness common sense could not prevail. It had gone too far now. Lefroy meant more to her than anything in the world, but she covered her eyes with her hands as she realised that she was treading in a mire of blood and tears.

CHAPTER SEVENTEEN

THE "terror" was abroad again. At eleven o'clock he had found himself in the neighbourhood of Seven Dials, mingling with the crowd of shoppers from the poor district in the immediate neighbourhood. He found time to reflect upon the strange change of environment that took place within a space of half a square mile. Ten minutes ago he had jostled with the crowd in Piccadilly Circus, had dodged luxurious limousines, had gazed with cynical and contemptuous eyes on women muffled in sables and bejewelled from neck to fingers. Now he turned a sympathetic eye on the poor mob that were counting their pennies, and besieging the stalls in the hope of making wonderful bargains ere the market closed.

Poverty and riches—side by side, half-starved creatures jostling overfed mistresses of bloated plutocrats. What a spectacle for those who boasted of Progress! He curled his lips as he reflected that these poor serfs had more virtue, more kindliness, more sympathy than were dreamed of in the homes of the rich and powerful, and a white flame seemed to strike through him while his unpivoted mind worked. This Jack o' Lantern *alias* Lefroy loved the dingy streets and the drab crowd. He thought they were his people—the oppressed mob. He imagined injustice built upon injustice. It was writ in his mind—as with letters of fire—that certain things were to be done—by him. At times he could not recall what these personal duties were, but there were moments when they flamed up—when the impulse to carry them out was overwhelming. He then became an automaton—a creature without volition, reacting to a mysterious stimulus. It was then that things were done, swiftly, silently. . . .

To himself he was a mystery, no less than to those who sought him in vain. He might well have been a Robot, manufactured in some underground laboratory, replete in every detail, but with buttons to press in place of Will—a sinister piece of mechanism, smooth-tongued, agile, the perfect machine controlled by some unknown hand. And there were the dreams—queer dreams of places and people—both pleasant and horrible. Periodically there came up with all the vividness of flawless photograph the image of a man in a wig—other men too, but this man above all others haunted him. It was Judge Wallington—that flattered and lauded emissary of the law. The man who gave no mercy to men driven to crime through human needs; the man who had sent Tobias Lantern to the scaffold; one who knew nothing of the lives of the under-dogs of the world. . . .

But to-night the image of the Judge was not in his mind. He had not the blood-lust. He was building up another picture—a pleasanter one. She was young and virile—a confection of blue eyes, and auburn hair; a rich voice whose timbre he could hear even in the noisy market. How she had come into his life he scarcely knew. Like many other things, she happened to be there. He was tired of working out "hows" and "whys." She was like the Universe—a going concern.

To find this woman was his chief desire, and it was not as easy as it should have been, for there were queer gaps in his memory that only time would fill up. He had to forge a whole series of connecting links, and this he did as he loitered amid the depleted hawkers' stalls. He bought a few articles—a knife, a lead pencil, a cheap cigarette case, and paid for them with a Treasury note which he produced from a well-packed wallet. Then he noticed a red-nosed child sniffing at a jar of candy. He gave the youngster a shilling and patted it on the shoulder. The mother smiled at him.

Such was Jack o' Lantern when his mind was comparatively calm—when the maggots lay dormant. He recalled that up a side street there was a certain place where he could get a drink—and other things necessary to him. He passed through the crowd and found the narrow staircase. A green door opposed progress. He rapped R R in Morse and the door opened. A wizened creature blinked at him, and then stood aside. The visitor strode in, humming an air. At the end of the long passage was another door. Again he knocked—as before—and after a slight delay he was admitted. It was a queer room with a flavour of the East about it. On the walls were crude drawings by Japanese artists, and in one corner was a big image of Buddha. There was a gas fire burning in the grate, and a low table before it with a divan on one side and a low lacquered chair on the other.

The woman who had opened the door was like a mask of death. She was obviously old, though her white thin face was devoid of wrinkles. It was like a sheet of ancient parchment, and barren of all emotion—all feeling. Her dirty tattered dress hung down to the floor, and there was a black silk scarf around her throat.

"Be seated!" she croaked.

He sat on the divan while she occupied the lacquered chair. They looked at each other—the man with amusement, the woman with dead seriousness.

"So you have come again, my friend?"

"Yes, and your welcome is cold."

"What do you expect?"

"A drink—and that quickly. It is cold outside—cold and beastly muddy. What day is it?"

"Saturday."

"Ah—that accounts for the crowd. Get that drink!"

She brought him a bottle of whisky, some water, and a tumbler. He helped himself liberally, and then sighed as he gulped down the almost undiluted spirit.

"And how are the spooks, Mother Gill?" he asked. "Do they still indulge in falsehoods?"

Her black, sunken eyes glinted.

"They never lie," she said. "You jest, but only because you do not know. A friend of yours came to-night. I do not like him. He breaks through—always he breaks through. I do not want him, but he comes."

"A living man?"

She shook her head slowly.

"One of your damned spirits! Pah, I have no faith in them. They tell nothing worth the knowing. They learn nothing worth revealing. His name?"

"Tobias."

His head came forward, and the sceptical expression changed to one of rising interest.

"What did he have to say?"

"That he is looking after you—until you have done—what you must do. He spoke of a message—a warning that you heeded in time. It was less than an hour ago,"

Jack o' Lantern laughed, but stopped abruptly. He felt in his pocket and produced a crumpled piece of paper. As he spread this out words danced before his eyes:

DON'T GO TO WATLING COURT?
DON'T GO TO
DON'T GO

"That is it," he muttered. "Sometimes he does not lie. Pah, he may have seen it. There may be eyes that can look across the grave. He takes the credit. . . . But he lied about the other matter. My life is to be long—full of adventure, of romance, of love. It was not always the same—not always. There must have been a time when—— That reminds me. I must have a place—a room, a den—now that I cannot go to Watling Court. There is such accommodation here. I will take it."

She shook her head.

"I am afraid of you. You tell me nothing, and much is not revealed to me. No."

"Yes," he rasped. "Have no fear—you shall be paid —handsomely rewarded. Money! Here is money!"

He produced his wallet and extracted a wad of Treasury notes. She clawed at them, hesitated, and then succumbed to the irresistible lure.

"Upstairs," she said. "I will show you—presently."

"Good! Now the powder—that is included."

    *   *   *   *   *

Half an hour later he stole away. The links were forged, and his objective was outlined clearly in his mind. He thought he saw the girl with the red hair and the forget-me-not eyes, waiting with arms outstretched. A singularly one-purpose creature was this, that made its way through back streets towards the house of Jim Banting.

He was about to enter the house from the front when his attention was taken by a solitary form loitering on the opposite side of the road. Instantly he changed his mind and turned the corner of the street. He found himself under a high wall. Without a moment's hesitation he scaled it. But ere he jumped into the garden on the other side, he caught a glimpse of the lone man in his rear. Leaping across the narrow garden, he scaled another wall and lay hid in the neighbouring property. Later he stood upon a mound and looked across at Banting's house, chuckling as he saw the sergeant interrogating the occupants of the sitting-room, into which he had a view.

Immediately the sergeant vanished he tore the flap from the back of an envelope and scribbled a message in pencil. Then, with the agility of a cat, he made his way to the window and affixed the note, returning posthaste to his late hiding-place.

Some time later he saw the woman of his dreams alone. He went to the window and tapped on the glass. Her face came round—a beautiful but startled visage. He tapped again, and she came to the window—and opened it.

"Lefroy!" she whispered.

He grasped the soft hand and kissed it.

"You—you can't come in," she said. "There's a police officer outside——"

But he stepped through, closed the window and pulled the curtains.

"Have no fear. That unimaginative fellow will have followed your father and the 'worm' on a wild-goose chase. At last we are alone. Aren't you glad to see me?"

"Yes—yes. But I'm afraid—for you. They are looking for you—everywhere. If anyone should come——"

"No one will come. And if anyone should——"

She shuddered at the awful expression that came to his face, but in a second it had vanished, and he was the perfect lover. He took her gently by the arm and led her to the couch, and she made no attempt to repulse him. Late as it was, he built up the fire and placed a cushion under her head.

CHAPTER EIGHTEEN

HE HAD put the light out to create a more romantic atmosphere, and now the blazing coals threw weird shadows on the wall behind them. The last remnants of Kate's fear had gone under the passion of his burning words. The guard that she had set upon her emotions was down, and she gave him her lips and wound her supple arms about his neck.

"Why have you stayed from me so long?" she murmured. "I began to think my intuition was wrong—my heart a lying thing. You might have sent word."

To this reproach he vouchsafed no answer, not caring to admit those queer lapses of memory that were a curse to him.

"If you love me don't leave me so much alone. I can do nothing but think of you, and I hate this house, and the people we meet. It is you who open up a new world, Paul. It stays when you are gone—for a while.

Then it vanishes into space and I wonder whether it was but a dream—and you but a man in a dream."

"I'm real—vitally real. Your father has been trying to keep us apart, hasn't he?"

"Yes. I don't know why—at least—— I want to ask you something. You must tell me the truth. What have you done to cause all this police activity? A short time ago they raided Brooking's. I was arrested—and my father. They questioned me about you, but I could tell them nothing. Thank God I could tell them nothing."

"The rats!"

"But I want to know. You must tell me. I want to be on my guard against them. You can trust me."

"There is nothing to tell. Don't worry your pretty head about it. They have their theories, their army of spies that persecute the poor sneak, and leave the millionaires to plunder unendingly. But me they will never catch."

"Are you sure?"

He laughed in his colossal vanity.

"One must discover their weaknesses and play upon them. They serve a good purpose too, for they weed out the fools, the inept, the cowards. But why talk of these things? Have we not bigger issues at stake?"

"Must I be kept in ignorance of—of what you are, where you live? Isn't love a business of mutual trust? My mind has been filled with awful thoughts. It isn't——" She clung to him. "It isn't possible that you have—that you have——?"

"No more," he said harshly. "That part is closed. We will begin anew. Hark! It is raining again. Rain —rain! Nothing but cold rain, fog and sunless skies. Love cannot be brought to fruition here. Suppose we fly—you and I—to some quiet spot where there are no prowling policeman, somewhere amid the hills in sunny

Provence? We could go to-morrow. It is only across the road—so to speak. A night's journey in the train— through the night to a new world. Isn't that a mighty idea? All the better for being spontaneous. I have money—we are young. Your excellent father would fly into paroxysms of rage, but you would be happy. I have the means to assure that. What do you say?"

"Do you—really mean it?"

"I never say what I do not mean. I will meet you at Charing Cross station—under the clock—and we will catch the Continental express. It is simple."

"But the passport?"

He stroked his chin.

"Ah, yes—the passport! That may take a day. We will make it Monday instead."

"But you dare not apply for a passport?"

"Dare not! My dear Kate, I shall procure a passport in less time than the average mortal. Shall it be Monday?"

She was trembling with excitement, for the prospect of escape from her lonely, monotonous, persecuted life was delightful. Borne up on passion's pinnacle she ceased to reason.

"Yes—yes," she said. "I will leave a note for my father. You will not forget?"

"Forget! You will need money to buy a few things. Better not bring them here. Buy a case to contain them and leave them at the cloak-room. I will do the rest."

He gave her four five-pound notes, and she slipped them into her handbag. Then she remembered something.

"Paul, are we to go as—as man and wife?"

"On the passport—yes. But we will make that relationship a reality when we reach the sunshine. I must go now, before that lynx-eyed servant of Scotland Yard comes back on the heels of your father. Until Monday!"

*   *   *   *   *

On Monday afternoon a telephone message reached Wrench at Scotland Yard.

"Silding speaking from Charing Cross. I saw Banting's daughter leave the house, and trailed her here. She picked up a suit-case at the cloak-room and is now waiting on the Continental platform. Looks as if she is expecting someone."

"Good! Hang on to her. If she meets a man—a stranger—arrest him. If she travels alone follow her to her destination."

At half-past five the same evening Silding turned up at the office in person.

"Well?" inquired Wrench.

"Nothing happened. But I'll wager anything she expected someone. She became agitated as the time of departure approached—walked up and down the platform —observing everyone. When the whistle blew she was mighty near to crying. She dumped herself on a seat for a few minutes, and watched the train steam out. Then she pulled herself together and made off. I trailed her back to the house."

"H'm!"

It was another disappointment following many. Wrench talked it over with his chief, and they both arrived at the same conclusion. The man for whom Kate had waited was Lefroy, and by some uncanny means he had divined the danger—in time.

"He deserves his sobriquet," mused Wrench. "It's like matching one's wits against a shadow."

"He probably saw Silding."

"It is possible. Rather leads one to surmise that he is an old hand, since he can pick out our men so easily

in a crowd. Silding is not the man to make himself
conspicuous. I propose putting a double watch on that
house of Banting's—night and day. If the woman stays
there Lantern will visit her again."

"He may fix another rendezvous—by letter or telephone."

"Quite. The woman must be watched. I find there
is a room just vacated in a house opposite. I intend
placing a man there at once."

"Good!"

As for Kate—she had suffered a fearful blow. Up to
the very last minute she had hoped, and then to watch
the train steam out—the train that was to have taken
her and Lefroy—— Her first reaction was insensate
rage against him, for playing this vile trick. But this
passed as she realised that something unexpected might
have happened. The police might even have cut short
his career! With that dread possibility in her mind
she hurried home, and reached the house in time to
destroy the note which she had left for her father. She
waited anxiously for a telephone message, but none came.

The following day brought no light. To her tremendous relief, the newspapers contained no such glaring
head-lines as she fully expected. No, Lefroy was at
large—barring some accident. Again she was faced with
the silence of old. This queer lover of hers was a riddle.
Had he really meant what he said? Or was she but a
plaything to him? She could not accept the latter conclusion. He had come to that house at great risk to see
her. He had given her money to buy articles of travel.
No—no, he was no conscious deceiver.

Banting divined that something was amiss, but he did
not fathom her secret, and at the same time he was
furious with Lefroy for making an appointment which
he did not keep. In addition, he was fully aware that

an even closer watch was being kept on the house. And he had the feeling that he was being trailed everywhere. His nerves were badly frayed, and his finances were low.

"Damn Lefroy!" he muttered in Kate's presence.

"What has he done now?"

"It is what he has not done. Well, I am through with him—and with this house. I am going to sell it, and get what there is to come when the mortgage is paid off. Kate, I'm tired—tired out."

"I know," she replied. "I feel like that too."

"Why don't you marry Sam?" he asked. "He's three parts an idiot, but he has means and he says he will start you in a small business. He is genuinely in love——"

Her scornful expression caused him to stop. He walked closer to her and regarded her keenly.

"Isn't Sam good enough for you?"

"He would drive me to suicide. What is he? A miserable sneak—a snatcher. I would rather——"

"You would rather risk life with a man like Lefroy, eh?" he asked harshly. "That shall never happen. I have warned you about him. You've got to stop that nonsense—do you hear?"

"I hear."

"And you will obey me."

"Am I not old enough to settle my own affairs?"

"You are a mere child in Lefroy's hands. I tell you, Kate, that to associate with him is dangerous. He must not come here again—or anywhere where we are."

"This is quite a new idea," she said coldly.

"Yes, but it is forced on me by circumstances. In future Lefroy will play no part in our affairs. I wish I had never seen him. Think over that proposition of Sam's."

She laughed scathingly.

"It needs no thinking over. It is as well that Sam should know where he stands."

He turned on her furiously.

"You are in love with Lefroy. I know it. I can read it in your eyes. It is no use denying it."

"I will not deny it. What then?"

"You are mad—demented." His attitude changed a little as he realised that wrath and threats made no impression upon her. "Listen, Kate. You're my only child —the only living being that I care anything about. I've always hoped that I might be able to settle you somewhere in comfort. For ten weary years I tried honest means. I was so damned honest that I refused to take a hand in a certain matter of business that would have brought me a certain five thousand pounds. What did I get for that display of moral rectitude?—two years' hard. I had no delusions after that. I couldn't have got back into honest employment if I had tried. Well, I didn't even try, but I still hoped to make your future safe by pulling off a big thing. I've never succeeded. Lefroy held out hopes, but he's a twister. We've planned and plotted, and always he has failed us. He's an egoist —full of himself. He works alone—in the dark, and he has no scruples. He tells us nothing—and laughs at us all the time. How he lives—where he lives I don't know, but I do know that one day he will make the fatal mistake that will send him to the gal——"

"Father!"

"You may as well know. There's a vast difference between larceny and—and the other. I would kill you with my own hands rather than you should live the sort of life that a woman lives with—a homicide."

"I don't believe it!" she cried chokingly. "Sam has poisoned your mind from motives of jealousy. You do not know Paul as I—as I do. It isn't possible."

"Are you blind? Why do you think half the police force is concentrated on capturing Lefroy? Do they take such pains with a common crook? Have you never heard of Jack o' Lantern?"

"Jack o' Lantern! Why, what——?"

He looked round cautiously, as if he dreaded that the walls might conceal the strange person that he feared almost as much as Sam Knudge.

"Lefroy is—Jack o' Lantern," he said almost in a whisper.

Kate opened her mouth and tried to protest, but no sound came. This revelation stunned her. She had never dreamed of that connection.

CHAPTER NINETEEN

A FORTNIGHT later Scotland Yard was startled by an urgent telephone message from a police station in North London. It notified them that a Doctor Ambrose Devinne had been found murdered in his consulting-room in Windsor Crescent. An inspector and a sergeant were instantly dispatched.

The victim was found lying on the carpet before an electric radiator, with a knife-wound in his heart. A doctor was in attendance and certified that life was extinct. There were certain remarkable facts about the crime—the outstanding one being that the maid had actually seen the murderer. She told her story intelligently and coherently. The doctor as a rule gave no consultations after seven P.M. But on this evening— shortly after nine o'clock—he was rung up on the telephone by a gentleman who gave his name as Sir Thomas Rant, who asserted that he was compelled to leave London on the midnight train, and begged for a con-

sultation before he left. The maid herself took the
message in the nurse's absence, and subsequently the doctor himself spoke to the caller. He informed the maid
that Sir Thomas would call later and intimated that he
would see him.

"And what time did he call?" inquired the inspector.

"It was one minute to half-past nine, by the hall
clock, which was put right by the wireless time-signal
this evening."

"Describe this man."

"He was fairly tall—about your size, sir. Clean-
shaven, with a very pale face—and sunken eyes. He
looked very ill—like a lot of the doctor's patients. He
wore a long, dark overcoat and a felt hat."

"Complexion?"

"I should call him sallow, sir."

"Hair?"

"I never saw his hair, sir. He had his hat pulled very
low down, and he didn't take it off. I thought he was
rather rude for a titled gentleman."

"What age?"

She hesitated.

"Forty. No—more perhaps. It's difficult to say."

"Go on."

"I showed him into the waiting-room, and then went
to inform the doctor. He told me to show him into the
consulting-room."

"He still wore his hat?"

"Yes, sir, until we reached the consulting-room. He
removed it then, but the hall was rather dark, and I did
not notice his hair. I closed the door after him and went
back to my sitting-room."

"When did you next see the doctor?"

"A long time elapsed. I was expecting to hear the bell
ring, but nothing happened. At half-past ten nurse re-

turned. I told her that the doctor was seeing a patient, and that he had been engaged with him for an hour. That's all I know, sir—until—until I heard——"

The nurse then gave evidence. She had gone out for the evening and had returned at ten-thirty. The maid had informed her about the patient. She was a little surprised at the length of the consultation, but thought it possible that the visitor was a friend of the doctor and that they were having a chat. But after waiting a little while longer she went to the door of the consulting-room and listened. She heard no sound of any kind and then grew apprehensive. She tried to open the door, but found it locked. Thereupon she went into the garden on to which the consulting-room looked. The casement window was open slightly, and on peering inside she saw the doctor lying on the floor. She telephoned the local police station.

"You know of no Sir Thomas Rant?"

"No."

"Does the description fit any of the doctor's patients?"

"It might. He has so many callers it is impossible to remember them in detail."

"He was an expert in mental diseases, was he not?"

"Yes."

"Did you look closely at the body before calling the police?"

"Yes. I saw immediately that he was dead."

"Nothing has been disturbed?"

"Nothing."

That the murderer had left by the window was fairly certain. The nurse had found the door locked on the inside, and also bolted. From the garden beyond the consulting-room there was easy access to a road, through a door which was normally bolted on the inside. The officer from the local station had found this unbolted, but had discovered no footprints of any kind, for a concrete path led down to it.

The inspector and his assistant made a minute search of the room, but no clue of any kind was forthcoming. He went through the evidence which his assistant had taken in shorthand, and ultimately returned to Scotland Yard.

By ten o'clock the following morning Wrench was in possession of all the facts. The name of Ambrose Devinne was not unknown to him, for he was considered to be an expert in mental cases, and was occasionally called in to give opinion. Wrench hunted through a pile of facts and statements in connection with the Tobias Lantern trial, and at last found what he wanted. He went to see the Assistant Commissioner.

"The theory fits, sir."

"You have found the name?"

"Yes. Devinne was one of the two doctors who examined Tobias Lantern, with a view to establishing whether he was mentally responsible."

"Who was the second doctor?"

"Cartwright."

"Ah, yes. I remember that. Well, Cartwright died in his bed two years ago. You have seen the corpse?"

"Yes. The doctor's opinion is that death was instantaneous. There was a deep knife wound clean into the heart."

"Not the old S type?"

"No. A straight blade. Undoubtedly the weapon we found at Watling Court was his customary tool. He has gone in for something more modern."

"This is bad business, Wrench. In a few hours all London will be shrieking about it. A cool customer to walk in like that, taking no precautions except the use of a false name. Well, it should make identification simple—when we get him."

Wrench nodded, but he scarcely knew what to do next. For over a fortnight Banting's house had been watched day and night, and both Banting and his daughter had been followed wherever they went. The old haunt at Watling Court was as empty as ever. It was a perplexing Chinese puzzle. The description of the murderer given by the maidservant agreed to some extent with particulars already in the possession of the police, and it enabled them to build up a fairly complete picture of the wanted man. This was broadcast to all police stations throughout the country, and published in the press.

Sonia read the details of the murder with horror and alarm. Apart from her natural repugnance, it meant that John would be unavailable to her; and already she was seeing little enough of him. To add to her depression, the Judge was indisposed again, and was confined to his room. As before, he was averse to her calling in the doctor, and for the moment she was indulging his whim. Late in the afternoon Michels called.

"The Judge is—not well," she said.

He raised his eyebrows, and displayed sympathy.

"But I have no doubt he would be glad to see you," she added. "He seems very depressed. Shall I tell him?"

"Do." He glanced at the newspaper which was lying on the table. "Horrible business, that!"

"Terrible."

She left Michels in order to apprise the Judge of his old friend's arrival. Michels scanned the headlines and winced. Normally he was a well-controlled individual— even phlegmatic—but now he was nervous, fidgety. He put the newspaper down and walked about—chin on one

hand. Nali entered to clear away some tea-things.
Michels glared at him.

"Did you enjoy yourself last night, Nali?"

The Hindu started.

"I—I do not understand the *sahib*," he replied slowly.

"It is not difficult. Think!"

Nali merely shook his head.

"I am old and cannot move with any swiftness, but
you are fleet of foot. Fleeter than I imagined. It was
nearly two o'clock—close to Marble Arch."

"The *sahib* speaks in riddles."

Michels laughed scornfully, and then Sonia came in
to tell him that the Judge would very much like to see
him. He picked up the newspaper as he left.

"Is—is that wise?" she quavered.

"He had better know."

"You know best. But I am afraid——"

He patted her on the arm, and smiled into her affrighted eyes.

"Trust me. It is all right."

At the door he narrowly averted his head. Nali had
the tea-tray poised on one hand, and was surveying him
strangely. He made no further comment, but went upstairs. The Judge was sitting in a chair before a blazing fire, wrapped in a thick shawl.

"Ah—Michels!"

Michels shook hands, and pulled a chair close beside
the Judge. Without a word, he handed him the newspaper. The Judge's eyes narrowed as he read the bold
headlines, and his hand trembled visibly.

"Devinne!" he exclaimed. "This—this is monstrous!
Yet I might have expected it. You know who Devinne
was?"

"Yes. Your theory was right, Wallington. Here is
a drama of vengeance—carried out with consummate

skill and deadly resolve. Perhaps vengeance is not the right word. It is a mistaken notion of justice."

"Justice! As if there——"

"I am looking at it from his point of view—the point of view of the man who believes that the jury, judge, prosecuting counsel, and medical advisers conspired to send to the gallows a man who was completely unaccountable for his actions. It may not be true, but this poor creature has deluded himself into that conviction."

The Judge nodded reflectively.

"And I am left until last," he mused. "But who is this person who takes upon himself the duty of righting a supposed injustice by perpetrating other injustices? Tobias had a brother, but Wrench is satisfied that this brother is a decent-living man. There are a mother and sister, but they can be ruled out."

"It may be no blood-relation."

"A fellow criminal?"

"A maniac—a creature who hides by day and stalks abroad by night, whose idiosyncracies are such that he may be the last person to be suspected. The police are looking for a criminal type. They may be wrong. This man—or woman—may normally be a quiet, well-mannered creature, a devoted husband, or wife, or servant, and homicidal only when completely obsessed."

"Why do you mention a woman, when the evidence is completely opposed?"

"Merely to cover every contingency. This is an uncommon case, Wallington, and one needed the knowledge of the psychologist and pathologist equally with that of the detective."

The Judge looked at his friend sharply. He was perceptive to an extraordinary extent, and was a fine reader of minds.

"You have a theory all your own, Michels?"

"Not a complete theory. There are considerable gaps in it, and it calls for caution—and secrecy. I want to ask a favour."

"It is granted."

"I should like to come here again, as your guest."

The Judge smiled.

"My dear Michels, nothing would please me more. Come whenever you wish. You will be good company for Sonia. Wrench is so infernally wrapped up in this mystery the poor girl is left too much to her thoughts. But do you expect your theory to be furthered by anything you may discover—here?"

"It may be. I can say no more."

The Judge sighed.

"What an air of mystery there is over everything. Sweeting had some mad idea about my being poisoned. It would have been perfectly simple for Nali or the cook to poison me, but neither of them did, and I am quite satisfied they will not. On the other hand, I am perfectly willing to admit that another individual may take it into his head to try his hand on me, and I fancy it it will not be poison."

"You are a brave man, Wallington."

"Tch! Think of the dangers we face every day. I may be mangled to-morrow by a London General omnibus. Take all the daily risks to life and limb combined, and they will be quite as great as the risk that Jack o' Lantern represents. It requires courage to live at all in this century, and yet we go on living, and laughing."

He laughed as if to prove his remark, but Michels did not laugh. What lay hidden in Michels' mind was something that put laughter clean out of court.

CHAPTER TWENTY

AGAIN came a comparatively uneventful period. The excitement, horror and agitation caused by the latest murder were reduced to their correct proportions. But at Scotland Yard there was no slackening of interest. Every man was on his mettle, and no single avenue that promised to shed light on the mystery was left unexplored. During a fortnight Sonia saw Wrench but twice, and even these meetings were of brief duration.

"I'm rapidly being reduced to skin and bone," he complained. "We're snowed under with all kinds of rubbish from well-meaning folk. Jack o' Lantern has been seen in Newcastle, Glasgow, Exeter, London—everywhere. A dozen landladies are perfectly certain that he is a lodger in their respective houses. Goodness knows how many innocent men have received notice to quit. We have followed up some of the information, but in every case it has proved to be of no value whatever. Phew!"

"Then things are just as they were?"

"Practically. This man is clever. He leaves no trail behind him—and he works alone. There are certain people who have seen him—talked to him—but they know no more of his real life than we do. Even the woman who undoubtedly loves him is left utterly in the dark as to his whereabouts."

"The woman you call Kate?"

"Yes—the daughter of an intelligent crook, named Banting."

"You have seen her—this woman?"

"Yes."

"What is she like? One reads of women who love murderers, but it is difficult to imagine such."

"I am not sure that she knows he is a murderer. To her he is Lefroy. She is decidedly fascinating, very self-possessed and proud in her way. It is rather a sad case—the Bantings. I have looked up his history, and I am convinced that he was unjustly imprisoned years ago. That is the ironical part of it. As an innocent man he received two years' hard labour. But when, from a sense of burning injustice, he resorts to a dishonest career he manages to steer clear of quod."

"Why do you think he was wrongly convicted?"

"I was mixed up with a forgery case. The culprit— an old offender—had reason to believe that a 'pal' had squealed on him, and in order to have his revenge he gave us certain information. It had reference to several old crimes, and, incidentally, it threw a lot of light on the case in which Banting figured. It made out Banting to be a scapegoat."

"So you do make mistakes?"

"Heaps. O that human wisdom were infallible!"

"This woman—she is young?"

"About your own age. Poor girl! What an appalling shock it will be to her when she knows the truth—if she doesn't know it already!"

Sonia shuddered. She tried to imagine herself in that terrible position—an awakening to the awful fact that the man she loved was a murderer—a creature outside the pale, who must live the life of a hunted thing for the rest of his days, or pay the penalty. She wondered if that would destroy love once it had been nurtured to full bloom?

"It's horrible," she said.

"Then let us not talk about it. How is the Judge?"

"Not at all himself. The last murder seems to have affected him deeply. At times I find him staring into space—in a kind of brown study—and it requires an effort to bring him to his senses. I think he is very ill, but is too proud and stubborn to admit it. Michels has been trying to persuade him to take a holiday, but he will not listen. He attends court when he ought to be in bed."

"So Michels is still staying with you?"

"Yes. The Judge enjoys his company. He is working on a book and——"

"The Judge?"

"No—Michels. Sometimes he works far into the night. He has stupendous energy for a man of his age."

"What sort of a book?"

"I don't know, but he seems utterly engrossed in it. The library is in a shocking state of untidiness—books all over the table and floor." She hesitated for a few moments. "John, isn't there something a little strange about Michels?"

"In what way?"

"He behaves in a queer way. As I told you, he stays up on the pretext of writing, but the other night I had occasion to go downstairs. The foolish maid had built up the boiler fire too high, and the water was making a hideous noise. I was afraid the boiler might burst, and went to attend to it. There was a light in the hall, and I looked into the library to see if Michels was there. He was not, but on the table was a small book—a diary, I think—and I could not help reading what was written on the open page. It was in German, with which I am fairly well acquainted. Roughly, it ran like this:

Cunningham's information is fairly conclusive, but I dare not accept it in toto. I must have ocular proof before taking steps. . . . If that should be forthcoming the gravest crisis will arise . . ."

Wrench pursed his lips at this.

"Who is Cunningham?" he asked.

"I don't know. But there is something else. I concluded that Michels had gone to his room for something, and therefore left the light burning in the hall. When I reached the landing I heard a noise from the direction of the hall door. I peered over the balustrade and saw the hall door open. Michels entered. He had a pistol in his hand, and was hatless. He bolted the door behind him and went into the library. I—I went to my room."

"Strange! He did not mention this matter to you the next day?"

"No."

"He may have thought he heard someone outside— a burglar."

"Or that man—Jack o' Lantern."

Wrench concurred reluctantly. But what engaged his mind more deeply was the writing which Sonia had seen. Who was Cunningham? And what had he told Michels to cause him to anticipate a grave crisis?

"I am not going to pretend that I understand half of what is going on," he confessed. "Detectives are just like other men. They have no miraculous inspirations. Things have to be sorted out and pieced together with a view to getting a coherent whole. Personally I find too many pieces missing. There is no reason to assume that Michels is acting in any way but in the interest of justice, but all the same I wish he would show his hand. This man Cunningham may well be an important factor."

"John, do you really think the Judge is in any real danger?"

"I do."

"Then he ought to be protected."

"He makes it very difficult. I had this house watched for some time, despite his objections. But recently he

apprehended one of our men, and wrote a snorting letter
to the Assistant Commissioner. The Chief humoured
him, but he is still protected to a greater extent than he
imagines."

"Shall we ever be free of this shadow?"

"Oh, yes. The darkest cloud passes. I am on night
duty again to-night. Cheer up, old girl! Despite all
the set-backs and queer factors, I believe we are very
close to getting our man."

But she thought his optimism was more apparent than
real. When he had gone she went into the library and
found Michels working. He packed up his manuscript
when he saw her and averred that he had finished for
the day.

"Are you writing it in German?" she asked.

"Yes. It will probably be published in Germany
first."

"And then translated into English?"

"If it is considered sufficiently important."

"It is sure to be."

"Thank you for the compliment."

"I presume it deals with some abstruse subject?"

"Yes—new light on old problems. Sonia, I am worried about the Judge. I have tried very hard to get him
to take a holiday, but he pooh-poohs the idea. I want
you to add your weight to the argument. I assure you
it is very necessary. He must get away from this house.
He needs a complete change."

"But it is necessary for him to be near the court."

"It is necessary for him not to attend the court for
some time," he replied seriously.

"He will not hear of that."

"We have to make him consider such a change."

"Are you—are you suggesting this merely because of
his health, or do you suspect that there is danger from

another quarter?" she asked in a quavering voice.

"There is grave danger—from several quarters. But the imminent danger is his health. For months he has been living on his nerves. It can't go on. Sir Henry called this morning when you were out."

She exhibited surprise, for she had no notion of this.

"It was intended to be a social call, but we had an ulterior motive."

"What—what did Sir Henry say?"

"Shall I confide in you?"

"Please—please!"

"Sir Henry is of the opinion that the Judge is still taking poison into his system. The Judge laughs at the idea. Have you ever known him take any sort of sleeping-draught?"

"No—never. But . . ."

"Go on."

"Perhaps I ought not to tell you this, since it is like a betrayal of confidence. But you are his friend, and I feel that you have the power to help us. The Judge would not dream of taking any kind of dope, but Nali does—or did. I found him in possession of a white powder. I admonished him and he promised to break himself of the habit."

"So he confessed to drug-taking?"

"Yes. I had discovered that he was in the habit of going out late at night. The drug was his explanation. John discovered this box of powder by accident. I had to explain how I became possessed of it. He told me later that it was cocaine."

Michels' eyes gleamed with interest.

"What was Wrench's theory?"

"I—I suppose he accepted Nali's story. What else could he do?"

"He might have doubted it."

"But you don't—you don't suggest that Nali lied to me—that he is capable——"

"That is what Superintendent Sweeting thinks. But it is not my theory."

"My brain is muddled," she confessed. "I cannot see the connection between that awful murderer and the alleged plot to poison the Judge."

"There is a possible connection."

"You mean that someone—someone in this house may be in league with that—that awful being?"

"I cannot tell you more at the moment. It is possible the Judge may make a swift recovery, in which case he will laugh to scorn the idea of taking a vacation. But if he should not get better, we must get him out of this house—even if we have to use force."

"Force! Why, that is incredible!"

"A good many incredible things may have to happen before we reach the end," he replied grimly. "I—I wish you were far away from here—out of this mire of horrible——"

"Mr. Michels! What are you concealing? You ask me to trust you—but you do not trust me. Haven't I heard the worst already? I know—we all know—that the Judge's life has been threatened by a monster who had already brutally murdered several people. If you have any information that will lead to the capture of this assassin, or if you believe that anyone in this house is aiding him, why not say so? Why not tell the police? Are you not on the side of the law?"

"Am I?" He wrinkled his great brow. "Child, you are young. Even to the aged there come new, ghastly facts about that queer set of conditions which we call Life. Justice is a man-made thing. It changes and must change as new things are revealed. There are occasions when a man finds himself up against a problem that sets all his experience at naught, and leaves him in mid-air, with no solid thing to cling to. That is where I am now —or shall be if—if certain things should happen. I wish I could believe they would not happen."

"What am I to glean from that?"

"Nothing yet. You must be patient. But it will be an incredible thing if we, with all the forces of the law on our side, cannot put an end to Mr. Jack o' Lantern before—before he commits much more damage."

She was impatient with this circumlocution—this web of evasion and verbiage. In return for her confidence he offered her a nebula. Yet she was compelled to recognise his undoubted intellect and reasoning. Both he and Wrench called for faith and trust on her part, and she divided what she possessed between them; but she thought it was a great pity that these two men could not work in harness.

CHAPTER TWENTY-ONE

AGAIN the Judge demonstrated his marvellous recuperative powers. One morning Sonia found him at breakfast, cracking a joke with Michels, who regarded him with wondering eyes. He was still pallid, but there was a look of new vitality about him.

"Why, Bunty!" she exclaimed.

"It is a fine day," he said. "It is such a rare phenomenon in this part of the world, that I decided it was an omen—a gentle hint on Nature's part to me. Come here!"

She went to him and he kissed her fondly, and wished her many happy returns of the day.

"So you did remember?" she said.

"My memory may not be what it was, but it works

—at times. I cannot ask you to look under your plate, but I fancy you will find your present outside—after breakfast."

"You dear! But I do not intend waiting that long. Excuse me, Mr. Michels!"

She ran into the hall, and almost collided with Nali, who gravely presented her with a small package, together with his best wishes. It proved to be a plain gold bangle. She took no exception to this offering from him, for in her eyes he was something more than a servant, and she knew that any display of embarrassment would have wounded him deeply.

"That is very nice of you, Nali," she said. "I had almost forgotten it was my birthday."

"Those who love do not forget," he replied, and vanished.

Outside the front door she found the Judge's present. It was a fascinating little two-seater car, with its new paint-work gleaming in the sunshine. A man—obviously from the garage from which it had been purchased—was in attendance. He informed her that he had been told to wait in order that he might give the first driving-lesson, if that was convenient.

"Yes," she replied. "In—in half an hour. Does it take long to drive a car?"

"Some never learn," he replied.

"That doesn't sound very encouraging."

"But some take to it as if they was born to it."

"Ah, that's better! Well, half an hour. If you will go round to the side door the maid will give you some breakfast."

"Thank you, miss, but I had mine two hours ago."

"Does the world get up so early?"

He grinned at her as she tripped up the steps, and

sighed as he thought of his last birthday present—two ties and a pair of socks.

"Bunty," she said, as she entered the breakfast-room, "you are a thought-reader."

"So it is what you wanted?"

"Yes. But in this Victorian house I dared hardly mention such a thing. What is the penalty for driving through a shop-window?"

"Ah, I shall live in fear and trembling from this moment onwards."

"Oh, no, you will not. In less than a week I shall be driving you to the court."

"You will not. Try your hand on Michels. He has a nerve of iron."

Sonia's first driving lesson was not associated with the horrors she had anticipated. Her wary tutor took her to a deserted road in the north of London, where she could do nothing worse than run into a ditch or smash a telegraph pole. But she came through the ordeal brilliantly, though she did cause him to indulge in facial contortions when she changed gear.

"That'll come," he said optimistically. "Women are always dud gear-changers—at first."

She was grateful for the qualification. It was abundantly clear to her that he had no great regard for the woman driver, and whenever she achieved anything she knew he was saying to himself "Not bad—for a woman." By the time the lengthy lesson was over she was in love with the dapper little vehicle, and had already formed the resolution that she would learn to care for it herself, even to washing it down!

The day's happiness was somewhat dulled by the reflection that John had sent no word of remembrance. She tried to make excuses for him, but they fell rather flat. At least he might have remembered that day, and have sent a card! But during the evening Wrench called, and subtly slipped a necklace over her head as he kissed her.

"Did you think I had forgotten?" he asked.

"Well, no; I—I——"

"You did."

"I tried not to."

"No doubt it looked bad. As a matter of fact I was on the verge of posting this to you when I was called away. I've been out all night on the trail of a man who is believed to be Jack o' Lantern."

"John!"

"Well, we've got him."

"You mean—you have got Jack o' Lantern?"

"We have got the suspected man. A woman lodged information. The man rented a room from her three months ago, and has been acting very mysteriously ever since. He came in at nights and left early in the mornings. Last night he entered the house earlier than usual. I received a telephone message, and we entered the place. Phew! he was like a cat. He leaped through the window on to an outbuilding nearly fifteen feet below and managed to make the street. He had a car waiting in the neighbouring square, and got away before we could reach him. We borrowed a parked car and went after him. Well, to cut a long story short, we finished on Salisbury Plain in the early hours of the morning. His petrol ran out before ours did. We brought him back, and in the meantime our men had located some stolen jewellry in his room. This has since been identified."

"But is he really——?"

"I have grave doubts. He gave the name of Grant, but of course that means nothing. We called in the maid from Doctor Devinne's house and also managed to collar

Sam Knudge. The maid, when asked to identify him from among half a dozen other men, hesitated, but lingered before him for a long time. Ultimately she said she wasn't sure. Knudge swore positively that none of the men was Jack o' Lantern."

"But mightn't he be nervous of telling the truth?"

"That is possible. But other facts rather bear out his assertion. It is fairly well established that the man we want is left-handed. This man is not. We had ample opportunity for observing that point. As yet there has been no time to prove his statements, but I shall not be surprised if he proves alibis, as he says he can."

"But why was the maid hesitant?"

"You have to remember that this man was arrested because of his resemblance to Jack o' Lantern—as published in the press. That resemblance would naturally cause the maid to be as dubious as his landlady. But we shall see. In the meantime he is safe. And whoever he turns out to be, he is certainly a crook. We can put him away on other charges, so our time was not entirely wasted. The worst he did was to cause you to believe that I had overlooked your birthday."

"Forgive me, John."

"Well, don't let it occur again," he said, pinching her ear affectionately. "Now what is the best news?"

"Bunty is better. He seems to be quite his old self again. But Michels—— No, I will relate nothing but what is pleasant to-day. Bunty has presented me with a wonderful little car, and I am fast developing into a speed maniac. If you are good I will take you for a run—when I can do so without risk of robbing the C.I.D. of the doyen of sleuth-hounds. Oh, and something else has happened. It is my own little secret, and by a co-incidence it has come to fruition on my birthday. Come and behold!"

She led him into the drawing-room and took a piece of sheet music from the piano. It was "The Hymn of the Soul" and it carried her name as the arranger from an old Hindu air.

"Well, I'm blessed!"

"It was just a crazy idea of mine," she said. "I was bored one day and started working out a pianoforte accompaniment. It went rather well, and I submitted it to a publisher. He offered me ten pounds for the copyright, but I refused, and now I am to receive a royalty. It was published to-day."

"Splendid! Play it to me."

The familiar weird air echoed through the room. Wrench had little knowledge of musical technique, but he was aware that she had modified the accompaniment since last he had heard it. It stirred him deeply, though as a rule he was not very susceptible to music.

"Uncommon thing," he mused. "I shouldn't be surprised if it goes like hot cakes. I had no idea you were so talented."

"Wait till Nali hears it. He hates me to play it on the piano. Seems to imagine that he has the sole instrumental rights. He will never forgive me. Are you free this evening?"

"Yes."

"Then you shall take me to the theatre."

"That's really what I came for. Don't trouble to dress up. Let's creep into the pit somewhere."

"I'd love to. But what is the idea—economy?"

"I'm saving up—in order to be able to support a wife." He took her by the arms and looked at her seriously. "Why should we wait any longer, Sonia? I had thought of waiting a bit in the hope of collaring Jack o' Lantern, for I believe promotion hangs on that, but now——"

"Now you have given up all hope?"

"Not a bit; but I realise that it is going to be a long and exasperating business."

"But the man you have in custody——?"

"Something in my bones tells me he is not the man. In the meantime the weeks and months are flying. Your husband may have to be a plain inspector instead of a superintendent. Could you bear that humiliation?"

"I might—try."

"Then let us put it to the Judge."

"Yes—yes. But he is not in at the moment. He and Michels went out together this afternoon. But they promised to be back to dinner."

"Then we will wait. How is Nali behaving himself?"

"I think he has kept his promise. At any rate I have not caught him at any of his nocturnal escapades. John, I had to tell Michels—about Nali."

"Why?"

"He put a leading question. I—I can't quite understand him. He seems very suspicious of Nali, and he acts as if he knows much more than any of us about—about everything. But I said I would not drag up——"

"We can't get away from it. I would give anything to see that diary of Michels'. I've a mind to pilfer it."

"John!"

"Well, I think that in the circumstances he is not acting in the public interest. Who is the man Cunningham? Why should Michels hesitate to confide in the police? Admittedly he is clever, but he cannot possibly have the knowledge that we possess as to the movements of criminals, and he may accidentally have hit upon a clue which would enable us to lay our hands on Jack o' Lantern. As for Nali—I think Michels is absolutely wrong."

"I am sure of it."

The Judge and his friend returned a little later. The

former was in high spirits, for he had been on the quest for two very desirable Baxter prints, and was now the proud possessor of them. He displayed them with a chuckle.

"I fear I have paid too much," he said. "But I had to have them, and that grasping dealer was evidently aware of the fact. But how are you, John?"

"Very fit, sir."

"Splendid! And you look it. I suppose you have come to the birthday party?"

"Yes."

"And dressed like a navvy."

"I hadn't time to change. I've been up all night, and frantically busy all day."

"And I like him best—as a navvy," put in Sonia. "We are thinking of joining the Socialist Party."

"That is so," agreed Wrench. "I should certainly like an eight-hour day."

"So should I," said the Judge. "But if we all had what we want, what an amazing place the world would be. There wouldn't be any incentive to do anything. All the criminals would be comfortably retired—probably in Parliament making laws for the incarceration of all policemen, and the slow torture of judges——"

"That is inconsistent," put in Sonia. "For you, too, would have had your wish granted. Of course it couldn't work at all. I suppose we must regard this world as the best of all possible worlds."

"There speaks care-free youth," said the Judge. "Well, it is something to be young."

After dinner Wrench had a few minutes with the Judge. He told him of his desire to marry Sonia without further delay, and Wallington pursed his lips. He raised no objections, but it was evident that he hated the prospect of losing his ward.

"You have spoken to Sonia?" he asked.

"Yes. She is quite agreeable."

"Then—then I have nothing to say—except to accept my fate. All I care about is her happiness, Wrench. My life has been somewhat drab—full of interests, but sombre interests. I will tell you a little secret, John. I was once in love—yes, deeply, passionately in love. It wasn't so long ago, and she was younger than I—full of life, of ideals. But it was all a nebula that never became a star. When she came to look into my life she found it—harsh, my nature unsympathetic. She expected me to share her erroneous pity and indulgence for creatures who were better not born at all. She saw good intentions, fine traits, where there were none. It was her sincerest belief that a criminal could be reformed and that kindness should take the place of punishment." He smiled wanly. "In short, she had all the sloppy dangerous sentimentalism that causes hundreds of thousands of people to sign a petition at the last moment for the reprieve of some cold-blooded monster to rid the earth of whom is a just man's prime duty. And she held such views with the finest motives. I had to go on my way—alone. As if by some merciful dispensation of Providence, Sonia came into my life. She took the place of the daughter who—who was never born to me. So if I indulge in a little of the sentimentalism which a few moments ago I disparaged, you must forgive me. Now run off and tell her I am relieved to shift the responsibiity."

Wrench shook hands with the fine fellow, and half an hour later he and Sonia were entirely occupied with their own future, while the Judge took his revenge on Michels in the form of chess, at which he was more brilliant than ever.

CHAPTER TWENTY-TWO

SAM KNUDGE was going through a crisis. For a week he had given his soul up to Bacchus without gaining much consolation from the protracted orgy. Now he sat in his lodgings with a violent headache and a murderous expression on his face. It seemed to him that Kate had gone out of his life for ever. Lefroy had got her, body and soul. In vain he tried to see her. In desperation he had written a letter, laying all he had to offer at her feet, and swearing he would give up drink— anything in fact—if only she would give him a trial. But no reply had come to him, and he began to contemplate suicide. He even tried to hang himself from a clothes peg in his room, but it was a ghastly failure. Sam was not destined to finish his life thus.

At nine o'clock he went out and visited one or two "pubs" in the neighbourhood of Leicester Square, but curiously enough the drink was bitter and nauseating to his palate. He left the last glass of it unfinished and wandered aimlessly for some time. Ultimately he found himself in the neighbourhood of Seven Dials. He thereupon decided to call on an old acquaintance, with a view to learning what the future really held, and a few minutes later he was rapping on the door of Mother Gill's flat. The door-keeper blinked at him and recognised him. Sam was shown into the sanctum sanctorum.

The medium-cum-fortune-teller was asleep on the divan, and snoring hideously. Sam shivered as he looked round the strange room, and then shook the arm of the sleeping woman. She opened her eyes and yawned.

"Hallo, Sal!"

"Who are——? Oh, it's Knudge! Why the h——!"

"Ain't you glad to see a client?"

"Why, yes. But I thought you had gone clean away."

"Not far. Rouse yourself."

She sat up and wrapped her shawl closer round her shoulders. Sam helped himself to a glass of whisky, but he did no more than sip it and pull a wry face.

"Ugh!"

"What's wrong with you, Sam Knudge?" she croaked. "You've been doping."

"You're wrong. It's a girl. She's driven me nigh to Hell, and I can't get her out of my mind."

"A woman, eh?" She chuckled mirthlessly.

"Get the cards," he said. "See if they can tell you anything—about me."

She peered up at him.

"You used to jeer at the cards——"

"Well, I'm not sure that you ain't a bit of a trickster."

"Maybe. It doesn't always do to tell people the truth. They mightn't come again. Some can face it and some can't."

She tottered across to a cabinet and extracted two dirty packs of playing cards. These she shuffled with the dexterity of a Monte Carlo professional despite her age and failing health. Sam had to cut them several times, after which she commenced to investigate the murky future.

"The Ace of Spades—that's death."

"Death!"

"Not for you—for someone who crosses your path. There's the woman—a fair woman. She eludes you—again and again. Hearts—what a mixing of hearts! Cut again!"

The manipulation seemed endless. All the time she talked—or rather chanted—and her whole attitude was so uncanny that Sam writhed in his chair. Whether by luck or some inexplicable faculty she told Sam his own story. It impressed him tremendously, and his head came nearer as she worked towards the end of the packs.

"She comes," she droned. "She comes closer—to him and to you. There! Well!"

"What—what do you make of that?"

"The luck is yours. You win—you win."

"Win? Garn!"

She looked mightily indignant.

"But she's chucked me—won't even look at me."

"I tell you she is coming to you—even now."

"My Gawd, if——!"

He reached out for his unfinished glass of whiskey, and this time it tasted well.

"You ain't tricking me?" he said hoarsely.

"There was no need to. The cards promised well. You're like my lodger. He sneers at the cards and at the voices, but in his heart he knows."

"So you've taken a lodger? That accounts for this display of the 'doings.' He's a good client, eh?"

Mother Gill looked uncommonly serious.

"He is strange," she confided. "There is one who knows him—in the spirit world. This spirit comes to me—when I do not want him. He is troublesome—pushes everything aside. I think he is causing great trouble on the earth-plane. Once he was called Tobias Lantern, and——"

Knudge started at the uncommon name and pricked up his ears.

"This Tobias, my guide tells me, is bad. She tells him to go, and brings greater spirits to dispatch him. He bellows, he roars, but they overpower him."

"Hold on,".said Sam. "I don't like this spooky business. Is he after your lodger?"

"I do not know—much."

"What is this lodger like?"

"A gentleman, tall, middle-aged."

"Is he—left-handed?"

"Yes. How did you know?" she demanded.

"Well—I guessed," he demurred. "And you like him, eh?"

"My God—I am afraid of him. But he pays well, and it is not my business. He lives upstairs, but he comes but seldom—like a ghost. I know when he is coming—for Tobias comes to me first—laughing and bellowing——"

Knudge took another drink, with a trembling hand. He felt he had made a discovery of considerable importance. The name "Lantern" was the link. He could not quite see the connection, but something within him told him that this strange left-handed lodger was his enemy Lefroy. When he left the place he went straight to Banting's house. There was no one at home but the maid, and she informed him that Kate and her father had gone to a music-hall. Sam went away and returned an hour later. He found Banting alone.

"Sit down," said Banting. "I've been wanting to see you."

Sam sat and waited.

"Sam, I'm clearing out."

"Eh!"

"I've sold the house, and I'll touch the money in two months' time. I'm going to America."

"Well! And Kate?"

"S-sh! She's writing letters—in the next room. It was Kate I wanted to discuss." He lowered his voice. "She knows all about—Lefroy."

"My God! You told her?'

"Yes. That affair was developing too fast. It knocked her clean out. But I think it killed her mad infatuation. She's more tractable now."

"You mean there's a chance—for me?"

"It depends how you handle things. I warn you she's not in love with the sneak-game. You once said you'd start her in a little business."

"So I would. I've got an offer of a business at this moment. It's a tobacconist-newspaper shop, with a pretty good connection. I can buy the whole thing, freehold and goodwill, for two thousand quid."

"Can you raise the money?"

"All of it. I haven't done so badly—on my own."

"But would you cut out the other stuff?"

"Yus—honest I would. Kate could hold her head high. I'd look after the newspaper side while she did the rest. There's living quarters, and I've already got some furniture of my own. Is it any good talking to her?"

Banting nodded. Socially Sam was outside the pale, but he was sincerely in love with Kate, and Banting believed that Kate's personality was strong enough always to override Sam. She would keep Sam in his place, and it was within the realm of possibility that she might find happiness with him. His great desire was that Kate should not be embroiled in any business of larceny, and suffer as he had suffered for years from the fear of detection and imprisonment.

"Talk to her," he said. "She is just in the mood now. Lefroy has neglected her, and what she has heard has turned her affection to horror. But don't start throwing bouquets at yourself. Exercise a little humility, and it may carry you a long way."

"I get you. Shall I barge in now?"

"Yes. But go warily. Don't try to force matters. It'll all come right if you show a little tact."

Sam gulped and went to the intervening door. He knocked softly and then entered. Kate had just finished her letter, and was sealing it when she looked up and saw Sam's nervous visage.

"Hope I ain't intruding," he said.

"You are. But you can come in."

Sam sat down opposite her, coughed, gulped, fidgeted with his collar and told her in a few brief moments exactly what was in his mind without uttering a word.

"Well?" she said. "You're unusually flustered."

"A bit," he mumbled. "Just a bit. It's not seeing you for nearly a fortnight, and not hearing from you——"

"Did you expect me to reply to your crazy letter? You're bad enough at speech, but at letter writing——! And I know you have been drinking yourself stiff, and uttering stupid threats."

"That's true," he said shamefacedly. "I went off the deep end when—— But that's all over. I'm not going to play the silly goat any more. Whatever happens I'm going steady. I'm sorry if I hurt your feelings in any way."

"You made me detest you—when I didn't want to."

"I know. My head ain't my strongest point. The old 'un was telling me he's sold the house—at last."

She nodded dolefully.

"Keen to go abroad, ain't he?"

"Yes."

"Well, he'd stand a better chance there. Too many narks round about here. Don't give a fellow a real chance. That's what he needs—a new start off."

"I wonder if a clean start is possible—after all these years of—of easy money."

"Easy money!" He laughed. "Not much of that about it. A fellow risks his neck for every cent he gets."

"You seem to have got away with it," she retorted with some bitterness.

"Well, yes. But I'm through with it all now. You

can laugh, but it's true. That's partly why I came to
see you. Kate, would you consider a straight business
proposition?"

"You don't really mean 'straight'?"

"Honest to goodness! You know Fletcher, who runs
the tobacconist business in the Gray's Inn Road? He's
giving it up and going to Canada to join his brother.
I can get the business and the premises for two thousand
quid. I've seen the accounts, and there's twelve quid a
week net profit—and rent free at that. There's a couple
of rooms I could let for another thirty bob. It's money
for jam, and on the level. What do you think of it?"

"I should take it."

"I want to, but one pair of hands can't run it."

"You can employ a girl—a pretty girl who will attract
new customers."

"Yah! I don't want no pretty girls making eyes at
men."

"Then get a man."

He shook his head impatiently.

"You know what I'm driving at, Kate, but you're just
teasing me. Wouldn't you like to make a clean start—
with me? We could make that business go like one
o'clock. Old Fletcher hasn't an idea in his head. The
shop is all dirty and untidy, and no decent folks will go
inside. I'd spend a hundred quid on it—put in a nice
new window, paint up everything. Maybe we could
employ a young chap who could look after it when we
wanted to go to the pictures. We could run a little
car, too. It would come in useful for the business.
Look, I'm asking you—will you think it over seriously?"

Kate was interested, for somewhere in her was the
business instinct. She was well aware that her father
desired to follow a lone trail, and she sincerely believed
that he was contemplating honest work in new fields.

The house was heavily mortgaged, and the most that Banting would get from its sale, when the incubus was removed, was five hundred pounds, plus whatever sum the furniture would fetch. With that very limited capital he could scarcely afford to pay her passage to America. She had been brought up to no occupation, and the most she could expect in the labour world was a job as a waitress, or domestic service. Even so, she was lacking references. On the other hand, she did not love Sam—at least not with the burning passionate love which she had experienced in Lefroy's case. But she was practical enough to realise that Sam was offering her something substantial.

"I'll think about it, Sam," she said after a long silence.

"Good! I don't want to worry you. But you'll understand that I can't delay too long, or that little business will be snapped up. Its a cinch, Kate. I'm all hot and excited about it."

"Give me—give me a day or two."

"Sure I will. I mentioned it to the old 'un, and he approves. It would solve all our problems, wouldn't it?"

"It might."

There was no enthusiasm on her part, but Sam did not look for that. He merely wanted her, and would have had her even had she told him that she considered him the most repulsive thing that crawled the earth. With most commendable wisdom he did not push the matter further, but left her and Banting together, and went home, rubbing his hands. Mother Gill was right. It was marvellous—stupendous!

And Kate? She saw herself being pressed into this cul-de-sac from sheer circumstances. The revelation concerning Lefroy had fallen like a knife on her heart. A cheat, a thief, a blackmailer, a receiver—it was possible to turn a blind eye to any of these, when love pressed, but a murderer! She had not come to that. It hurt her, too, to reflect that Lefroy had played a trick on her at the station. He had not meant to turn up. That was like him—to indulge in a cruel practical joke. No, she pushed his imaginary figure to the back of her mind.

On the following day she walked into the Gray's Inn Road, and saw the shop which Sam had mentioned. It was as he had said, untidy and dirty. Fletcher was dirty too. If the business was making so much profit in such circumstances, how much more could be made under proper management. Her fanciful mind conjured up pictures of more shops, a great extension of the business, and profits in proportion. Sam was clever in his way—and ambitious. Between them they might build up a considerable fortune. At any rate there was a chance. It was better than the present life of lurking fear—the shadow of the prison bars. And there might be children. She wanted that, for she was aware that she was missing much.

She made up her mind that night, and wrote a note to Sam to tell him to buy the business without delay. After that she felt more at ease.

CHAPTER TWENTY-THREE

THE improvement in the Judge's health was maintained for nearly a month, during which time Michels prowled about the house and acted as if he were thoroughly mystified. Then suddenly a change came. The Judge's old symptoms returned. He crept down to breakfast one morning, looking more like a ghost than his real self. He played with his toast and ate nothing else. Sonia was alarmed at his appearance, and begged him to go back to bed.

"It is—impossible. I have an important case—this morning. I—I must go."

He went despite her appeals. Michels watched the car depart, and his expression was one of mingled anxiety and bewilderment.

"How stubborn he is," said Sonia. "As if one case can matter as much as his health matters! What makes him come over like that intermittently?"

Michels shook his head.

"It was a pity I was out last night," he mused.

"Why?"

"I should have liked—— Did he retire at his usual hour?"

"Yes. He seemed to be quite well. We had some music, and he even sang a song."

"How strange it all is!"

"Why is it so strange? Do you think his illness is not a natural result of—of overwork—worry?"

"It may be so but——"

"You doubt it. Oh, we are back again to the old impossible theory, and just when I thought he was better than he has been for years. Mr. Michels, couldn't you go to the court and try to persuade him to adjourn the case early? You could see him at the luncheon interval. I'm terribly apprehensive. He has such will-power, and I fear that that may cause him to carry on until—until a complete collapse comes."

"I will do my best."

"Thank you."

But before Michels could carry out his promise the Judge was brought home in a car. He had collapsed in court, and the case had had to be adjourned. Fortunately Sonia was out when the car arrived, and she did not see him until he was put to bed. Sir Henry was telephoned for, but an hour passed before he arrived.

"Heart," he confided to Michels. "Heart—and something else."

"A long job?"

"He must be careful. I think he should have a nurse."

Sonia agreed. It was clear to her that the Judge was breaking up, but it seemed rather strange after his recent remarkable recovery.

"What did he mean about 'something else'?" she asked when the doctor had gone.

"The old mystery. You must get a nurse in."

This was accordingly done. For days the Judge lay helpless, and gloom lay over the house, but slowly his trouble vanished and new hope was born in Sonia's breast. The long spell of filthy weather broke, and brilliant sunshine came to breathe messages of arriving spring. When at last the nurse was dismissed Michels came forward with a suggestion.

"I have been your guest long enough, Wallington," he said. "Now you are going to be mine. Sir Henry strongly recommends a change of air, and I have recently rented a furnished house in the Chiltern Hills. I insist that you spend a few weeks with me."

"It would be too far from the court."

"Nonsense! Sir Henry has absolutely forbidden you to think of resuming your duties for at least two months. You must be reasonable."

"Please, Bunty," begged Sonia. "No man can go on working and working for ever, without a respite."

"What about this house—and the servants?"

"It can stay open," she argued. "It is better than closing it and letting the damp get in. This time you are going to do as you are told."

"Very well. You have me in a corner."

Within a week Sonia, the Judge and Nali were transferred to Randon Hall. The servants of the owner had stayed on, and proved entirely satisfactory. That Michels should have been willing to take Nali was a little surprising to Sonia, for she had the feeling that Michels' real motive was to get his old friend away from certain sinister influences and threats, and she believed that in Michels' mind Nali was a sort of evil genius.

The Hall was a commodious place—a Tudor mansion that had recently been renovated. Around it was a spreading park, containing many splendid trees and some deer. The old moat was still in existence, and most of the original surrounding wall. The interior was comfortable, if not luxurious, for the present owner was fabulously rich, and had let the place to Michels purely as a favour.

"I met him in Germany some years ago," explained Michels. "And was able to do him a small service. What do you think of it all?"

"It is rather—unreal, and I am not sure that I love a great rambling place—and suits of armour. But the grounds are wonderful, and the quietness a glorious change after the eternal rumble of the London traffic. It ought to do the Judge a power of good. May I ask John to come down next Sunday?"

"Of course. Have you fixed the date of your wedding?"

"Yes. In two months' time."

"The Judge will miss you."

"That is the only regret I have. Mr. Michels, why did you let Nali come?"

"The Judge wanted him to. He hates being fussed upon by anyone else."

"But you—you don't quite trust Nali?"

"I have never said so."

"One cannot help observing facts."

"It is not exactly mistrust."

"I wish I could understand you."

He did not attempt to elucidate his remark, and she was discreet enough not to press for an explanation. After a long walk among the hills she wrote to Wrench and told him about the place, begging him to come and see her on the Sunday.

Wrench arrived on the early train, and Sonia met him at the station and drove him back to the Hall in her car, which she now handled fairly well. She pointed to two dints in the wing and a lamp which was askew.

"My only mishap," she said. "A lamp-post exercised a fatal attraction for me. I—I lost my nerve and put my foot on the accelerator instead of the brake. Shall I show you what speed she can do?"

"Thanks, but don't bother. I am quite prepared to take your word for it."

"Coward! Look, there is the Hall! It's a marvellous place. This is the old road along which came knights in armour—at least I like to think they did."

"Is the Judge settling down?"

"Yes, astonishingly well. He walks in the park, and I think that in his heart he is thoroughly enjoying himself. Oh, did I tell you that a gramophone record has been made of my most marvellous composition?"

" 'The Hymn of the Soul'?"

"Yes. It is really good. Fortunately there was a gramophone in the house, and the record arrived yesterday. I tried it—when Nali was in the room. He—he looked almost murderous."

"Perhaps he thinks he should share the royalties."

"There may be something in that. Here we are! The drawbridge used to be there. It's a pity they took it away."

The Judge welcomed Wrench warmly. He showed

little sign of ill-health, for the fresh air of the hills was fast giving him quite a youthful complexion.

"So you haven't broken your neck?" he said. "Well, your trust is more profound than mine. And how are things at your end of the world?"

"About the same. Sweeting has been on another wild-goose chase, and is out of temper. The man—Banting—whose house we have been watching without any sort of success, has sold it. I suppose he finds his normal occupation more hazardous than ever. He is a clever scoundrel, and will probably seek new fields for profit—if we don't nab him before he gets out of the country."

"But can you?" asked Sania.

"Not at the moment. But there is always a hope."

Wrench and Sonia spent a delightful day together. It was impossible to conjure up spectres in the refulgent light of a perfect day, when Nature was striving to burst into new life, and birds sang in the trees, with the full knowledge that the winter was past. They saw little of Michels, but Sonia understood that he was working furiously at his new book in a room at the back of the house.

"I shall not be able to get down again until next Sunday," said Wrench. "Why not run up to town on Thursday, and have a bit of dinner with me? We could go to a show after."

"I'd love to, but there is no train back, and I should not like to drive the car so late at night."

"Couldn't you put up at Regent's Park?"

"Yes. I never thought of that. I'll come."

"Splendid!"

He stayed to dinner and Sonia drove him to the station afterwards. The Judge and Michels repaired to the library to engage in a bout at chess, and when she returned they were so immersed in complicated problems that they were scarcely aware of her existence.

"I will play the piano until you are more sociable," she said lightly.

"Do, dear. We will come and talk when I have convinced Michels that his fifth move was fatal."

Michels chuckled and shook his head. When she entered the sitting-room Nali was there, stoking up the fire. He did not hear her tread on the thick pile carpet, and turned from the fire to the gramophone, which was on a small table in the recess. Amused, she watched him turn the handle and start the machine. The weird air of the Hindu song rose high. He uttered a cry of rage, stopped the machine, and snatched the record from it. She saw it about to be shattered to atoms.

"Nali!"

He turned round sharply.

"Put that down! Why are you so foolish?"

"It is bad," he said. "I tell you——"

"Put it where you found it, please."

He did as he was bid, and then passed by her, his shoulders drooping. At the door he stopped and turned round.

"Very sorry," he said. "Very sorry."

It seemed to her that his action was due to a stupid sort of vanity. He looked upon that queer song as something sacred, that was only defiled when played on any other instrument than his Indian pipe. But her annoyance wore off as quickly as it had arisen. After all, he had so many excellent traits. At the worst his behaviour was only childish.

CHAPTER TWENTY-FOUR

SONIA kept her appointment with Wrench on the following Thursday. They dined in a quiet restaurant in the neighbourhood of Piccadilly, and afterwards visited a theatre. She had left word at the house that she would be home late, and her bedroom was prepared for her.

"The Judge didn't object?" asked Wrench.

"Oh, no. I told him that I should be back early in the morning. He is getting remarkably fit. It was a splendid idea of Michels to get him away from all worry."

"And have you made it up with Nali after the gramophone incident which you wrote about?"

"Not quite. Nali is behaving most strangely. We used to be such friends, but now he seems to have taken umbrage. Of course he is polite—he couldn't be anything else—but he avoids me, and when he does meet me he is silent. It is impossible to get a word out of him."

"A queer fellow. What will he do when you are married?"

"Stay with the Judge, of course. Nothing would persuade him to leave—except getting sacked, and that is not likely to happen."

"The Judge is fond of him?"

"He is a most devoted servant. The Judge hates new faces. He has got used to Nali. Nali does everything for him, and seems to anticipate his every requirement. I doubt if any English valet could be found to equal him."

Wrench nodded, but remained very reflective.

"I hate to drag up the spectre," he said at length. "But you know we have never solved the mystery of that dagger that was once hanging in the hall of the Judge's house. There is no doubt whatever that it was the in-

strument originally used by Jack o' Lantern. The shape
of the fatal wounds, and the fact that it was found in
that house in Watling Court are, taken together, very
conclusive. Who removed that weapon, and why did
Nali pretend to be ignorant of it?"

"That has been worrying me, too."

"There is another fact of which you are unaware. I
have kept it from you because—well, chiefly because I
was not quite sure whether I should regard it as a professional matter. But I have been thinking it over, and
I see no harm in telling you now. You remember the
note that was sent to the Judge, on the morning of the
trial of the 'Slasher'?"

"Yes."

"It was written on a rough piece of brown paper—
evidently torn from a larger sheet."

"Yes."

"Sweeting found the parent sheet—in the house."

Her eyes opened wide at this totally unexpected piece
of information.

"That—that isn't possible!" she gasped.

"There is no doubt about it. Sweeting behaved
abominably. He entered your bedroom when you were
absent and found an incomplete paper bag in your wardrobe."

She went pallid.

"Do you recall that bag?"

"Yes. It contained some—some things. But it was
pushed behind all kinds of things. I—I had forgotten
it. John—you don't mean that he suspected——"

"It gave him a theory—a hopelessly wrong theory.
Be patient, dear—try to be amused. If that message was
sent to the Judge by some member of the household it
was naturally deduced that the sender had a very distinct motive. He looked for the motive. He suspected

either you or Nali, because he divined that both of you would benefit——"

"This—this is horrible!"

"I know."

"Why—why did he not tell me—accuse me?"

"He played the subtler game of watching you—and Nali. And when the Judge fell sick, and poison was suspected—even asserted by Sir Henry—things looked bad."

"But you—you did not believe that?"

"No. But the mystery is still unsolved. The person who sent that warning to the Judge went to your room and tore a piece of paper from that millinery bag. Can you throw any light on that extraordinary fact?"

"No. But the writing! Doesn't that help?"

"That is where Sweeting scored over me. The letter found on the 'Slasher'—bearing the true writing of Jack o' Lantern—was shown to the Judge. It might have been seen by—by others, and copied. Also there was another message—sent years ago. That corresponded with the 'Slasher' writing."

Sonia saw all too plainly the grounds for Sweeting's suspicions, and the cause of his frequent visits to the house. Even now she wondered whether John was positive as regards her innocence in the face of these inexplicable facts.

"Have you never had a doubt—about me?" she asked huskily.

"Never! That is an absurd question."

"And Nali?"

He hesitated.

"You do—you do suspect Nali!"

"Not of conspiring to murder the Judge. But sometimes I feel he knows more than he cares to reveal. And then there is Michels. What lies hidden in Michels' mind?"

She passed her hand across her brow wearily. Wrench gave her a hug and forced a smile to her face.

"You must leave it to us," he said. "What I would give anything in the world to achieve, is the full and satisfactory solution of this mystery before we are married."

"Ought we—ought we to get married in the circumstances?" she quavered.

"What are you saying?"

"Well, I am under a cloud. Yes—yes, that is true. What Sweeting has suspected might be true—it might. You know it is not. The Judge knows. But look at the facts as they stand. I am not related to the Judge. I come from India to live on his charity. At my express wish Nali comes too. We worm ourselves into the Judge's affections—and are probably mentioned in his will. I have heard that he is rich. Oh, wait—wait! The Judge suffers from mysterious illness, and poison is suspected. Think of the cases where apparently docile women had plotted to murder for gain. Why not I?"

He caught her firmly and looked into her eyes.

"None of that. I wish to God I had not told you. I didn't quite realise the force of that argument. But we are not going to have our happiness wrecked because of certain things which at the moment we cannot understand."

"But are you sure—in your heart of hearts? Do you sincerely believe that I love the Judge more than anyone in the world—except you—and that money, riches even, means nothing to me?"

"I am sure," he said tensely. "And I am equally certain that before very long something will happen that will shed a ray of revealing light over everything. Now cheer up, and thank God that we are together."

But throughout the evening she was reflective, and he rather blamed himself for choosing so unsuitable a moment to confide in her.

"I'm on duty to-night," he said on the way back to the house.

"But it was only a few days ago——"

"It is not really my turn. A man has gone sick. Sonia, you aren't going to worry about—about what I told you?"

"Not more than I can help. But I'm glad you told me. It helps me to understand the situation. And, John, you will come down to the Hall on Sunday?"

He promised to do so, and shortly afterwards bade her good night on the doorstep. She went straight to her room, and was soon in bed. But her mind was far from being composed, and she got out and picked up a book. It was a *de luxe* edition of Shelly's "Sensitive Plant," and the smooth flow of the thing was like a narcotic. . . . Ultimately she had to exert herself to prevent falling to sleep with the light on. She closed the book, with her mind full of flowers and pleasant creations of the poet's imagery, and switched out the bedside light.

Almost simultaneously there came a knock on her door —an agitated tapping that was followed immediately by louder noises, as if a whole fist were being used. She switched on the light and gulped.

"Who—who is there?"

"Me, miss—cook!"

She jumped out of bed, slipped on a kimono and went to the door. Upon opening it she saw the cook, in a voluminous garment and her hair in "crackers." From her expression it was evident she was suffering from some kind of shock.

"What is the matter?" asked Sonia.

"There's—there's someone in the house, miss."

"Someone in—— I don't understand."

"Did you—did you come to my room just now and turn the handle of the door?"

"No."

"Then someone did. I'm a light sleeper. Someone tried to get in. I heard the door creak as if—as if a body was pushing it."

"Nonsense! You have been dreaming. It was just an ordinary nightmare. Or it may have been Ann."

"It wasn't any dream, and Ann was asleep. I could hear her snoring in the next room. I'm sure there's someone walking about the house, miss."

Sonia did her best to pacify her. It might have been the wind—anything. She begged her to go back to bed and forget all about it. The cook looked round nervously, and ultimately inclined her head. Sonia watched her walk along the corridor, and was about to shut the door when from somewhere below there came the sound of smashing glass. The cook turned and ran back.

"I told you so!" she gasped.

Sonia felt a cold shudder run down her spine, but she pulled herself together, for it would have required little help from her to send the cook into shrieking hystericals.

"Calm yourself," she whispered. "If it is a burglar he must be in the rear part of the house. The telephone is not twenty yards away. I will go——"

The cook clung to her.

"Don't go! You'll be murdered——"

"Don't be foolish!"

A sudden idea came to the cook.

"Oh, the pistol! I forgot the pistol."

"What pistol?"

"I found a pistol—in a drawer in the library. My brother called to see me, and seeing as there was only me and Ann left in the house he advised me to keep it in my bedroom. It's loaded, too."

This was rather strange, for Sonia had no idea the house possessed such a weapon. She decided it might be advisable to arm herself with this, if only to scare off any possible intruder.

"Stay here," she whispered. "Where is this pistol?"

"In—in the drawer of my dressing-table."

"I'll get it."

Despite the cook's protest at being left alone, she went along the corridor, and found the pistol in the place indicated. From the next room came the noise of a snoring woman, and she thought it best to let Ann sleep on in ignorance. But to make sure the maid was safe from harm she tried the door of her room. It was locked. She joined the trembling cook.

"I'm going to the telephone," she said.

"Oh—be careful!"

She trod lightly down the stairs, and reached the telephone. Having often rung up Wrench, she remembered his number, and made a whispered request to the operator. She had to repeat it twice before she was understood. Almost immediately she was on to Wrench himself.

"Wrench," she whispered. "Come—come here at once, or—or send someone."

"Yes, yes—but what is the matter?"

"It's——" She got no further, for the light was suddenly extinguished. She put up the receiver and reached for another switch opposite. There was no response, and she deduced that someone must have pressed the main switch in the basement, unless a fuse had gone, which was less probable.

An idea came to her ere she flew up the stairs. By closing the door at the end of the hall, and also that leading to the domestic part of the house, the intruder could be kept out of the rest of the building. She blundered in the darkness, and managed to find the door to the kitchen. She locked it from her side. Then she made for the door that gave direct access to the basement, and as she reached it she heard distinctly the sound of footsteps on the other side. She fumbled for the bolt, and pushed it home as quietly as possible.

CHAPTER TWENTY-FIVE

FROM the window of her bedroom Sonia saw a car entering the drive. It stopped just inside the gate, and the lights were dimmed. She saw two men get out, but could not recognise either of them in the very faint light. It seemed to her incredible that Wrench could have reached the house in the short time that had elapsed, but it proved to be true. She called from the window as they were about to pass, and shone down an electric torch.

"Sonia!"

"Oh—it's you, John! Thank God! Shall I come down and open the door?"

"Yes."

She was immensely relieved when she reached the front door and slipped the bolt. Wrench had left his assistant outside. He blinked at the torch.

"The lights are off," she whispered. "They must have been switched off from the basement."

"Tell me what happened—as briefly as you can."

This she did, as rapidly as a woman can use her tongue, and Wrench nodded grimly.

"Have you heard any further sound?"

"None. But I have been watching from my window, and I have not seen anyone leave the house."

"Good! He may be here."

"John, you don't think it is——?"

"It would be interesting if it were. My luck would be in."

"Why didn't you bring more men?"

"We have a big thing on to-night—elsewhere. I must get these lights going. Where is the basement?"

"I'll show you."

"Wouldn't you prefer to go to your room?"

"No. I'm armed, too. See!"

She showed him the pistol, and he raised his eyebrows. But he was not keen that she should expose herself to any possible danger. It might, of course, prove to be a mere attempt at burglary, but, on the other hand, there was always the other possibility—an attempt on the Judge's life by someone who did not know that the Judge was elsewhere.

"You would be safer——" he argued.

"I am coming," she said determinedly.

"Very well."

They reached the door to the basement, and he pulled back the bolt. A series of stone steps led down. Wrench's powerful electric lamp threw a brilliant beam of light forward. In his right hand he held a pistol. They went along a narrow passage and finally reached the electric light meter. Beneath it was a big switch. It was up.

"See!" whispered Sonia.

"You were right. Someone——"

He suddenly withdrew his hand from the switch, as if it were red-hot, and brought the ray of the light to bear full upon it. Sonia saw what it was that interested him.

A very light dust had settled on the ebonite handle, and impressed on this were fairly good finger-prints. Wrench switched on the light by manipulating the extreme end of the switch.

"Careless of him—that," he mused. "I ought to be able to take a good photograph to-morrow."

"There is no one here."

"Where do those steps lead?"

"Up to the kitchen."

"Let us go up."

They finally entered the kitchen. To all appearances it had not been disturbed, and the door along the passage which led to the hall was locked on the other side.

"I did that," explained Sonia, "after I had telephoned you."

"Then it is certain he has not passed that way. He must have gone out through the basement area."

"But the breaking of glass, and his means of entry?"

"We will go back."

They retraced their footsteps into the basement, and Wrench found an old door which led into the garden. This was unlocked and slightly ajar.

"He—he must have possessed a key," said Sonia.

"A smart housebreaker doesn't need keys of the usual kind. Where does this passage lead?"

"It divides farther on. The right branch goes to the back of the hall—where I heard him approaching. The other leads to an old secondary staircase which we never use."

"That is the one we came down—the right-hand one?"

"Yes. But we took the short cut. This is a rambling sort of place. The servants used to live down here before we had the house modernised."

"H'm! It looks as if he has got away. But we will try the secondary staircase."

It was here they discovered the breakage of glass. There was a door on the landing, glazed on the upper half. One of the panes was broken—obviously in order that the intruder might reach the bolt on the other side.

"He evidently did not enter by the basement," whispered Wrench. "The bolt is on this side. He must have come down the staircase from an upper part of the house. His movements seem to have been undecisive."

The stairs led them to the end of the landing on the first floor. Wrench entered and examined three rooms, and then came to Ann's room. She was still snoring.

"The maid," whispered Sonia. "She sleeps like a log."

"Whose is the next room?"

"Cookie's."

"Is she there now?"

"I think not. I left her in my room. She was badly scared."

"Well, it looks as if we have missed him. He must have got away before we arrived."

"It was possible for him to slip through the shrubbery on the north side of the garden and climb over the wall, but I heard no sound."

"You probably would not."

"Do you—do you think it was a burglar?"

"Yes. Those finger-prints may help—if he is an old offender, which most of them are."

They had reached the door of Sonia's room. Beyond that were several other rooms.

"The end one is the Judge's," she explained.

"I may as well look, in order to put your mind at rest."

When he entered the Judge's room he suffered a surprise. The bedclothes were dragged from the bed and were lying on the floor in a heap. A photograph of the Judge which had stood on his dressing-table was torn in halves and lying on the mattress. One of the two pillows was gashed with a knife, and various articles of furniture were disarranged. These grim facts provided a new motive. Sonia's face went pallid as she realised this.

"It—it was no burglar," she said hoarsely.

Wrench agreed with a nod of his head. He opened the window and looked out. There was a century's growth of thick ivy on the wall, with abundant foothold for a normal man. Below he saw his assistant.

"Have you seen anyone, Caffy?"

"No, sir."

"Keep your eyes skinned."

He was shutting the window when out went the lights again. Sonia gasped, and Wrench grasped her by the arm.

"Stay here! Lock the door after me. He must be down there again."

"John——!"

"I can't wait a second. Do as I say—please!"

He ran off at once, descending the stairs at breakneck speed. On reaching the basement his heart bounded. Before him was a spectral form, enwrapped in a big coat. He caught but a glimpse of a face—from the nose upwards.

"Hands up!" he cried. "Quick, or——!"

A pistol cracked and the electric torch was shattered in his hand, a piece of the metal penetrating his flesh. He cursed and fired blindly. A hand gripped his leg and he fell with a crash on the hard stone steps. He made a wild grab and caught hold of a piece of cloth, but the injured hand which held it was weak, and he lost his grip. . . . There was a scuffling—a short laugh and silence. He picked himself up and groped for the switch which was near at hand. The place became illumined, and he ran through the door which led into the garden.

"Caffy!" he yelled.

There was no response from the sergeant, so he ran to the front of the house. There he noticed that the car was gone. He kicked himself in his bitter disappointment, and ran down the drive. He thought he heard the sound of a car in the street at the back of the garden, but it might have been any car but the missing one, for London was not yet completely asleep. After a futile search for the sergeant, he came to the conclusion that it was he who had taken the car, on which hypothesis he must have seen the intruder escaping. With hope renewed he went back to the house and rejoined Sonia. She stared at his bleeding hand.

"I—I heard a shot," she quavered.

"I've seen the brute."

"Jack o' Lantern?"

"Yes—I am certain."

"He—he got away?"

"My infernal luck. He had me at a disadvantage. I suppose I should have let loose at him without a moment's hesitation."

"But your hand?"

"He got in a lucky shot, which hit my torch. My hand is scratched—this is all."

"Then—then he is gone?"

"Yes. But Caffy must have seen him from a distance. At any rate the car is gone. Caffy may have luck. We shall see."

"John, it may be imagination, but I thought I heard a noise from along the corridor—when I opened the door just now."

"What kind of noise?"

"A groan."

"But there is no one in the house—excepting the cook and Ann. Is Ann still in your room?"

"I think so."

Wrench opened the door and walked in the direction indicated by Sonia. He opened the first door he came to and switched on the light. The room was empty.

"Nothing there——"

He winced as a distinct groan came from farther along the corridor.

"There!"

"It must come from the end room."

"That is Nali's."

He walked to the door and opened it. The light was on and a figure was huddled up against the bed, groaning intermittently.

"Great Scott! It is Nali!" he exclaimed.

"But——!"

The Hindu gazed vacantly into Wrench's face. Across his brow was a big protuberance where some heavy missile had struck him, but there was no blood. Wrench, with compressed lips, lifted him into a chair and gave him a drink of water. The bed was not disarranged and Nali was fully dressed, even to his overcoat.

"What does this mean?" demanded Sonia. "Why are you here?"

Nali shook his head, and Wrench curled his lip in a strange manner.

"Pull yourself together," he said gruffly. "There is a whole lot that must be explained."

Sonia looked at Wrench appealingly.

"Give him a little time," she begged. "He is evidently badly hurt."

"I'll come back—in ten minutes," said Wrench to the Hindu. "But I shall want the truth—you understand?"

It is doubtful whether Nali did understand, but he

inclined his head in a dazed manner, and Wrench and Sonia left him.

CHAPTER TWENTY-SIX

THE cook, having been assured that the burglar was gone, went to her room. Immediately afterwards the sergeant returned with the car. Wrench interrogated him, and learnt that he had seen the housebreaker running across the garden towards the wall. Realising that he was making for the back street, Caffy had started the car and gone in pursuit.

"I overhauled him pretty quickly," he said. "But he turned off into a narrow passage and gained time on me, as I had to stop the car and get out. It's a regular maze of turnings at the end of the passage. I had to decide quickly, as he wasn't in sight. Of course I took the wrong one. I ran into the constable on patrol, but he hadn't seen anyone answering the description of the fellow. I'm afraid he's gone, sir."

"Did you see his face?"

"No. Only his back—and that only for a few seconds."

Wrench told him to wait, and then rejoined Sonia, who was racking her brains to solve the mystery of Nali's presence. It looked bad—she had to admit that.

"We'll see him now," said Wrench.

Nali had recovered from the first stunning force of the blow, and his dark eyes shifted uneasily as Wrench and Sonia entered the room.

"Now," said Wrench. "Why are you here?"

"I miss the last train, and have nowhere to sleep, so I came here."

"What do you intend to convey by that? Is the

Judge aware that you came to London this evening?"

Nali shook his head slowly.

"You broke out, eh?"

"Yes."

"For what purpose?"

"Someone telephoned me—a friend. The master was asleep. I feared to wake him so—so I came."

"Who was this friend?"

Nali hesitated and then shook his head. Wrench shook his finger at him threateningly.

"This is a serious business," he said. "Who is the man who telephoned you?"

"The—the mistress knows," mumbled Nali.

Sonia bit her lip at this.

"You mean you went to that place—to get drugs?" she demanded.

He nodded and hung his head as if in shame.

"Where is it? Give it to me!"

"I have nothing," he said. "It was only to smoke."

"Nali—are you telling the truth?"

"I would not lie to the mistress."

Wrench took up the questioning with a crispness that clearly conveyed the fact that he did not believe this story.

"You say the Judge was asleep when you left the Hall?"

"Yes."

"What time was it?"

"Half-past nine."

"And was Mr. Michels also in his room?"

"No. He was working in the library—writing."

"You did not tell him you were going out?"

Nali shook his head.

"Well, you caught a train from the station. At what time did that train leave?"

"At ten-twenty."

"Then you did not reach London until past eleven o'clock. And yet you have had time to go to the East End, smoke opium or hashish and come back here?"

"I did not stay long."

"You did not stay at all. You did not go to that house that you have occasionally visited. Moreover, you must have known that the last train to the Hall leaves London at half-past ten."

"I did not know."

Wrench laughed scornfully.

"Well, go on," he said. "Let us hear the rest of the story. You came here to sleep? I presume you had a key?"

"Yes—have key to front door."

"You did not knock or ring?"

"The house was dark. I did not wish to awaken anyone."

Wrench took him up in a flash, and Sonia at the same moment realised the flaw in this argument.

"If the house was in darkness," said Wrench, "Miss Pelling must have come in before you, and she would have locked and bolted the door from the inside." He turned to Sonia. "Is that not so?"

"Yes," she replied. "Nali, what are you concealing?"

"The door was not bolted," he said stubbornly. "Only locked."

"Continue!" rapped Wrench.

"I went to my room. But as I closed the door behind me I heard another door close. I thought it was my master's door—because that is nearest. Then I heard the sound of feet. I opened my door just a little and—and saw a strange man. His eyes—his eyes were terrible. He leapt straight at me . . . there was a pistol in his hand. It hit me here. I—I know no more."

"So you saw this man face to face?"

"Yes."

"Describe him."

He gave a description which tallied exactly with the person seen by Wrench in the basement. But Nali added that he had a scarf wrapped round his neck and chin, and that his hat was tilted over his forehead.

"Do you remember in which hand he held the pistol?"

Nali reflected.

"Yes, *sahib*. It was in his left hand."

"You would know this man again?"

"Yes—yes. Among a million."

Wrench paused and cogitated. The latter part of the story had all the semblance of truth, but the explanation of Nali's presence was palpably fiction. It was difficult to know what to do—at the moment.

"I will see you in the morning," he said ultimately. "But I warn you to reflect upon your deposition, for this is a serious matter. To-night there has been an attempt at murder."

Sonia flinched and Nali's eyelids flickered.

"It pays to tell the truth," resumed Wrench.

"Nali tell the whole truth."

Wrench shrugged his shoulders and turned from him. The door closed on Nali.

"Why does he lie?" mused Wrench.

"Are you sure he is lying?"

"He must be. How could he possibly enter by the front door when you had bolted it?"

"Suppose—suppose someone had unbolted it?"

"Yes, I had thought of that. But do you realise the significance of such an act? It would make Nali an accomplice."

"Isn't that what you suspect?" she asked in a quaking voice.

"I should do, but for certain hard facts. He certainly received a stunning blow on the head. That was no ruse on his part. In addition he knew perfectly well that the Judge was not in this house, and so could not be involved in any attempted murder. The whole business is a mass of contradictions."

"Unless for some reason the intending murderer did unbolt the front door, and Nali entered as he said he did. His story might be true, after all."

"The time factor is against it. But I hope to settle that point to-morrow morning. In the meantime I will leave Caffy in the house. That will give you a greater sense of security."

She thanked him, and a little later they parted, while Caffy made himself comfortable in the library. Her head ached from the confused thoughts that passed through her brain, and she was horrified to reflect that if the Judge had been in that room he would now be a stark corpse. When at last the morning came she thanked God for the daylight.

*　　　*　　　*　　　*　　　*

Wrench called at eleven o'clock. In the meantime he had made certain inquiries, some of which upset his theories. He had found that it was just possible for Nali to have carried out his programme as stated— although improbable. He had visited the house of ill-repute and interrogated the owner. This worthy—a Chinaman—admitted that he knew Nali, and on the promise that anything he might divulge would be strictly confidential he confessed to having supplied the Hindu with a pipe of hashish. The only descrepancy between the two versions was in regard to the telephone call. Whereas Nali asserted that he had been rung up, the

Chinaman swore that Nali had merely called in, and had stayed but a short time.

"I've made one blunder of omission," said Wrench. "I should have put the telephone out of order."

"Why?"

"There was nothing to prevent Nali from ringing up his drug-provisioner, and coaching him in what he must say in the event of my making inquiries."

"Do you think he would be smart enough to anticipate such a thing?"

"I do. But as matters stand at this moment, his story is vouched for. Even if I wanted to arrest him I haven't enough justification. He possessed a key to this house, and I presume the Judge was quite aware of it?"

"Oh, yes."

"Then any charge would fail."

"Yes. And it would not do," she argued. "We must accept his story. There is nothing else to do."

"And what will the Judge say when he hears of this exploit of his faithful valet?"

"I don't know. Of course he will be angry, but I hope he will not discharge him. He ought to have another chance."

"Have you rung up the Hall?"

"Not yet."

"I should do so. Nali's absence must be explained."

Sonia put the call through, and was told that she would be rung later.

"Are you going to see Nali?" she asked.

"Yes. He may have changed his mind and decided to tell the truth."

"I am inclined to believe that he is telling the truth. But may I speak to him first? I—I think I have some little influence over him.

"Do."

She found the Hindu sitting in his room, with a bandage round his forehead. He seemed to be sunk in thought and gave a visible start when she entered.

"How is the wound, Nali?" she asked.

"There is a pain, mistress, but it will go."

"Nali, I am very worried about last night—about your being found here in such strange circumstances. Inspector Wrench doubts your explanation. Will you not make a clean breast of everything?"

"I have spoken, mistress."

"You have nothing to add—or withdraw?"

He shook his head.

"Well then, if there is something you do not wish to tell the inspector, will you tell me in strict confidence, for my own peace of mind? It shall go no farther."

"There is nothing more to tell, mistress. I crave the mistress's forgiveness for leaving the other house without permission, and for breaking the promise which I gave her. But the urge was on me. It gave me no rest."

It was abundantly clear that nothing would move him, and she was still doubtful about his veracity. The ringing of the telephone bell caused her to hurry downstairs.

"That must be the Hall," she said.

Wrench, who had taken up the receiver, gave it to her. She recognized Michels' voice at the other end. Before she could give him her message he told her something that caused her face to go pallid, and her hand to shake.

"Anything wrong?" asked Wrench.

"Yes—yes. The Judge—the Judge is missing."

"What!"

"It is Michels speaking. You had better——"

Wrench took the receiver and fired off some questions

rapidly. Ultimately he rang off and faced her with tight lips.

"We shall have to go there at once—you and I and Nali. You came by car?"

"Yes."

"Then Nali can come in the dickey-seat. What new deviltry is this?"

Before they left, Wrench went to look at the electric light switch which had carried the finger-prints, but as he fully expected, the second use of the handle had obliterated these. That clue had vanished for ever.

CHAPTER TWENTY-SEVEN

SONIA broke records on the road to the Hall. The miles were reeled off at fearful speeds, and in less than an hour they were inside the Hall. Michels had heard the car approaching and came to the porch to meet them. He glared at Nali, and the Hindu slunk off.

"This is a terrible affair, Wrench."

"Bad enough. What has happened—exactly?"

"At breakfast time the butler informed me that the Judge was still in his room. I thought he was tired and that Nali was attending to him, and had my breakfast alone. Later the butler came to say that the chambermaid had informed him that Nali's room was empty, and that his bed had not been slept in. I thereupon went to the Judge's room."

"Well?"

"The bedclothes were very disarranged, and the window was wide open. I looked in the bathroom, but that, too, was empty. It looked as if it had not been used."

"When did you last see the Judge?"

"Before he retired last night. He seemed rather fatigued, and even declined a game of chess."

"At what time was this?"

"Soon after nine o'clock."

Wrench pursed his lips, for here at any rate Nali's statement was borne out. He expressed a desire to see the Judge's bedroom, and found it exactly as Michels had said. Disordered as the bed was, there was no sign of a struggle. Wrench picked up the bedclothes, and suddenly came across a streak of blood on one of the blankets. He tried to conceal it from Sonia, but it was too late.

"Steady!" he wispered, catching her hand. "It may not signify anything serious."

"But it does! The other house was broken into—with intent to murder. And here——"

"What is that?" asked Michels.

Wrench told him briefly what had taken place in London, and Michels seemed greatly perturbed.

"It looks—it looks as if the fellow came here—later," he said. "After the failure——"

"And dragged the Judge away with him?" put in Wrench. "It is too fantastic. You heard no sound of a car—during the night?"

"No."

"And the servants?"

"Not a sound. They are all stricken with amazement."

Wrench rang the bell, and the butler entered. He asked him to send Nali to them, and a minute later Nali entered.

"You know what has happened here?" asked Wrench.

Nali was in a state of great agitation. They observed his efforts to conquer this. Under the swarthy skin was a queer pallor. He nodded and passed his hand across his brow.

"Did you see your master last night—after he had gone to his bedroom?"

"Yes. Nali take him drink."

"The usual drink—whiskey?"

"Yes."

"Was the window left open?"

"No—Nali close the window."

"Did you fasten it?"

"No."

"You are sure?"

"Quite sure."

"And then you left him, and saw him no more?"

"That is so."

He was dispatched, and Sonia, too, left the room, for she was near to a nervous collapse. Wrench swung round on Michels, who was nursing his chin in an attitude characteristic of him.

"What do you make of this, Mr. Michels?"

"What do you, Inspector?" replied Michels in a low voice.

"To be frank—I'm baffled. But I know that the Hindu is playing some game of his own, and I would arrest him if I had the smallest tangible ground."

"That might be a—mistake."

"What do you mean?"

"I can say no more."

"Are you acting wisely yourself, Mr. Michels?" rapped Wrench with some asperity.

"What am I to infer from that?"

"What you please. But there was an attempt at murder last night—in London—and the intended victim is now missing. The man I saw in the London house was Jack o' Lantern—without a shadow of doubt. It looks—it looks as if he had succeeded. With that awful possibility staring us in the face, are you justified in withholding from the police certain information?"

"You think I possess such?"

"I have every ground for believing it."

Michels walked up and down, his shoulders hunched and his big hands closing and unclosing.

"You must give me time, Wrench," he said. "Too much damage is done by premature acts. This case is not so simple as you——"

"Simple! Great Heavens! It is the most complicated, baffling mystery imaginable, because it is bung-full of contradictions. On the face of things it is easy to believe that Nali tried to poison the Judge. It is equally easy to arrive at the theory that he is in league with Jack o' Lantern. But in both cases there are serious flaws. And why—if Jack o' Lantern came here to murder the Judge in his bed—why did he depart with the body?"

"He may not be quite accountable for his actions."

"That doesn't harmonise with what we know of him. No, this man is fiendishly clever. I can only assume that he took the body in order to dispose of it completely, and render conviction impossible."

"And the other murders? Can he clear himself there?"

"Who can say? You know the legal loopholes that a great mind might make use of."

"Yes—yes. It is difficult."

"And yet you might help."

"You credit me with a kind of super-intelligence, Wrench," said Michels. "But, believe me, I am baffled too. The first thing is to find the Judge—or at least his body."

Thereafter commenced the hue-and-cry.

*　　　*　　　*　　　*　　　*

In the meantime Sam Knudge was living in a perfect

paradise. Acting on Kate's advice, he had bought the tobacconist business in the Gray's Inn Road, and was already planning extensive alterations, most of which had not been contemplated, for Sam in the interim had found some additional "easy money." This had come about through his association with Philton, and the magic sesame was related to a small press in the basement far from the busy thoroughfares, where a perverted genius turned out quite excellent specimens of one-pound Treasury notes. The passing of these was a simple matter—at first. Sam found the easiest means on race-courses, where money changed hands rapidly and regularly. The danger lay in being caught with a parcel of spurious currency on his person, so Sam employed a "go-between," who carried the stock-in-trade, and who casually passed a note or two only when they were required.

Marvellous business resulted, and Sam congratulated himself on his astuteness. It was certainly getting one back on the bookies, but the bookies, in their turn, passed a large proportion of these counterfeits back on the long-suffering public. Sam, once out of the race-course, had nothing but good coin on his person.

"Good biz!" he said to Philton. "Them things would pass a bank manager."

"Don't you try," warned Philton. "Keep 'em up country—among the crowd."

Kate knew nothing of this matter. She was fully aware that Sam had amassed his little capital by processes which would not have commended themselves to honest citizens, but all that lay in the past. She was prepared to close the door on that and to accept the tobacconist business as an opening to a new and blameless life—with Sam.

The idea thrilled her—as a business proposition, but

when she looked at it from the emotional side, she had grave doubts. To see Sam every day—to listen to his appalling accent, to be known as Mrs. Knudge for the rest of her days, unless some merciful providence took him off first—these were disturbing thoughts. But the alternatives were equally distressing. Banting had indulged her love for easy ways of life. There had been no luxuries, but equally there had been few hardships. She was essentially a creature of environment, not very good, and not very bad. A rather romantic, kindly girl, forced to knuckle down to hard facts. Her life had been made for her to the extent at which there is no unmaking.

"Sam's a good sort," said Banting. "He has business ability too. You can improve him a lot."

"He needs it."

"Now—now!"

"And you, daddy," she said, using a term that he had not heard for a long time. "What are you going to do?"

"I'm going straight—if they will let me. Does that sound comical to you?"

"No. Why should it?"

"Well, it does to me. I've developed a kind of second personality that sits up and leers at me. It reminds me that when I did lead an honest life they clapped me in jail, and that to talk of going straight when one has gone crooked is an ostrich kind of philosophy that is best shattered by a brick at one's head."

"Don't be cynical, daddy—not to me."

"I won't. You see, Kate, I'm getting on in years. Either I go down and down into the mire until I become nauseous in my own eyes and despicable in yours, or I make an eleventh-hour effort to be decent—as I once was. I may fail—I don't know. But it's worth trying —don't you think?"

"I do. I admire you for your resolution."

"And you," he said tensely. "If you're not happy, write and tell me so. I won't have you unhappy, if I have to——"

She put his fingers across his lips.

"Don't worry, dad. If Sam starts any of his non-sense he'll regret it. I can take care of myself."

This was true as regards Sam, but she reflected that she had not that certitude where Lefroy was concerned. There she was the primitive woman, ready to sit at the feet of her master, to obey him, to venerate him. It was strange that it should be so, and she was incapable of understanding the cause. She tried to rid her mind of that sinister figure. He, too, must be buried with the past.

It was on the following morning that she had cause to realise that Lefroy was not so easily buried. Sam had brought her home from the first house of a cinema show, and had gone out with Banting on some mysterious mission, promising to return in an hour. She was playing the piano when a missile was pitched into the room through the half-open casement window. It was a stone enclosed in a piece of white paper. She looked through the window but saw no sign of a human form. Nervously she unwrapped the paper. On the inner side was written:

I must see you—corner of Roberts' Avenue. Come at once.—Paul.

She went pallid, crumpled up the note and flung it into the grate. It hit the bars and rolled to safety. Again she looked into the garden, but everything was perfectly still there. She was determined not to obey that command, and went back to the piano. After a few bars she stopped. What had he to say to her? What could he say in the face——? No, it was impossible. He was a threat to her happiness—to her safety.

She could not play. It was no use pretending. Some invisible, subtle force seemed to be dragging at her very soul. She envisaged him, waiting there for her. Perhaps he had something of great importance to say? At any rate, she ought to tell him that she was done with him. Poor, flimsy excuse! Anything rather than admit to herself that this passion for Lefroy was a flaming reality even yet. She thought she saw him through a blood-red mist, but notwithstanding every nerve in her body was trembling. It might be love—it might be madness. But there it was. This fight with her better nature—her natural repugnance—was of comparatively short duration. Ultimately she crept out; put on her hat and coat and went towards Roberts' Avenue.

CHAPTER TWENTY-EIGHT

"KATE!"

She found her hands gripped tight, saw those dark, hypnotic eyes staring into her own. Before she could utter a word he had kissed her passionately.

"Wait!" she said chokingly.

"I have waited, all alone under the moon," he replied lightly. "I came to the house, but it seems to prove an extremely interesting antique to certain people. I have a natural sense of self-preservation and avoided the regular mode of visiting. God, it's good to see you again!"

She gulped and choked, and wrested her hands free.
"I only came to tell you——"

"Not here," he interrupted. "It's cold and bleak and altogether unsuited to lovers' confidences."

"Lovers! No—no! I was mad to come. This is the last time. You and I must never meet again."

He looked at her with his burning eyes, and shook his head slowly.

"We shall go on meeting while life runs," he said. "Because it is our destiny. We have found each other among all the teeming millions——"

"I tell you——"

He seized her by the arm and propelled her forward.

"This district is unhealthy. I love the crowds. Either the crowds or the solitude. There is no compromise."

"Listen," she said. "I—I know everything."

"Everything! Fortunate woman. To know even the merest shred of reality would make one a sage. To know everything is to aspire to Deity itself."

"Will you not be sensible?" she pleaded.

"I am eminently sensible, to a degree which you may fail to realise. I am sensible that I am madly, passionately in love with a woman called Kate. And that, at the moment, is all that matters. Look! A taxi in this insalubrious neighbourhood."

He stopped the vehicle, laughed at her protests, and bundled her inside it, after giving the driver his instructions. She felt she was being smothered. Worse than that, her repugnance was being smothered too. He put his arms round her and drew her close to him. She wanted to shriek, but did not. All that Sam was incapable of arousing was being aroused. He was talking to her, almost crooning, stopping her tongue with endearments. . . .

The taxi stopped. It seemed to be but a few seconds since she had entered it. She took no note of where they were, and had but a vague notion that they were mounting some stairs. A man opened a door . . . there were

more stairs. . . . She found herself sitting on a couch
in a small and poorly furnished room, with Lefroy beside
her, chafing her hands.

"Cold—cold," he murmured. "We will soon warm
them. This is my mansion. Regard those works of
art, and weep for the future of humanity. But love
gilds the scene. The woman over there who was so
horrible to look upon an hour ago, is now transfigured.
You are reflected there—an angel who should not have
walked this mundane earth——"

"Paul, I believe you are mad!" she cried.

"Perhaps we are all a little mad. That is the cost of
existence. But let me remove your coat."

"No—no!" She suddenly stood up. "What am I
doing here? How dare you bring me here? I—I am
engaged to be married. Let me go. For God's sake
let——"

He looked at her with his head on one side.

"Engaged to be married! Now that is queer. I do
not remember that we——"

"You! No, not you."

"You are distraught," he said abruptly. "You need
a stimulant. I'll get you a drink."

She might have escaped while he got the drink, but
she did not. It was long and strong and pleasing to her
dry palate. He drank with her, and took a sip from her
glass.

"What were you saying about being engaged?" he
asked quietly.

"It is true. I am engaged to marry Sam—Sam
Knudge."

His whole expression changed from calm to fearful
storm, and in this paroxysm of rage the glass which he
held was crushed in his hand. The broken pieces fell
at his feet.

"That diseased rat!" he snarled. "But you are lying to me. Why do you say such ridiculous things?"

She lowered her head, for it did seem ridiculous now. Shrink as she might from him, it was nevertheless a fact that her inner passion was unaffected. He sat down beside her, and at the touch of his hands she was lost again.

"Why did you play that joke on me?" she asked. "I waited at the station, and you did not come."

"The station!"

"Have you even forgotten that?" she asked bitterly. "We were to go to France—to be married."

"Why, yes. I——I was taken ill. For weeks I have been oblivious to everything. By God, you are right. But it was no senseless jest. You poor little girl. I have wounded you without the slightest intention. And in desperation—in a fit of pique—you made some sort of foolish promise to—Knudge? Well, it is nothing. You must tell him you were mistaken—that you are going to marry me."

"Paul!" she protested helplessly.

"Of course you are."

"But they tell me—— I have heard——"

"You should not listen to anyone but me. We will make new plans, and this time there shall be no hitch. I remember now. We were to go down into the sunshine. And so we will. In some quiet spot we'll build our home, and never come back to this cold and dismal climate. I'll forgive Knudge for falling in love with you. The fool couldn't help himself. But your beauty is not for such as he. You shall have life in abundance, amid the colour and flowers of a southern clime. All my life I have waited for this—this consummation of a dream. . . ."

And so he rambled on, weaving a spell about her, until

she saw nothing but the picture which he built up with consummate verbal artistry. Poor Sam faded into the mists, and the horrible picture of Jack o' Lantern faded with him. She was with her lover. That was enough— for the moment.

*   *   *   *   *

Banting returned home with Sam Knudge, after what Sam termed a "pub-crawl." Sam was in the best of humours, for his name was already coupled with Kate's in the office of the registrar, and he was waxing eloquent about the future.

"You needn't worry none, Jim," he said. "I'll warrant Kate and me will run in tandem fine. I've got my eye on a dinky little car that's for sale."

"Well, stick to the business and you'll be all right," advised his prospective father-in-law. "And don't get too thick with Philton's crowd."

Sam winced at this.

"What's wrong with Philton?" he asked.

"He'll overreach himself one day. I don't want Kate mixed up with the old gang. Cut 'em clean out."

"Well, maybe you're right," agreed Sam.

Both men were very surprised when they found the sitting-room empty, and the fire very low.

"Can't have gone to bed," said Sam.

Banting shook his head and rang for the maid. The girl thought she had heard Kate go out—two hours ago —and a visit to Kate's room bore out this statement.

"She knew we was coming back," said Sam dolefully. "What did she want to go out for this time of night?"

"It was our fault," replied Banting. "We promised to come back early. Well, she can't be long."

They sat and smoked for some time, but still Kate remained absent. Banting looked at his watch and moved uneasily, and Sam yawned and shuffled his feet impatiently.

"I s'pose she's got the spike," he mused. "Lumme, ain't women the blue limit!"

Banting refilled his pipe, and stooped to pick up a small roll of paper from which to fashion a spill. He was about to ignite it when he noticed some writing on it. He pressed it out flat, and then uttered a low cry of alarm.

"What's the matter?"

Banting passed Sam the paper, and Sam squealed like a rabbit as he read the few words it contained.

"That—that swine!" he gasped.

They were both on their feet now, staring into each other's faces. Of the two, Banting was the more controlled, but even he looked murderous. Sam whipped out an automatic pistol.

"Put that away!"

"I'm going to kill him," he fumed. "He's got Kate. He's got your gal. If I swing for it I'm——"

Banting clapped his strong hand on Sam's wrist and forced him to pocket his weapon.

"Don't be an hysterical idiot," he growled. "We don't even know where he is."

"Don't we! I know. I found out by a bit of luck. He was chased out of one hole, but he found another. Do you remember Sally Gill?"

"In Soho?"

"Yes. That's where he is. She let on to me that she had taken a queer lodger. It was him—I know. She described him all right. And there was a spook mixed up in it—a fellow named Lantern—Tobias Lantern."

"It might be——"

"No doubt about it. Lord, what's going to happen to her? Why, by this time she may be——"

"Shut up!" snarled Banting. "It's bad enough without you drawing on your imagination. We'll go to that house."

"Better still, put the cops on to him," suggested Sam. "He's wanted for murder. If they knew——"

But Banting was not of that disposition. In the event of anything having happened to Kate he was quite capable of shooting Jack o' Lantern dead, but his rather proud spirit revolted at the idea of "squealing" on an accomplice.

"This is our affair," he said. "And we've got to settle it. If you're nervous——"

"Nervous!" Sam shuddered and bolstered up his hate. "I'm ready. I'm not scared of him. Come on!"

Banting went to a bureau and took a pistol from a drawer. He slipped it into his pocket quickly. Sam saw the older man's grim expression, and rather wished that they were more than two. And as they made towards Sally Gill's house his old fear returned.

"We ought to get the cops," he said. "Two ain't much against a killer like him."

Banting said nothing, but hurried on—a good yard ahead of his craven companion. At the top of St. Martin's Lane a newsboy was exhibiting a placard. On it was inscribed in large red letters:

STRANGE DISAPPEARANCE OF EMINENT
JUDGE. MURDER SUSPECTED.

"Who's the judge?" queried Sam.

"Judge Wallington. 'Nother of them Jack o' Lantern murders. My Gawd—ain't he awful!"

Sam overtook Banting and grabbed him by the arm.

"Did you hear that? He's got Judge Wallington. Jack o' Lantern's done in the Judge. Can't you wait a bit?"

Banting flung off the detaining arm and glared at Sam. "Wait?" he said in a voice that was choked with emotion. "You can talk of waiting when Kate is with that scoundrel? You week-kneed cur!"

"But the police——!"

"Damn the police!"

Sam gulped. To him every policeman was now a desirable friend. He had no guts for this kind of thing. Terror had even frozen out the first passionate desire for personal revenge. But not so Banting. He would have faced Hell itself in the circumstances. Ultimately they stood before the house in the narrow dark street.

"Is this it?" asked Banting.

"Y-yes."

"Then come on, if you've any spunk left. If not, you can stay where you are. Better still, go and drown yourself. What is it to be?"

Sam gulped and trembled in his shoes.

"I'm—I'm coming," he quavered in a weak voice.

CHAPTER TWENTY-NINE

KATE had forgotten everything save that she was with the man she loved. Always his influence over her had been tremendous, but to-night it was hypnotic. All the horror and dread that had been generated by her recent knowledge of his terrible deeds had gone. The new life that he offered her drugged her better self. Now she knew that she could never marry Sam—that an hour of life with Lefroy was worth an eternity without him, and all the time he was pouring love's portion into her ears. The battered clock on the mantelpiece ticked on noisily, but it did not strike and the hour of midnight passed quite unobserved.

She was awakened from a beautiful dream by the sudden opening of the door and the intrusion of a hunchback. It was the man who had let them in, and she recalled him vaguely. His ugly face was now full of excitement. He put his finger to his lips and waved his hand behind him.

"Two men come," he said to Jack o' Lantern. "Break in—one have pistol."

"What are they like?"

"Police, I think. Go to——"

Jack o' Lantern became alert, and Kate gathered her wits together. There was a noise from below—a creaking of the stairs under heavy boots. Jack o' Lantern pushed the dwarf outside and locked the door. He turned to see Kate's affrighted eyes fixed on him intently.

"Most inopportune," he muttered quite calmly. "Most inopportune."

"What—what are you going to do?" she gasped.

He laughed softly, and then pointed to the bedroom.

"You had better keep out of this," he whispered. "Go in there, and stay quiet."

"But——"

"Do exactly as I say."

She obeyed him, for her brain was yet too confused to work things out clearly. He turned the key in the lock after her, and pocketed it. Simultaneously there came a banging on the other door. He took an automatic pistol from his pocket, made sure that it was loaded, and crept to the right of the door. Again there came the banging.

"Who is there?" he asked calmly.

"Open—open!"

He turned the key and then leapt aside, with the pistol ready for action. Banting broke in, with Sam slinking at his heels. Jack o' Lantern laughed and slipped his weapon into his pocket unobserved.

"What a pleasant surprise!" he said. "I had a notion it was someone much less welcome. How the devil did you find out my humble abode?"

Banting glared at him.

"I've come for Kate," he snapped.

"Kate! Do you expect to find her here?"

"I do."

"My dear Banting, by what mental process you arrive at such a conclusion is beyond me. And why is the valiant Sam gulping like a goldfish? But have a drink. Never let it be said that I was lacking in hospitality—even after midnight."

Despite Banting's muttered refusal he poured out some drinks and offered them to his visitors. Neither of them touched the glasses. Jack o' Lantern looked hurt.

"What is all this nonsense?" he asked.

Banting walked up to him and looked him squarely in the eyes. His was a masterful personality, but it never for one instant dominated the other man.

"She met you to-night," he said. "We found your note."

"Well?"

"She did not return."

"Surely!"

"You know she did not. You took her away. You brought her here."

"You are quite mistaken. But you flatter me."

"Listen!" said Banting grimly. "We've been good friends up to now. I know who I'm talking to, and I've never been fool enough to meddle in things that do not concern me. But this *does* concern me. Kate's life and yours lie far apart. I have made plans for her, and they are going through."

"Quite right! Quite right!"

"I know that you brought Kate here by force."

"You are utterly wrong."

"Well, she is here, and cannot be anywhere else. Don't play with me, Lefroy, I am a desperate man."

"Quite dramatic, that! I always thought you had a dash of the stage in your make-up. Come, have a drink——!"

He made to pick up a glass and Banting seized his opportunity. A pistol suddenly appeared and was thrust into Jack o' Lantern's side.

"Try that door, Sam!"

Sam was jerked into action. He tried the door.

"Locked!"

"I thought so. Search him, Sam!"

Nervously Sam came forward, but Jack o' Lantern suddenly produced the key.

"You are both mad," he said. "Satisfy yourselves, and then clear out. You bore me horribly."

Sam took the key and opened the bedroom door. He found the room empty. There was a gas-bracket beside the bed, and he lighted it. Eagerly he looked under the bed.

"She ain't here," he said.

Jack o' Lantern chuckled, and Banting joined Sam in the next room.

"Maybe she escaped through the window?" suggested Sam.

Banting opened the window and looked out. So far as he could see there was no means of escape. Certainly none that a woman would care to take, for there was a drop of some forty feet into an alley below, and nothing but a narrow coping to left and right which few but an acrobat would have risked walking along in order to reach the roof of a half-demolished building some fifty feet away. He shut the window and turned round. Jack o' Lantern was in the bedroom, laughing at him scornfully.

"Are you quite satisfied?" he asked.

"No. There must be another room—— The wardrobe! Sam, open the door of——!"

Sam was about to obey when Jack o' Lantern turned on him and seized him by the throat. Sam went hurtling through the door. Banting drew his pistol, but his wrist was caught as in a vice and he saw Jack o' Lantern's burning eyes within a foot of his own.

"Sam!"

"Drop that——!"

"I'm damned——!"

The pistol went off with a reverberating report, but the shot went wide. Fighting desperately the two men fell against the bed. They rose again, clasped in each other's arms. Banting still held the pistol. He wrenched one arm free, but the weapon hit against the gas-bracket and shattered the glass globe. Sam came in, holding his throat. He gasped as he saw the disturbed curtains make contact with the soaring gas flame. The next moment the inflammable material was alight. He shouted and tried to get near, but a heavy boot caught him in the ribs. Like lightening the conflagration spread. Sam found his pistol and levelled it at Jack o' Lantern. But the intended victim saw the danger just in time. He broke away from Banting and leapt at Sam. That worthy dropped his pistol and sprang through the door. The fight went on.

The pungent smell of smoke, and the strange, low roaring of flame brought Kate from her hiding-place. She gasped with horror to see the bed ablaze and the two men fighting furiously, and ran at them.

"Paul! Father! The place——!"

She was knocked down, and two heavy bodies fell on top of her. Then she heard a loud report and the struggle ceased. . . . She became aware that her father was lying still on the floor and Jack o' Lantern was holding his wrist and wincing. He gave her his uninjured arm and pulled her to her feet.

"Quick! There is no time——!"

But she wrested herself free and dropped by the side of her father. To her surprise, he still held the pistol in his hand. By some means he had managed to shoot himself. Jack o' Lantern dragged her from the spreading flame.

"Accident!" he said. "It's no use——!"

Half suffocated, she reeled away from the dense smoke. He caught her and took her firmly into the next room. As they reached it the hunchback's shrill voice shouted "Fire!" and "Police!" Jack o' Lantern opened the door and saw two helmeted figures running up the stairs, with Sam Knudge behind them. He slammed the door at once, and locked it. Then he wedged the back of a strong chair under the handle, and commenced to pile heavy furniture against it. Kate sprang up.

"Why——?"

"The rat has squealed."

"But we——!"

He caught her in his arms and looked at her fondly.

"The test," he said. "Are you afraid now? Is this love you boast of as big a thing as you imagined?"

"Let me—let me go!" she gasped.

"So it fails in the test?" he said scornfully. "I can save you by giving my own life—by opening that door. Shall it be that?"

"Yes—yes. We shall be burnt alive."

The constables had reached the door. They smashed at it with their truncheons, but it was stoutly built, and the lock was of the good old-fashioned order.

"Open, in the name of the law!"

"The fools!" he laughed. "As if the name of the

law were a greater terror than the song of the flames."

She broke from him and commenced to remove some of the furniture. He sat down on the end of the couch and watched her.

She was weak from fright and her recent mauling, but she managed to shift one piece of furniture a few inches. Then a great flame broke through from the bedroom, and the air grew almost too hot to breathe. She grew faint and reeled towards him. He caught her and looked towards the door, which was being savagely attacked from the other side.

"All right, he said. "You shall go."

He placed her on the couch and commenced to move the furniture. In a flash she seemed to see the future—him and a rope, and—and hopelessness. Half mad from her mental agony, she ran at him and caught his arm.

"No," she said hoarsely. "I was a coward just now. Life means nothing to me—without you. They mustn't take you. They mustn't take you. Barricade! Barricade!"

So they pushed the obstructions even closer to the door, while the encroaching flames blackened everything, and sang their hideous song. He kissed her, and swallowed a glass of neat whiskey hastily.

"It isn't the end—yet," he whispered. "Get in that corner—quick!"

He ran to the window and opened it wide. The incoming air fanned the flames even higher, and Kate cringed before them. He came back to her.

"Now is the time for courage. Trust me!"

He dragged her to the window, and pointed along the coping to where the half-demolished building offered a possible descent to mother earth. But her courage failed her at the prospect of that awful ordeal.

"I—I—couldn't——!"

"You—must!"

He climbed through the window on to the nine-inch coping, and offered her his hand. The crashing of the dividing wall of the room was the deciding factor. Trembling with fear, she reached the coping, but one hand still held the window sash.

"Shut your eyes, and fear nothing," he said.

She was glad to do so. He lifted her in his arms, and with firm steps walked along the coping. In one place a broken piece of the cement became dislodged and went smashing down into the alley. Jack o' Lantern smiled to himself. Utterly without fear, he made his way forward, and ultimately laid his burden among a pile of old bricks on the top of the half-demolished building. There he chafed her hands.

"Safe so far! The place is burning like tinder, and the fire brigade his arrived. We must not tarry."

"No, no. But my father—— O God!"

"There's a ladder. I'll go first."

Ultimately they reached the ground, and flew swiftly through a maze of alleys and back streets until they emerged in a main thoroughfare.

"Where now?" she asked plaintively.

"I know a safe place. Look!"

He pointed behind her, and she looked and saw a ruddy glow in the sky. Evidently the fire was spreading to adjacent premises, and in that awful conflagration was the dead body of her father! Dazed and heartbroken, she permitted him to lead her away. The past was severed for ever, and the future——!

CHAPTER THIRTY

THE country was being scoured for the body—dead or alive—of Judge Wallington, and so far without any success. Sonia lived literally from minute to minute, dreading every ring of the telephone bell. In her heart she believed that she would never see her beloved benefactor again. Jack o' Lantern had taken his toll as he had threatened. Michels strove to bring a gleam of hope.

"He may have lost his memory," he said. "We must remember that he has been ill of late."

"But the blood on the blanket?"

"That might be accounted for in many ways."

"Oh, no. The other house was broken into. The pillow was gashed. The—the murderer must have discovered that the Judge was here. I fear at any moment——"

She started as she heard a knock on the door, and then uttered a little cry of welcome to behold Wrench.

"Any—news?"

"None—so far as the Judge is concerned. But a strange thing happened last night. There was a big fire near Seven Dials. The alarm was given by Sam Knudge——"

"Knudge!"

"We have detained him. He found a constable at the top of St. Martin's Lane and stated that Jack o' Lantern was in a certain house, and that the place was on fire. The latter part of his statement was certainly borne out. When the constable arrived the place was burning furiously. The fire brigade was rung up, and the constable, with a fellow officer, attempted to force an entry into the top part of the premises. They found the door locked and barricaded. By the time the brigade arrived it was impossible to get up the staircase. A whole block of buildings is completely razed to the ground."

"And Jack o' Lantern?" asked Michels eagerly.

"Knudge swears that Jack o' Lantern took the woman Kate to this place—his lodgings—and that he and Banting went there with the object of getting her away. There seems to have been a fight between Jack o' Lantern and Banting. Knudge, like the rat he is, ran out in the middle of it and squealed."

"Yes—yes."

"Late this morning a body was found among the ruins."

"Whose body?"

"That is the problem. There was nothing but a charred skeleton—no article of any kind that would lead to identification. The only thing that is certain is that the body is either Lantern's or Banting's. Every other person in the house has been accounted for."

"But Knudge——?"

"He says it looks like Banting's, but he is not sure."

"But if Banting is alive, wouldn't he come forward?"

"It is unlikely, because it can be proved that the corpse really died from a gunshot wound. His skull was perforated."

"That would account for the door being barricaded against the police?"

"Precisely."

"And Kate—was she really in the house?"

"That is another mystery. Knudge swears that it was upon his going to the wardrobe with a view to looking inside that Jack o' Lantern sprang at him, and the fight commenced. So whichever of the two men survived has good cause to hide himself away."

"But presuming the woman was hidden there, how did she and the man get away?"

"That was possible by means of a narrow coping at the back of the house, but it was a most hazardous task. We have visited Banting's house, and there is no one there but the maid."

"And what do you think personally?" asked Michels.

Wrench shook his head.

"It can only be a guess at the best, but I am of the opinion that Jack o' Lantern is too clever to get shot by Banting. In which case he and Kate are at large."

"But would she go with him after he shot her own father?" asked Sonia in a horrified voice.

"She might. You have to realise that we are not dealing with ordinary people. If she was really in that house she must have gone there voluntarily, for it is inconceivable that he could have taken her there by force at a time when the West End of London is full of people."

"She may have been lured there."

"No. A note was found in Banting's house. It was a peremptory message, and she obeyed it. She went to meet him even though she was aware of his real identity. That being so, I deduce she would be capable of staying with him in any circumstances. But it makes our task easier."

"How?" asked Sonia.

"Two persons are easier to run down than one, and three easier than two, and so on *ad infinitum*."

Michels seemed very perturbed. Ever since the disappearance of the Judge he had displayed signs of great agitation. Sonia had seen him prowling in the park, searching everywhere. Then he would vanish for half a day and return home, silent and reflective. She drew Wrench away.

"Are—are you staying long, John?"

"No. I want to have another look round here. There is a tremendous to-do at the 'Yard.' I wish I were as sure of the Judge's existence as I am of Jack o' Lantern's."

"You—you believe the worst?"

"I'm sorry to say I do. Be brave, dear. It is better

to face the grimmest possibility. If I could give you a word of hope I would, but everything points to murder and concealment of the body. There is a big force searching the coutry-side, and every pond is being dragged."

She shuddered at these awful words, but she thought that he was right to prevent her from hoping where there was no grounds for hope. The only inconsistent point was the disappearance of the body, when in every other case the supposed murderer had not gone to all that trouble. Wrench had tried to explain that, but it was not a good explanation.

"How does Nali take this?" he asked.

"Badly. It is difficult to get him to do anything. He is silent and takes scarcely any food. Sweeting came here yesterday, and questioned Nali. I—I thought he was going to arrest him, but he didn't. Of course it is all wrong. Nali knows no more than we do about these terrible events."

"You are wrong."

"What do you mean?"

"I mean that both Nali and Michels are concealing something. Although I cannot prove it, I am convinced that Nali told us a lie to explain his presence at Regent's Park, and Michels has learned something that he prefers to keep to himself. Well, they are both playing a very dangerous game, and I wish I could make them realise it."

"Do you mean it is possible they may be ar——?"

"It is not impossible. Any concealment of information is not in the public interest, and the tracking of criminals is best left to the police."

"Yes—yes." She wrung her hands. "When I think of poor Bunty I—I can't control myself. They said he was harsh, but he wasn't. To me he has been an angel—ever since I first came here. I—I don't know what to do now. Ought I to go back to the other house? I was only invited here because the Judge came, and somehow I hate the place. What shall I do?"

"You must do what appeals to you most—until we are married, and I can look after you."

"I—I wish it could be to-morrow."

"It can be in three weeks. Shall I arrange that? But for this case we might have been married weeks ago. I have let that foul murderer rob us of some happiness. Whether the Judge is dead or alive, let us lose no more time."

"Would it be right if—if he is—dead?"

Wrench bit his lip. He saw her point, but could not quite fall in with her ideas. There need be no display— just a quiet affair at a register office—and then the right to take care of her and banish this great shadow from her life.

"Don't you think he would approve—if he knew?" he asked quietly.

"Yes. He would not want mourning. Do—do as you suggest, John. I shall go mad if I am left to myself much longer."

He was greatly relieved and went off by himself to hunt over the ground for the nth time. On the edge of the plantation he met a sergeant from the local police force.

"Hallo, Jenkins!" he said. "Any luck?"

"A bit, sir."

"What?"

The sergeant produced a collar. It had once been highly starched and polished, but was now damp and stained with blood in one place. Wrench looked at the maker's name. It was a Bond Street address.

"Where did you find this?" he asked.

"Over there—where I have placed the small stake. But I've been all through the plantation and found nothing."

"Make another search in that direction. Better get some help. I am going to the house, but will come back soon."

Wrench rounded up Nali and showed him the collar. He nodded his head as he examined it, and admitted that it belonged to the Judge.

"Can you say whether it is the collar which your master wore on that evening?"

"Yes."

"How do you know?"

"He call Nali to fasten it before he come downstairs to dinner. Nali notice little brown mark inside—there."

"Good! Now think! You have already stated that on that night you took your master a drink—into his bedroom. Is that so?"

"Yes."

"Was he undressed—when you left him there?"

"N—no."

"Isn't it your custom to help him undress?"

"Sometimes—not always. He did not want Nali to stay—that night. Nali just take off his shoes and he tell Nali he may go."

"That is—the truth?"

The Hindu bowed.

Wrench let him go, but he was considerably perplexed. Here was new light on the time factor which complicated matters. He said nothing to Sonia of his discovery, but hurried back to the sergeant, who had been joined by two other men. A long and minute search failed to provide any further clue, and Wrench ultimately returned to the "Yard."

He and Sweeting and their chief held a conference,

and went over the ground again. The collar played rather an important part, since it served to indicate the time of the tragedy.

"If the Judge went to his room soon after nine o'clock, and was left by Nali at, say, nine-fifteen, it is inconceivable that he would sit there with his collar on for any considerable time," said Sweeting.

"Quite!"

"Then we can time the affair as between half-past nine and ten o'clock?"

"That is reasonable."

"Unless he went to sleep in his clothes—sitting in his chair, for instance," suggested Wrench.

"That is possible but not likely," snapped Sweeting. "A man does not fall asleep in a chair with his bed close by. No, it is more reasonable to conclude that the tragedy took place round about half-past nine. From the blood on the collar I should say he was knocked on the head first."

"And taken through the window?"

"No. That would have been impossible. But the murderer might have waited in that room until everyone had gone to bed, and then taken the body out of the house by an easy route."

"And the collar?"

"The Judge may have recovered consciousness near the plantation, and put up a fight—ere he was put to death. But I am coming to the point, sir. If the Judge was taken from the Hall by the man who entered the place somewhere about half-past nine the affair at Regent's Park was a subterfuge."

"On whose part?"

"The murderer's. We know he must have gone to Regent's Park after he did the crime and not before, and therefore there was no object in entering that house except for the purpose of making it appear that the murder at the Hall was subsequent to the entry of the Regent's Park house."

"For what purpose?"

"In order that he might prove an alibi."

Wrench started, for he saw at what Sweeting was driving.

"One moment, Inspector," said Sweeting. "We have been puzzled to know what the Hindu was doing in that house. I submit that he went there immediately after he had disposed of his victim, because he knew that Miss Pelling was there. He inflicted that wound upon himself for two purposes—firstly to make it appear that he had been attacked, and secondly as an excuse to draw her attention to the fact that he was there."

"Rubbish!" said Wrench.

"Inspector!"

"Sorry, sir, but that theory cannot be supported, for I saw Jack o' Lantern with my own eyes, and my assistant chased him down a side street."

"I have never said there was no accomplice," urged Sweeting. "I am sure there is. You must see that we have piled up evidence against this trusted servant, and we have only refrained from arresting him because the Judge was dead against it, and believed in him implicitly. But now——"

"You are not suggesting that he is Jack o' Lantern?"

"No, I believe—and have always believed—that this old enemy of the Judge's is being used as a scapegoat."

The Assistant Commissioner demurred. Plausible as Sweeting's theory sounded, there was not enough evidence to bring a charge against Nali. It was a difficult, tantalising business. He turned to Wrench.

"What is your opinion, Wrench?"

"At the moment, sir, I cannot explain the anomalies in the time factor, but I am convinced that the Hindu is innocent, and that the Judge's life was threatened by Jack o' Lantern and no other person. If the Hindu is keeping back any information, we shall learn more by keeping him under observation than by arresting him. He had a perfect right in that house, and I will never believe that his wound was self-inflicted. The man I saw in the cellar was Jack o' Lantern—as sure as I'm standing here."

In the end the Chief held his hand so far as Nali was concerned, and Sweeting was furious to reflect that once again his subordinate officer had got his way.

CHAPTER THIRTY-ONE

A few days later Sonia returned to Regent's Park. The house had never been a bright one, but now it seemed sunk in gloom as was her very soul. Wrench had made arrangements for the wedding, and she tried to draw pleasant thoughts from that. So far she had not dealt with the problem of Nali. It might be possible that John would engage his services, but she could not help feeling that Wrench was very suspicious of the Hindu.

The charred human remains found among the débris of the fire had not been identified. Whether it was Banting or Jack o' Lantern no one could say. As the days passed she gave up all hope of ever seeing the Judge again. The efforts of the police and public had proved vain. It was the element of uncertainty that tortured her, and she knew she would be happier if she could finally accept the conclusion that Jack o' Lantern had taken his revenge.

Michels called one morning, and paid his respects.

He had heard about the arrangements for her marriage and gave it as his opinion that she was doing the right thing. It was, he believed, what the Judge would have desired.

"You have lived too long in a gloomy atmosphere," he said. "Youth should be gay."

"I am getting over the worst effects," she said. "At first it stunned me. It is all so horrible."

"What shall you do about Nali?"

"I don't know. We are scarcely friends now. I suppose—I suppose I shall have to discharge him. But Mr. Michels, do you believe that the Judge was really murdered by Jack o' Lantern?"

"No."

"Then——!"

"Don't ask me anything—yet. When the time is ripe I may tell you something. But think of yourself—of your future happiness and let time solve your problems."

"I don't understand you."

"It is better you should not. Where is Nali now?"

"Out. I can do nothing with him. He is not disrespectful, but he is disobedient. I am certain he was out all last night, for he looked tired and ill this morning—an utterly changed man. I think he will not believe the Judge is—is dead, and goes out searching for him. Poor Nali!"

While they were talking Michels saw the Hindu coming up the drive. He seemed to be in a state of great excitement, for he ran and walked at intervals, and was breathing heavily—laboriously. Sonia did not see this, for her back was towards the window.

"I think I saw Nali just then," said Michels. "Do you mind if I have a word with him?"

"Not in the least. I will send him in to you."

She left the room, and a few minutes passed before Nali entered. He halted in front of Michels.

"You send for me, *sahib?*"

"Yes. Where have you been?"

"An errand."

"On whose behalf?"

"It was to do with the house."

"Your hands are shaking. You have discovered something. What is it you have discovered?"

Nali's piercing black eyes read something in the face of his questioner.

"What does the *sahib* know?" he lisped.

"I know Jack o' Lantern, and I want him before—before the police get him."

"If I could trust——"

"There is no one you can trust but me. Tell me all you know, or we may be too late."

"You swear——?"

"You must trust me. I alone can help you. Do you know where he is—at this moment?"

Nali inclined his head.

"Good! Where is he?"

"In an empty house—not far away. The woman is with him. Last night he went for the drug which he needs, and they tell Nali on the telephone. I have seen the house."

"You can take me there?"

"Yes."

"We will go to-night. I will have a car outside the house. Join me at ten o'clock."

"And then?"

"I shall find a way to save the situation."

Nali's eyes gleamed with hope. He bowed and left the room. Michels sat in deep reflection for a few minutes and then went to say good-bye to Sonia.

"So quick?" she asked.

"I have an appointment."

"What was the matter with Nali?"

"He is very distressed. There is no doubt he had a great regard for his master."

"Yes—I know. But he causes me to worry deeply."

* * * * *

At ten o'clock that night a closed car drew up in the side street. Nali had slipped from the house and was already in the neighbourhood. He went to the car and saw Michels reclining inside. The door opened and he entered.

"The driver is a trusted friend," said Michels. "You must direct him."

Nali did this through the speaking-tube, and the car moved away. It sped through a maze of streets and ultimately drew up in a dark thoroughfare that was lined on both sides with tall houses of Early Victorian type. In the centre were gardens very much run to seed, and all the houses were in a bad state of repair.

"That house," said Nali, pointing to the second one.

They got out of the car and walked through a short garden, past a board inscribed. "To Let," until they reached a flight of stone steps. Here Nali hesitated, and finally pointed to another flight of steps which led down to the area. They traversed these and found a window at the bottom. The Hindu produced a table knife from his pocket, and inserted the blade between the sashes. In a few seconds he had slipped back the fastening.

"Nali go first. Have torch," he whispered.

They entered the basement, with Nali's electric torch as pilot. It was empty and very damp, and a rat or

two scuttled under their feet. Some stairs brought them
to the upper part of the building, and here they stopped
and listened intently. Michels heard nothing, but Nali
did.

"Up above," he whispered. "I hear the woman's
voice. You have a pistol?"

"Yes."

"There may be great danger. I cannot say."

"I understand."

"Softly then."

They mounted the main staircase, treading as lightly
as possible on the bare boards. When they reached the
landing Michels could hear voices—very low and very
tense. They came from the room on the left of the
corridor. Cautiously they went forward, and reached
the door.

Here they halted for a moment, muffling the sound
of their breathing as much as possible. Nali displayed
a knife and Michels' hand closed on an automatic pistol.
A glance and a nod, and the door was pushed open.
On a mattress in the corner were seated a man and a
woman, eating something by the light of two candles
stuck in black bottles. Michels gasped as he saw the
livid face of Jack o' Lantern—set with two piercing
cruel eyes. But time was of the utmost importance.
Nali realised that and leapt like a cat across the room.
Kate screamed and tried to grab him, but he succeeded
in gripping the two arms of Jack o' Lantern. Michels
acted swiftly. He took from his pocket a round pad
and held it over the nose of the resisting man. There
was a choking sound, a gradual slackening of resistance,
and then stillness.

"Good!"

Kate tore at Michels' arm.

"Don't hurt him!" she wailed.

"S-sh! Be quiet. We are not police. Who are you?"

"I'm—— What are you going to do?"

"Take him away. You must leave this place and go to your home. You must forget—him. You understand?"

"No—no!"

"Yes."

"Quick, *sahib!*" pleaded Nali.

They paid no more attention to the hysterical Kate, and between them they carried the inert body of Jack o' Lantern downstairs, and finally got him into the car.

"You must come with me," said Michels to Nali. "I may need you."

Through the night the car sped, out into the country towards Michels' rented house. Once the prisoner showed signs of reviving, but Michels put him off again with a whiff of the chloroform. At last they reached the Hall. On the north side of the big building was an old tower, containing a single room, with a stout door. The driver was directed there, and they carried Jack o' Lantern up the steps and dumped him on a trestle bed. The car was sent away and Michels proceeded to bring the prisoner to his senses by the use of a small blue bottle of chemicals. At last the eyes opened and stared at Michels and the Hindu.

"My God!"

Michels winced, but said nothing. He seemed to be overwhelmed with horror. Jack o' Lantern's finger came out and pointed to Nali.

"I know you. I've seen you before."

"Nali is a friend."

"A friend!" he laughed scathingly, and then looked about him eagerly. "Where is she? What have you done with her? If any harm has come——"

"Silence!" rapped Michels. "I have much to say to you. Look! Do you recall this man?"

He held out a small portrait of Judge Wallington, replete in wig and robe. Jack o' Lantern took it and a murderous expression came into his eyes.

"I know him—the swine! But I didn't kill him. It is all a lie—a trick. I went for him—in that house, but he wasn't there. He had run—run for his life." His voice sank to a sinister whisper. "I shall find him yet."

He clasped at his throat and seemed to be suffocating. Michels saw long scars beneath the "choker"—the marks of finger-nails.

"Do you remember me?" he asked.

"No. Who are you?"

"Try to remember where you saw me last."

"Is it necessary? No, I have never seen you before. But the Indian, yes. He has followed me at times—like a dark phantom." He looked about him, and twisted his mouth cunningly. "This is no police prison. What is your game, eh?"

"To save you—to save you from yourself," said Michels tensely. "We must go into the past. Do you remember Tobias Lantern?"

The prisoner shut his mouth so tightly that the thin lips almost vanished.

"He was—my brother—no, not my brother. He was— Why in God's name do you ask me that?"

"It means much to you—and to us. You once met Tobias Lantern. You looked into his eyes. You saw into his very soul. You took upon yourself——"

Jack o' Lantern suddenly leapt forward. His hands reached Michels' throat, and it took the combined strength of the two men to fling him off. He fell across the bed, gasping.

"It is useless now," said Michels. "We must leave him for a while. Come!"

They left the room and made the door secure behind them. As they made for the house they heard a hideous laugh from the direction of the tower. Nali looked at Michels.

"Master, it is too late," he said.

CHAPTER THIRTY-TWO

A WEEK later Michels was writing somewhat laboriously in his diary—as if each word caused him mental agony. Small as the writing was, the fairly thick volume was now almost full. He read over his recent addition:

> *Nothing seems of any avail, and I fear that the case is hopeless. Seven days have passed since I brought him here, and he is exactly the same—if not worse. There is little doubt that the servants suspect that something is amiss, and but for Nali's vigilance they would have discovered the truth before now. It is impossible to take them all into my confidence, and yet one word of alarm would bring the police down upon us. What is one to do in the face of such a gigantic problem—unique in my lengthy experience? Only the sense of his own peril prevents him from raising a fracas. That at least I have dinned into him. There is no doubt about the depth of his passion for Kate. Poor girl! I can find time to pity her. Unquestionably it is this passion that ties him down—that and the cumulative effects of the drug. Conti is of the opinion that the key to the riddle lies in some comparatively simple recurrent event. But what?*

"Ah, what?" he mused, and closed the book.

The door opened and an angular man entered. He was as thin as a lath, with a perfectly bald head and lashless eyes. His clothes fitted him badly, and were creased and dusty. In all he was a remarkable figure. He was Adolphe Conti, a professional hypnotist and a well-known writer on psychological subjects. He hailed from Budapest, and had come post-haste to England at Michels' request.

"He is in a bad mood," he said. "Vicious and sullen. I could do nothing with him."

"Is he eating?"

"A little—but not enough. And the heart—it will not stand the strain much longer."

"You think it is a hopeless case, Conti?"

"No—but difficult. We are working amid unfavourable conditions. He has no comfort and is burning with hate. That is bad for him. We need a different environment. Could he not be brought into the house?"

"It is impossible. Already I am running a great risk."

"Then he must be got away."

"To where?"

"Budapest—to my clinic. I think I could promise a cure—in time. The woman is the chief drag upon him. He cannot rid his mind of her. She holds his brain. But in Budapest he would forget her—eventually, and then we might reach the seat of the trouble."

"Yes—yes. I had thought of that. But can it be achieved? The police are watching the ports. Everyone is on the alert. Half England is after him."

"It could be done—by aeroplane. In any case I hold a doctor's diploma and could certify him as an urgent case. My clinic is well known. You, too, have some influence."

Michels walked up and down in a state of great agitation. What he was doing was outside the law that he loved so much, but there were occasions when the law could not apply—and this was one. He thought he saw his way to fall in with Conti's plan, and ultimately he nodded his head.

"We will risk it, Conti."

"The ends may justify the means. It is an interesting case, and one that I do not want to abandon. It may be necessary to put him to sleep."

"Let us make our plans."

*   *   *   *   *

At Regent's Park Sonia was in a dilemma. Nali had disappeared and a week had now passed without her receiving any news from him. Wrench was a little startled, for he had not expected this.

"There wasn't any quarrel?" he asked.

"No, but for some time we have been at loggerheads. I was ready to forgive him for breaking his word to me, but he did not seem to want to be forgiven. Can it possibly have anything to do with—with Jack o' Lantern?"

"Who can say? You told me that Michels saw Nali on the day of his disappearance?"

"Yes."

"You don't know what transpired?"

"No. I left them together. Afterwards Nali seemed rather—excited. He disappeared the same evening."

"Has Michels been here since?"

"No."

"H'm!"

"What are you thinking, John?"

"Nothing—definite. I have come to the conclusion that I am a rotten policeman."

"Are you fishing for compliments?"

"No. I was thinking of our failure to land that murderer. We have been near to him—very near, but always he slips through our fingers. This morning I saw an old friend—Kate Banting."

"You—you have located her?"

"Yes. She went back to her father's house. She made a long statement—a fake one."

"Are you sure?"

"Yes. She swore that she did not go to the house that was burnt down, and that she knew nothing about the fire until two days ago, when she saw Sam Knudge. She admitted that a note had been thrown into the room on the night of the fire, and swore that she refused to meet Lefroy—or Jack o' Lantern, as she now knows him to be."

"But how could she explain her absence?"

"She didn't try. She said she had a reason for going away—suddenly, and she took advantage of the opportunity that offered itself that night. Of course it was a pack of lies. She was in that room where the fight took place, but we have no possible means of proving it."

"Then it *was* her father who was burnt to death?"

"Without doubt, or he would be living there with her. She is distressed—on the verge of a breakdown. We can do nothing but watch her in the hope that she may lead us to Jack o' Lantern. But it is a thankless job."

"But if she loves him, why has she left him and come back to that house?"

"I don't know. He may have sent her away because he realises that her companionship is dangerous. Alone he stands a chance of wriggling through the net, but with a woman——"

"It is all so involved. You told me that Kate was engaged to marry Knudge, and yet she goes off with that —that murderer, hides in his flat, sees her father murdered, or discovers that he has been shot, and then makes her escape with the man who killed him. Isn't it all illogical—unreal?"

"The murderer is unreal. Who can say what sort of fatal fascination he has for that girl? There have been other men like that, and no normal person can explain them. From what I can gather she became engaged to Knudge out of pique. Jack o' Lantern had apparently deserted her, and Knudge got in at a moment when she was lonely and miserable. The little rat has made some money, and has that to lay at her feet."

"They are reconciled now?"

"I don't know. But don't worry your head about these people who are outside your world. In a fortnight you and I——"

She smiled and they dropped the gloomy subject. When Wrench had gone she played the piano—the first time for many days, and derived some measure of forgetfulness from it. But under the copy of Schumann was "The Hymn of the Soul," and that brought back the Judge very clearly. She remembered how he had loved that weird Hindu air, and how they had argued as to its real merit. She put it aside, with tears in her eyes.

A few miles away another girl was similarly engaged. She was Kate Banting, and her trouble was very similar to Sonia's. She, too, was alone, and reflecting upon the past. Since Jack o' Lantern had been snatched from her so mysteriously she had had time to think clearly over things. It was always the same when he was not present. She could be logical—eminently practical. Free from the spell of his presence, she saw that no happiness lay in that direction. She blamed herself for the death of her father—not Jack o' Lantern. There was no doubt in her mind that that affair was an accident. But there were the other tragedies that were no accidents. Under the magic influence of his power she could forget those, but not now.

She had lied to Wrench from a desire to be loyal to the man she loved and always would love—though that love could never be consummated. Whatever might happen she did not want him on her conscience. It must be Sam again—Sam, the pitiful sneak. That or nothing!

Well, it had been her father's wish, and she really believed she was doing homage to his memory by carrying out that wish. Perhaps Sam might be licked into the semblance of a decent man by a woman of will—perhaps!

He called an hour later, having been invited by post card. It was clear he did not know quite what to expect, after the incident of the flat, and he was inwardly furious with her for the part she had played. But Banting's death had sobered him. He had received a rude shock.

"I—I got your note, Kate," he said.

She came across and sat down beside him.

"I wanted to explain, Sam," she said. "That story I told the inspector was a lie."

"I knew that."

"I went with—with him. I can't tell you why. You'll never understand. Poor daddy was shot by accident. He—Lefroy—barricaded the door. We escaped through the window, and stayed the night in an empty house— two nights, no, I can't remember how long it was. But there was nothing wrong—nothing, I swear. He was taken ill there—and I dared not call a doctor. He just crumpled up and—and was like a child. But he revived again—as if by a miracle. I had to creep out and buy food. Of course he is mad—mad. There were occasions when he didn't know me. His voice changed—and he

was fighting—fighting against something. The second
night he must have gone out. Anyway, he got hold of
a box of powder—dope. That gave him new life—new
strength. My mind seemed to have gone. I had to hold
myself to save going mad—like him. When—when I
had made up my mind to leave him, a strange thing
happened. Two men broke into the house. One was
oldish—looked and spoke like a foreigner, and the other
was a Hindu. They sprang at him, drugged him, and
took him away."

Sam's eyes opened wide with amazement.

"Not the cops?"

"No."

"Lumme, that's funny!"

"Well, now he's gone—for ever. And father's gone
too. I don't know how I stand about the proceeds from
the sale of the house, for until Jack o' Lantern is captured it will be impossible to have my father's death
assumed. And there isn't much to come to me, either."

"Never mind that," said Sam. "I'm just as keen as
ever—if you are. I bin in hell since—since that night.
But I can understand better than you think. He's like
that—a kind of snake; when he looks at you—right
through you, and when he talks in that queer way, and
laughs, you don't know what's come over you. He's
the devil—that's what he is—something out of Hell."

"Let us forget him, Sam."

"Can *you* forget him?"

"I'm going to. Father was right. I was mad ever
to get—to get to care about him, but nobody told me
just what he was, and when I did hear the truth it was
too late. I—I had to let off steam. But it's all over—
all over now."

Sam rubbed his hands together in his inward joy. His
jealousy was quite a shallow thing and he preened him-

self as having beaten Jack o' Lantern in this intriguing game of love. Here was Kate, genuinely regretful, almost ready to eat out of his hand. That was indeed a stupendous triumph for a plain-faced, illiterate sneak-thief.

"Let's go somewhere," he begged. "A bit of food, and then the movies."

Kate was quite agreeable.

CHAPTER THIRTY-THREE

MICHELS had made all his preparations. An aeroplane and a competent pilot had been commissioned, also a closed car wherein to convey the prisoner to the aviation ground. Nali was to go back to Regent's Park and fabricate some excuse, which Michels left to his quite capable imagination. Shortly after dark the car arrived.

They found the prisoner eating his heart out in the room in the tower. He scowled as Michels and Conti entered, and seemed surprised that they were fully dressed. Conti had more influence over him than Michels, and it was left to him to explain what was in prospect.

"We are taking you away," he said. "I beg of you to come quietly, for it is in your own interest."

"Quite altruistic. What is the idea behind all this?"

"You are ill."

"Ill! Is my health of moment to you?"

"Yes, and it is not safe here. The servants are becoming more and more suspicious."

"Who the devil are you, and what do you want with me? I had rather be in a proper prison than in this miserable room."

"Prison is not the worst," hinted Conti. "Will you put yourself in our hands?"

"Anything to get out of this damned place."

"Then come!"

Jack o' Lantern went with them down the steps, and a cunning smile passed over his face as he saw the waiting car. But he displayed no sign of excitement, nor even interest. When Conti opened the door of the vehicle he stepped inside. The two men sat one on either side of him, and both of them were armed, for Conti at least knew with what kind of creature they were dealing.

"Whither away?" asked the prisoner sneeringly.

"You will know—in due course."

The car made towards London at a great rate of speed, and every few minutes the prisoner's expression changed. Now it was calm—reflective, now sullen, now aflame with hate. Conti was quite impassive. To him Jack o' Lantern was just a "case"—an interesting case. Michels, however, displayed signs of emotion. He was uneasy— nervous of the outcome. From time to time he looked through the window to see exactly where they were, and occasionally he would gaze at the prisoner sadly.

They were skirting the metropolis when the car suddenly swerved and all but ran into a ditch. All three were jerked forward by the sudden application of the powerful brakes. The car stopped dead. The driver left his seat and came to the window.

"Burst tyre. I'll have to change a wheel."

"Hurry, then!"

"Aye, sir."

"Must we get out?"

"I'm afraid so. I can't jack up the wheel otherwise."

Michels was against that, for the road was dark and deserted, and there was a dangerous light in the eyes of the prisoner.

"One of us will get out," he said. "Try to——"

The prisoner saw his great hope in process of being

blasted. He suddenly pushed Conti through the door—projecting him on to the road full length. Then he jumped over him and ran swiftly towards the opposite hedge. He vaulted this like an athlete and sent back a mocking laugh.

"After him!" cried Michels. "He mustn't get away."

Conti was pulled to his feet, and the three men started in hot pursuit. They caught a glimpse of a running form—ere it vanished behind some farm buildings. Michels was too advanced in years to be a harrier, and Conti was none too fit. The chauffeur displayed a reluctance to go on alone, and in a very short time defeat was obvious.

"That is bad!" gasped Michels. "We ought to have put him to sleep."

"Is he a lunatic?" asked the chauffeur.

"Partly."

"I'd better get that wheel changed and drive you to the police station."

Michels nodded, but he had no idea of going to the police station. He cursed his own folly in not taking adequate steps to prevent such a happening.

"What is the next step?" asked Conti.

"I am at my wits' end. It is possible he may go to Regent's Park. He did that on the last occasion, and now he is madder than ever. Yes, I must prevent that. The girl is probably alone."

"The Hindu has gone back."

"He could not deal with that creature single-handed. We must go there—at once."

"On what pretext?"

"I will find an excuse."

The delay gave the fugitive his opportunity to get clear away. The moonless, misty night favoured him, and he kept to the fields until they merged into the fringe of

outer London. As before, his goal was clearly marked
in his mind's eye. His one yearning was for Kate, from
whose side those mysterious personages had dragged him.
He was now in a badly lighted, poor suburb—a narrow
street with shops on either side. The sight of a barber's
pole caused him to halt and pass his hand over his chin
and cheeks. For a week he had gone unshaven. They
had not trusted him with a razor. The result was not to
his liking. He could not see Kate in his present state.
Calmly he walked into the shop and took a seat while
the barber attended to another customer.

"Your turn, sir!"

He reclined in the chair and sighed as the warm lather
was spread over his face.

"Bit of a crop, sir."

"I meant to have my money's worth," he replied.

The barber laughed and began to talk about football,
adroitly changing the subject when he perceived that his
customer was not interested in the slightest.

"Haven't got that Jack o' Lantern fellow yet."

"No, and they won't."

"Well, you never know. There's not many murderers
who get away with it. Never was such a case since
Charlie Peace. And to finish up with a Judge too!
Queer they haven't found the body arter all this
time."

"Whose body?"

"The Judge's. They've had the boy scouts out, and
bloodhounds and Lord knows what else, and not a
bloomin' sign. Oh, he's clever, he is. Fine stuff for the
newspapers. Why, he's worth ten thousand a year to
them."

To this Jack o' Lantern made no response. He was
puzzled. The past was always hazy with him, except
in its relation to Kate. He recalled going to the house

at Regent's Park, and finding no one there but women.
. . . Stay! There had been others. There had been
the man in the cellar and—and the Hindu. That part
came clear now. The Hindu whom he had "floored" in
that house was the same fellow who had dragged him
from the empty house; and he had seen him before—
many times. That strangely dislocated memory of his
was his bugbear. It was worse than ever to-night. He
needed certain things—the drink and the white powder.
After that, Kate and the thrill of her embraces.

"Thank you, sir!"

He jumped up, surveyed his image in the mirror and
smiled back at it. He felt in his pocket, and was relieved to find that they had left him his money. Mag-
nanimously he proffered a shilling and waved his hand to
indicate that he expected no change.

"How can I get to Charing Cross?"

"Tube—round the corner."

He went out, but he did not take the Tube. This
defective memory for details—and everything was a detail now, except Kate—did not affect his cunning. For
him the dark ways, or the jostling crowds. And there
was nothing inconsistent about this, for both afforded
shelter. It was the middle path that was dangerous.
He avoided that.

At the end of the street he found a motor-bus ter-
minus, and a double-decker was waiting marked "Strand."
He mounted the stairs and wedged himself in a seat beside an enormous woman. . . . On reaching the Strand
he got out. The open door of a public-house attracted
him, but he passed by it. There was a better place—a
more congenial place farther east, where both his urgent
needs could be supplied. . . . The Chinese proprietor
looked terrified when he entered, but quickly switched
him into a back parlour.

"You big fool," he lisped. "Pleece come here. You no stay—velly dangerous."

"Get me what I want—you know. Hurry!"

He stayed but ten minutes, with the Chinaman waiting in a state of nervous terror. Now he felt better, stronger, ready for anything. In that short time he had consumed nearly half a bottle of whiskey and had snuffed the intriguing powder that was slowly eating out his soul. He gave the Chinaman a Treasury note and made to walk past him, but the man caught his sleeve.

"Not that way. Fu know. Man watch—long time."

"All right."

He left the place through a rambling cellar which gave him access to a back alley. Like an automaton he moved towards his objective, humming an air to himself. The proper sequence of the notes eluded him. He tried and tried again, but never got beyond a certain bar. It was "The Hymn of the Soul"—that strange, weird melody that brought up from the hidden depths of his mind faint images. . . .

At last he saw the house he sought, and his heart throbbed with joy. His first impulse was to run across the street, mount the steps and pull the bell. But his cunning never failed him. He walked away from the house and crossed the road farther down the street. Under the shadow of the wall he came back, then climbed over it. He was at the bottom of the garden, and a pang of disappointment came when he perceived that the sitting-room was in darkness. It was yet early, so he concluded she must be out and not asleep in her bedroom. He tried the window fastening, but could not gain entry to the room. At the side was a smaller window of the old-fashioned type, but this, too, was secured on the inside. Michels had taken away his knife, but he remembered there was a gardener's shed a short distance away in which he had once noticed a few old tools. He went to the shed and after some searching found a short-bladed knife. With the aid of this he entered the house, switched on the light and made himself comfortable in an arm-chair.

To kill time he had recourse to his pernicious drug. The maggots scampered in his brain. Some of the events of the past came up in vivid perspective. He saw before him a gallery of portraits. But they were all dead men —save one. That one wore a wig—he was the infamous Judge Wallington, who they said was missing. But he knew better. It was a hoax—a hoax to mislead him— throw dust in his eyes. He extracted a wallet from his pocket. It was still packed with paper money, and in the small pocket were several folded newspaper cuttings, much tattered and torn. One was the portrait of Sir Randolph Cantler, another the portrait of a Dr. Devinne, and there were others—all bearing a great red cross and a date. But the last one bore no cross, and carried the hateful, memorable features of his *bête noire* —Judge Wallington!

He placed this flat on the table, gloated over it for a long time, and then found the stub end of a red crayon. He drew a cross from corner to corner and tried to remember the date. At last a small calendar on the wall gave it to him. He added this and also the words "to-night." He thought he saw the game being played by the police and by his intended victim. They wanted to saddle him with a crime not yet perpetrated. He would teach them a lesson! So his tormented mind ramped on, like a machine that has lost its governor. Then he felt ill, and everything around him seemed to dissolve into a blood-red mist. Outlined in this was a form—a vague creature that grinned at him. He knew it and nodded.

"To-night," he gasped. "I understand, Tobias. It shall be to-night, after—after——"

The door suddenly opened, and he turned his head and saw Kate. He was not aware of the fear and horror that sat on her face. All he saw was her gleaming hair, her blue eyes, and the curving red lips. He pulled himself together.

"Kate!"

"You?"

He moved towards her, and she seemed powerless to move. Softly he caught her hands and kissed them.

"Come!"

"No—no. Why—what——?"

He pulled her towards the couch. At last she resisted and flung him off. His weakness astonished her, and she stared blankly at his almost inert form leaning against the table. Then she saw the newspaper cutting—the red cross and the date.

"You have—you have—?" she gasped.

He saw the object of her gaze, and again hate overrode his love passion. He raised his eyes from the print and stared past her.

"Of course!" he muttered. "I was almost forgetting. That—that comes first. I'll go—I'll go."

He made towards the window, but she ran at him and caught him by the arm.

"Where are you going? What are you going to——?"

He thrust her away from him, and this time his arms were strong. But he seemed to be in a kind of trance.

"Stay there!" he said harshly. "I'll come back—later. I have—business—on hand."

He went through the casement window before she could prevent him and disappeared from sight. She collapsed on to the sofa. But again her gaze went to the portrait of the Judge. Obviously he had been found and was living, or Jack o' Lantern would not— Murder was intended. She could not sit there and let it happen. Determined to prevent it at all costs, she went to the telephone, looked up the Judge's number and put the call through. She got the "engaged" signal. Again she tried and again received the signal. The girl on the exchange believed that the telephone receiver at the other end had not been replaced. In the meantime a crazy murderer was on his way——

Kate hesitated for a few moments, and then put on her coat and hat, and made out of the house. She ran along the street and ultimately found a taxi. A few moments later she was being driven towards Regent's Park.

CHAPTER THIRTY-FOUR

WRENCH had spent the evening with Sonia, and they returned from dining in town to have the door opened by Nali. Sonia was completely flabbergasted.

"Why, Nali!" she gasped. "What does this mean?"

"Nali come back," he replied nervously.

"I will see you later on."

In the drawing-room she looked at Wrench blankly.

"Isn't that extraordinary?"

"It is certainly unexpected. What do you intend to do?"

"He must go," she said slowly. "It is impossible to continue in this way. Besides, we shall be married soon, and then——"

"You had better see what excuse he gives."

"I am tired of his excuses. It is fairly evident that he has been indulging his old vice. But you don't know how hard it is to tell him that I have no further need

of his services. Since he was a boy he was my father's
faithful servant."

"I know. But some explanation is necessary."

She nodded and very reluctantly pushed the bell. The
Hindu entered and stood before her.

"Now, Nali—please explain the meaning of all this.
Why did you run away and stay away for a whole week?"

"I go—I go to seek the master."

"But you know—you must know——"

To her amazement Nali shook his head.

"What do you mean?"

"Nali think the master lives. He ask the mistress to
forgive him—for going away. But when the master
needs him——"

Wrench intervened.

"Now listen, Nali. These hints and evasions will not
do. If you believe the Judge is alive you must tell us
what causes you to hold that opinion. This is a very
serious matter."

"Nali's lips are sealed."

"This is preposterous. I warn you——"

The front door bell rang very loudly, and Nali averted
his head.

"Yes, answer it," said Sonia. "Whoever it is, say I
am engaged and can see no one."

Nali bowed and left the room.

"I am going to wring the truth from him," said
Wrench. "If he is obdurate I shall arrest him."

"John!"

"There is really no alternative. In this queer business
we need every scrap of help that the public can give us.
Nali is concealing something which may be of the utmost importance. It is——"

Nali knocked and entered. He looked flustered.

"Mr. Michels—and a friend, lady."

Sonia looked at Wrench, who like herself was obviously surprised at this late visit.

"Better see him," he said.

"All right. Ask Mr. Michels in here, Nali."

Michels made profuse apologies. He introduced Conti as a very old friend and patron of the arts. He had mentioned a particular picture which the Judge possessed and this turned out to be a work which Conti had been endeavouring to locate for some years. Had she any objection to his seeing it? His friend was obliged to leave England early in the morning—hence this very late call.

"You are perfectly welcome," she said.

The picture in question was in the library. She took them there and left them discussing the masterpiece, begging them to take some refreshment when they had finished. She found Wrench walking up and down reflectively.

"A somewhat flimsy pretext," he said.

"What do you mean?"

"He didn't come to look at pictures. He was annoyed to find me here, and if I am not mistaken he will stay on in the hope that I shall go."

"I can't see——"

"He made one very serious omission. Nali let him in. He knew that Nali had been missing for over a week, and yet he made no reference to that. Isn't that a little strange?"

"Well—yes."

"An oversight—due to some kind of excitement, but not an oversight that would have taken place had he not known that Nali had returned."

"But he may have questioned Nali in the hall. He was rather a long time coming in."

"Yes. He had something to say to Nali, but not what you imagine."

"But why should he call here at a late hour—and tell an untruth?"

"That is precisely what I intend to discover. I propose to leave almost immediately. But I shall return in half an hour—for something I have left. This unposted letter, for instance."

He took a foolscap envelope from his pocket and placed it on the mantelpiece. Sonia shook her head uncomprehendingly.

"I am anxious to find out if in my absence he finds some excuse for staying here—in this house."

"All right," she said. "I will tell Nali to bring some coffee. You will stay for that?"

"No. Tell him I have had to leave."

"But you will come back?"

"Oh yes. There is something strange going on."

She let him out and then gave Nali her instructions. The Hindu, too, wanted to be very sure about the number of cups, and she was obliged to point out that Wrench had gone. He seemed to derive some comfort from that. Michels and Conti returned to the drawing-room a little later.

"My friend is crazy about the picture," he said. "But I have assured him it cannot be bought. Has Inspector Wrench gone?"

"Yes. I think he has business on hand."

"H'm! He must find his time fully occupied these days. I have been showing Mr. Conti all the sights of your wonderful city. It is his first visit to London."

Coffee was served, and Michels chatted on various subjects and seemed in no great hurry to leave. He seemed to be constantly on the alert, averting his head at the slightest sound. Ultimately he looked at the clock on the mantelpiece.

"Surely that is not the correct time?"

"No. It is ten minutes slow."

"Slow! Why, we have missed the last train to the Hall." He consulted his watch. "Confound! It stopped over an hour ago. How shockingly careless of me. I must telephone an hotel."

Sonia saw the subterfuge. John was right, but she reflected that he had not told her whether she should fall in with the suggestion so clearly made. Common hospitality decided the point.

"Why worry?" she said. "We have plenty of room here. This house has always been at your disposal."

"But I wouldn't dream——!"

"Please do. I will tell Nali to prepare two rooms for you. I have no doubt he can fix you up with all that you need."

"If you are sure——?"

"Perfectly sure."

Nali was told what to do, and at Michels' request she played the piano for them, choosing his favourite German masters. But she was conscious of the fact that neither of her two guests was really listening. Wrench interrupted.

"I left a letter here," he explained. "It must be posted to-night. Ah—here it is!"

Michels moved uneasily.

"Was the picture genuine?" asked Wrench.

"Quite—quite."

"Mr. Michels and Mr. Conti are staying the night," said Sonia. "They have missed the last train."

"Really!"

"Frightfully careless of me," said Michels.

A look of antagonism passed between the two men.

Wrench bade them good night, and Sonia apologised and escorted Wrench to the door.

"I was right," he whispered. "Clever devil, Michels. I wonder what his game is?"

"You don't doubt his—his friendship?"

Wrench turned his head at the sound of scurrying feet on the gravel drive. A woman came into the ring of light. It was Kate Banting, breathless and obviously agitated. She started at the sight of the man who had once arrested her.

"Good evening, Miss Banting!" said Wrench. "This is rather unexpected."

"This—this is Judge Wallington's house?"

"Yes."

"Is he—is he inside?"

Sonia trembled, but Wrench touched her arm warningly, and she remained silent.

"Why do you ask?" demanded Wrench.

"He is in danger—great danger."

"You had better come inside."

Kate hesitated, but finally accepted the invitation. Wrench piloted her to the library.

"Now then—what is wrong?"

"He—he is coming here—Jack o' Lantern."

"What!"

"Yes—yes. I know what I am saying. He came to my house—broke in. He is crazy—mad with drink and drugs. He has planned to murder the Judge to-night. I tried to get through to this house on the telephone, but something was wrong with the line. I took a taxi, and——"

She was interrupted by a prolonged ringing of the front door bell. A few moments later a plain-clothes man entered the room. Wrench's eyes lighted up.

"Anything wrong, Hunter?"

"Yes, sir. A man has just entered the premises. I saw him climb over the garden wall and make towards the back door. At the same time Sergeant York entered the drive. He followed this young woman from the house which he was watching. I have left him posted at the other entrance."

Wrench became active. He took a pistol from his pocket, examined it, and replaced it.

"See York, tell him not to move from that door, then come back and guard the main entrance. We want this man—dead or alive, you understand?"

Hunter went off and Wrench turned to the two startled women.

"I think it would be wiser for you two ladies to join the men in the drawing-room," he said. "Quickly, please!"

He conducted them to the drawing-room and introduced Kate curtly. But Kate stood and stared in amazement at Michels.

"Why, you—!" she commenced.

"Miss Banting and I have met before," said Michels. "Is anything amiss?"

"Much," retorted Wrench grimly. "I must ask you all to stay here. It is unlikely you will be disturbed——"

Out went the lights, exactly as on a former occasion. Sonia uttered a little cry, and Michels poked the fire into a blaze. Wrench had gone off like a shot.

"He's here," said Conti in a low voice.

"So you knew," said Sonia. "But I don't understand it. Why should he come—why?"

"The Judge," whispered Kate. "He means to——"

"But the Judge is—is not here."

"Not here? Thank God!"

"I must go," said Michels, in a strangely agitated voice. "Conti, will you——?"

"It is hopeless," said Conti. "Quite hopeless. We had better stay where we are."

Suddenly the silence was broken by the wail of a pipe. It rose in strange cadence, fell and rose again.

"What——!"

"Nali!" said Sonia. "It came from upstairs. What is he doing up there?"

The music went on for a minute or two, holding them spellbound. Sonia knew it well. It was "The Hymn of the Soul," played as only the Hindu could play it. At last it faded away. She saw Michels' face in the red glow of the fire. It was curiously contorted.

"That air," he muttered. "Great Heaven! It may be——!"

He opened the door and ran from the room. Outside he came under the ray of a torch. Wrench was behind the light, with a pistol in his hand.

"I told you——" he commenced.

But Michels' eyes were turned upwards. Over Wrench's head—on the half-landing—he saw very faintly a human form. It was enveloped in a long coat, and was engaged at the window. There was a noise as the wide sash was raised. Wrench swung round and the ray from the torch fell upon the form.

"Halt!" he cried.

The pistol cracked as the form sprang forward. Wrench ran to the front door, opened it and bounded down the steps. He saw Hunter outside, on the alert.

"Round there!" he cried. "He jumped through the window. There he goes!"

The piercing blast of a whistle brought the other officer from the rear of the house. They had the fugitive penned into the corner of the garden, which part was enclosed by a quite unscalable wall.

"Don't shoot!" said Wrench. "We want him alive."

The fugitive turned and made to cut across the garden to where the wall was lower. But York interposed his figure and levelled a pistol at him. Swiftly all three men closed on him. They bore him down, and a pair of handcuffs were snapped on his wrists.

"Good! Let's have a look at him!"

Wrench gave vent to an ejaculation of amazement, for the ray of the torch fell full on the face of Nali.

"You!" he said incredulously.

Nali smiled back at him.

"Tch! There is a mistake. It is all wrong! Bring him into the house!"

Nali was taken into the drawing-room, and the light was got going. Sonia stared at the Hindu as if she could not believe her eyes. The sergeant produced a short-bladed knife which he had wrested from Nali's hand.

"Surely it can't be—it can't be possible!" said Sonia.

"This woman can tell us. Miss Banting——"

"That is not Jack o' Lantern," said Kate. "I ought to know him. No—no!"

"Damn! Where is Michels?"

"I—I don't know."

"Wait here!" said Wrench. "There is some funny work going on. Let no one leave."

He switched on the lights in the corridors, and mounted the stairs. There came to him a kind of murmur, and he moved towards the spot where the sound originated. It came from the Judge's room. He turned the handle and went in. On the bed lay a figure, coatless and collarless, with mud on the trousers and boots. Michels was leaning over it. He turned and saw Wrench.

"S-sh! He's going!"

Two pained eyes looked up at Wrench.

"Why—John! Just in time. *Sic transit gloria*—Have I been—unconscious—long? Horrid dreams—horrid, and then soft music that—drove—beasts——"

Wrench heard the death-rattle ere he touched the grimy hand. Sorrow and amazement overwhelmed him. He sat down on the bed and stared woodenly at the fine head of what had been Judge Wallington.

"Perhaps it is as well," said Michels.

"He—he was Jack o' Lantern?"

"Yes."

"And you knew all the time?"

"Not all the time."

"But did *he* know?"

"No—thank God! He thought he had been ill and dreaming. For what Jack o' Lantern did, Judge Wallington was not responsible. That foul ursurper of his soul even threatened his own life. It is one of Nature's evil jokes."

"It is the one solution I never dreamed of."

"There is a strange story behind it all, but that must be told later. We had better ring for the doctor."

CHAPTER THIRTY-FIVE

THE will of Judge Wallington had been proved. He left to his beloved ward all his possessions, after the payment of certain legacies to servants and friends, and he prayed that his ward might take into her service his most admirable servant, Nali.

"I am still in the dark about many things," said Sonia to Michels. "Please tell me everything now. I want to know."

"It all started over seven years ago. The Judge ought never to have taken the Tobias Lantern case. He was just recovering from a stubborn illness, and should have rested for a much longer period. Tobias was an extraordinary character. It took three juries and three judges to send him to the gallows. The Judge had a theory that Tobias was able to influence the minds of people at a distance. He himself was badly affected. In his weak state of health he feared that man. He saw into his inner life—he loathed and detested him. Yet he believed that Tobias should not have been hanged. But he was bound to act on the medical report. Something happened at that trial of which the Judge was totally unaware. The soul of Tobias Lantern was grafted on to an already existing second personality."

"But he was always—himself," argued Sonia.

"Yes—in later life. But to get to the bottom of these things one must go back to youth, when the emotions are given free play. I had not known the Judge in his early days, but I knew a man who had been to school with him—a man named Cunningham."

"Ah—the name I saw in your diary?"

"Yes. He was in Paris at the time when I suspected the truth. I had a long talk with him, without divulging my reasons for wanting an intimate account of the Judge's youth. He told me what I half expected to hear. The Judge as a boy exhibited distinct signs of dual-personality. As a light-hearted, lovable boy he would suddenly change into a morose person—a little cruel at times, and suffering from the hallucination of persecution. He seemed to outgrow this as he matured, but that little root was not dead. On to it Tobias grafted the being we called Jack o' Lantern."

"Did he imagine himself to be Tobias?"

"Possibly—at times. At any rate, he carried that grievance of Tobias against all the people who contributed to his conviction and death, and I believe that he sincerely justified his actions in his own unbalanced

mind. He appears to have carried over with him the
one thing to which he devoted his normal life—his in-
nate sense of justice. But in the transit it became warped
into fanaticism."

"When did you hit upon this theory?" asked Wrench.

"When no other theory would meet the case, and after
I had most carefully watched Nali."

"So Nali knew much earlier?"

"Yes. He is loath to speak about it even now. But
for Nali's assistance the Judge could never have lived
this double life. It was Nali who obliterated the trail
all the time. I think he did not at first realise what
was wrong with his master. It looked to him like ordinary debauchery, and when he did suspect the truth he
did everything in his power to prevent it from leaking
out. It was he who took the drug from the Judge's
pocket and who hid the soiled clothing."

"How did the Judge leave the house?"

"Through the back staircase. On most occasions Nali
followed him. That was how he came to know most of
his haunts."

"It is almost incredible."

"Yes. And a curious fact emerged from the phenomenon. In his second personality the Judge was left-
handed. It changed the character of his handwriting.
Also there seems to have been a period in the change-
over when he was aware of both personalities. I found
some roughly-written notes in his pockets. One warned
him not to go to the house in Watling Court, another
told him facts that enabled him to steer clear of danger.
He wrote those himself, when in the agony of the transi-
tion he realised that the process could not be checked.
As Jack o' Lantern he never guessed who wrote those
notes, but he was cunning enough to act on them. That
was what made your task so difficult, Wrench."

"I can see that—now. But have you any idea of the average duration of this second existence?"

"It varied. At first it was short—a few hours. Then a new factor crept in—love. It was love for Kate that caused him to cling more and more to his underworld life, until at last his better self was swamped. I suspect the drugs and drink to which he was addicted held him back."

Sonia shook her head sadly.

"You found him at last?" she said.

"Nali had traced him. I found myself confronted with a big problem. Consider the position. Here was a man, of great talent, a man of incalculable value to his country in his normal mentality. The revealing of the truth would have sent him either to the gallows or to a criminal asylum. I believed that it was possible to eradicate the second personality for ever, and bring back permanently the wise administrator of the law. Some might not uphold that motive, but I could only act as I saw the thing. After painful reflection I decided to do what I believed was right. Conti is a great mental expert and hypnotist. Well, we tried to get to the seat of the trouble and we failed. Conti was of the opinion that the second personality became dominant through some comparatively simple cause. He was inclined to suspect drugs, but that was not the case. It was only on the night of his death that I hit upon the truth."

It was the first time he had mentioned this, and his auditors were keenly interested.

"Don't you realise it even now?" he asked.

"No."

"It was a musical air—a thing he loved. It had a strange effect upon him——"

" 'The Hymn of the Soul'!" said Sonia.

"Yes. You may recall that on several occasions when

that air was played he exhibited signs of great lassitude, and hurriedly retired. I did not realise the significance of that until the night of his death, when we heard Nali playing it upstairs. The truth suddenly burst upon me. Nali had captured him by some means and was making a frantic endeavour to awaken the first personality by the employment of the same means that had put it to sleep."

"Then—then Nali knew?"

"Yes. I asked him why he didn't tell me before, but he did not appear to realise what an important point that was. As a matter of fact, I have had the greatest difficulty in getting any details from him. He feels it all very keenly, and calls the second personality 'the Jinn.' I think it is best not to question him further on the matter."

Sonia agreed. She wanted to hear no more. Like Nali she laid all the horrors to the account of the "jinn," and still carried in her mind very pleasant pictures of the wise and benevolent Judge. Later Wrench told her about the Judge's early unfruitful romance, and she fully understood Jack o' Lantern's burning passion for Kate Banting, and pitied the pale-faced, red-haired girl who had crept into the church before the interment.

"Let us look to our own lives, John," she said. "So you are getting promotion after all?"

"Yes. But I don't deserve it."

"You do. It wasn't an ordinary case. Of course we shall take on Nali?"

"Rather! Jove, I admire that last act of his. I all but put a bullet through him. Loyalty! You find it everywhere. That is what makes life such a glorious adventure. Sweeting was so disgusted he decided to retire."

"And now let us go and see about that furniture. I am certain you are wrong about the curtains. They must be blue, or we shall have the colour scheme completely ruined. John, I fear you are colour-blind."

"I must be," he said seriously. "At least there is something wrong with my eyes, for wherever I look I see nothing but you."

THE END

THE MYSTERY OF BURNLEIGH MANOR

By

WALTER LIVINGSTON

CHAPTER I

"BURNLEIGH MANOR——County seat of the Earl of
————, located on the edge of a cliff overlooking the
North Sea, fifteen miles N. by E. of King's Lynn, Nor-
folk, and one hundred and fourteen miles N. by E. of
London. At one time ranked among the show places
of England, it has stood empty for some years and is
now in a state of disrepair.

Upon the death of Edward, it became the property
of Cecil. Upon the death of Cecil it will in all prob-
ability pass from the direct line of succession for the
first time in its history, inasmuch as Robert, younger
brother of Edward and Cecil, disappeared over fifteen
years ago, and Lord Cecil is a bachelor.

For further details, see the Register."

*   *   *   *   *

I give you the above just as I copied it into my notes
some years ago. I can also tell you that it will avail
you nothing to turn to the Register. You would find, as
I did, that there are no further details.

To be sure, the whole interesting history of the Burnleigh family, beginning somewhere in 1100, is there, with a great deal of furbishing and fanfares; but you will find that when the Recorder reached Edward, Cecil, and the youngest, Robert, his pen had run dry—or else he felt that what could be entered would be better left unsaid.

Figuratively speaking, Cecil Burnleigh walked into my office with the manor tucked under his arm. There was nothing unusual in that, for I was with an internationally famous firm of American architects, and Burnleigh Manor was presented to me much as the ordinary reconstruction commission. Lord Cecil seemed to be a quiet but pleasant enough old gentleman of rather indeterminate age.

It did seem to me that Lord Cecil was a bit reluctant to speak of Edward Burnleigh. Evidently the present condition of the Manor was the fault of this older brother. Cecil was perfectly frank in saying he had allowed it to run down prior to his death. Early in our conversation I learned that Edward's manner of leaving this World was a matter of quite some disgrace to a very proud family. On a Christmas Eve, sixteen years before I came into this World, he had died by his own hand, surrounded by what was left of his home.

Until the beginning of the reference work, of which the quotation previously given is a part, I had not heard of Robert. His mysterious and unexplained disappearance was apparently another blot on the family record which Lord Cecil found it hard to discuss. I think I dismissed these family details from my mind at this time because they formed no real part of the architectural and historical background of the old place. I was being retained by the last of the Burnleighs to restore his ancestral house to its original condition, so it was quite natural that I should consider only the architectural features. The peculiarities I began to notice in my client I attributed to the peculiarities of his family, and I found later that, in the main, I was quite correct.

However, they did not enhance my first trip abroad. I was made comfortable enough in a suite adjoining that occupied by Lord Cecil, and for the first time in my life I knew the luxury, but rather doubtful enjoyment, of a valet. Personally I still prefer chasing my own collar buttons under beds and bureaus. Irrespective of my preferences which I was not ungracious enough to mention, my every want was ministered to by Burnleigh's own man, Glome. Odd name, that, and at our very first meeting I changed it to Gloom, a much more appropriate designation. He impressed me as the perfect model for an undertaker's assistant.

It would seem to be the height of callousness to make any complaint of a trip which one made at no expense whatever, in a luxurious suite on a fast, comfortable liner, especially when one is provided with a shadow that hovers about the entire day anticipating each wish as it is born. Ungrateful and blasé as it may seem, I can truly say that I have had far more pleasure from trips made later and under far more humble conditions. No matter how sumptuous one's surroundings are they become irksome when they constitute too steady a diet. Let me explain what I mean.

We sailed at twelve, and my luncheon was brought to me shortly after by "Gloom." On the tray with the delicious looking food was a note written in rather a shaky hand. I give it to you here:

"My dear Mr. Riker,
You may set this all down to an old man's whims if you wish, but I hope you will be kind enough to humor

them. Would you mind remaining in your rooms as much as possible—in fact I would appreciate your leaving them only in the evening.

And a still heavier burden on your good nature is the request that you do not associate with any of the other passengers for the present, at least.

I hope you will pardon this seeming intrusion of your affairs until I have an opportunity to explain the reasons that seem to justify it.

Sincerely,
CECIL B.

P. S. I have taken the liberty of keeping both our names from the passenger list."

Certainly he was entitled to say what disposition was to be made of my time from nine in the morning until five at night, and when one is listening to a client with a million dollar commission, his requests with regard to the evening hours are likely to become orders inviolable.

Not that I sank back into the tufted chairs in resigned submission. As I came on board I had seen one or two very attractive young ladies and I had made quite definite, if tentative, plans for those evening hours. Instead I was to be a semi-prisoner in my rooms because of the foolish whims of an old man. I say foolish because at this time it had not occurred to me that there might be anything of a serious nature behind them. At least I felt that my case was the first on record. There were probably many people who would like to lock their architects in far more unpleasant and hotter places than these quarters of mine, but up to the present I have never heard of it being done.

After luncheon I roamed about the suite and found on the table beside my bed quite a collection of magazines and books. On top of them lay a card. I seemed to be surrounded with correspondence if not company.

"Perhaps these will partially repay you for the part of the trip of which you have been deprived by my peculiarities.

CECIL B."

At least the old fellow was thoughtful. The periodicals were recent and diversified. After glancing idly through one or two I turned up the books and read their titles. There was not a novel among them. If and when I absorbed their contents I would be well versed in some odd phrases of architecture. I cannot remember them all now, but two do stand out clearly from the rest,— Thenaud's, "Notes on the Detection of Hidden Spaces" —and Wilson's, "Studies of Ancient Architecture." These two were as fascinating as any novels could have been, and were destined to be of some assistance to me later. They were delightful companions and the first two days were spent with them except for an occasional stolen and cautious trip to the rail for a glimpse of the sea and a snatch of sunshine.

Burnleigh was confined to his room for reasons unknown and entirely indeterminate, for the sea was a great smooth lake. I began to wonder if these chaps who had written about "the bounding main" had not been a bit facetious.

Gloom flitted in and out of my quarters, but he was far from a pleasant traveling companion. As a conversationalist he was an excellent running mate to a sphinx. I recall one of my efforts to broaden my knowledge of Burnleigh Manor with his assistance. He had brought in my dinner tray and I opened the conversation along general lines.

"Nice sailing weather, isn't it?"

"I couldn't say, sir."

I found out later that there were two words left out of Gloom's vocabulary, "yes," and "no." He avoided using them even when sailing weather was the topic of conversation on the grounds that they might be incriminating. I do not believe that in all my acquaintance with him I have ever heard him make a statement that could not, somehow, be made to point north and south at the same time. Undaunted, I tried a fresh start.

"Been across often?"

"A few times, sir."

You see? That might mean two or twenty-two.

"Have you ever been in Burnleigh Manor, Gloom?"

He stiffened as if I had touched him with a hot poker. It was only for a second, and as he relaxed and opened his mouth to speak, I knew instinctively that he had thought his way out of that one, too.

"Glome is the name, sir, begging your pardon."

With the tongs suspended over my tea-cup he turned the tide by asking a question himself.

"One or two lumps, sir?"

Ordinarily I take one lump with lemon, but with an idiotic idea of annoying him by selecting something he had not mentioned, I answered him.

"Three lumps."

His eyebrows went up a fraction of an inch which was quite a dramatic gesture for him to make, and he carefully—almost maliciously—counted out three lumps of sugar. For no good sound reason the man irritated me. He had evaded my question and I was determined he should not do it again.

"I asked you if you had ever been in Burnleigh Manor."

"Why do you ask that of me, sir?"

"Idle curiosity I suppose."

"Oh, yes, to be sure, sir."

And that was that. To be sure what? I certainly was not going to humiliate myself to the extent of asking whether the "Oh, yes" referred to my curiosity or to Burnleigh Manor. I thought I could get him to discuss himself a bit. The most astute and taciturn of men will become quite loquacious when afforded as fascinating a subject as themselves.

"Been in the family long, Gloom?"

I knew that I was irritating him by calling him Gloom, but this time he made a valiant effort to hide his feelings.

"For years, sir, I might say for a good many years."

With this running start I turned the conversation in an abrupt movement against his flank designed to catch him off his guard, to one point on which I really wished enlightenment.

"Then I suppose that you knew Lord Robert?"

He glanced up at me quickly and I was quite surprised at the expression on his face. It was one of the few times that I have ever seen anything on Gloom's face which could be dignified by the term "expression." It was only a flash, but when he spoke again it seemed to be with an enormous effort.

"Begging your pardon, sir, His Lordship asked me to convey his apologies to you and to tell you that as soon as he is feeling well enough he would see you. I—I hope you enjoy your dinner, sir."

With a bow and what, I suppose, was meant to be a smile, he was gone. His attitude, together with the conditions under which I was travelling, began to get on my nerves. I think it was here that I began to suspect that something more than architecture lurked in the atmosphere. The next evening my suspicions were confirmed.

CHAPTER II

I HAD come in from a short evening stroll. There is not a great deal of enjoyment to be derived by a young bachelor in strolling about empty decks, listening to the seductive strains of an excellent dance orchestra from somewhere below. Everything was so far from normal that I caught myself giving wide berths to the very shadowy corners that I might otherwise have been seeking, and glancing over my shoulder occasionally as if half expecting something to jump at me from each dark niche.

When I returned to my stateroom I found Gloom waiting there.

"Lord Cecil would like to see you to-night, if you would care to step into his cabin."

"Care is hardly the word, Gloom. An explanation is long since due me."

"I am repeating his Lordship's words, sir."

"Is this game of hide and seek over now?"

"I can't say, sir."

"You mean you won't say!"

"I mean I can't say, sir."

"Oh, go to the devil!"

And Gloom went. Naturally I mean out of the room. I tagged along at his heels for all the World like a blustering little bull pup. Without any further words he led me to Burnleigh's quarters which were duplicates of mine. As I entered, the old man looked up at me from the comfortable depths of his chair with the ghost of a smile. Smiles were a rare thing with him, and when they did come they actually seemed to be the ghosts of others that had died on his lips centuries ago, when smiling came more easily.

"Good evening, Mr. Riker. I know that I could spend the rest of the evening with apologies and not make up for your discomfort. Sit there, will you please?"

He indicated a chair across the table from him. I am afraid my replies to his preliminary remarks were not any too gracious, but being the very acme of the English gentleman he did not seem to notice it.

"It has been quite lonely for you, has it not?"

"Well, I have had better traveling companions than Gloom."

"Gloom?"

"I prefer Gloom. It is more descriptive."

Again that flicker of a smile crossed his face.

"He intimated that your solitude was beginning to be—well—a trifle irksome to you."

"He was putting it mildly."

"Putting it? Ah, yes—will you have one?"

His cigarette case was passed across the table.

"I do not smoke cigars and I do not like them smoked in the room with me. Another whim."

When he had lighted up, he leaned forward in his chair.

"Mr. Riker, instead of expressing my gratitude to you for the splendid way you have granted my silly requests, I am going to ask you to do still another thing for me. When I have finished telling you a bit of a story to-night, you may not care to go any further. That is your privilege, but before I start I must have your assurance that what I am about to tell you will be kept a secret by you as long as I live. Will you give me your word on that?"

I did. I had reached a stage where his affairs were not of the slightest interest to me. Enticing as the restoration of an old English Manor was to my architectural heart, I regretted coming. But I have kept my word, for until Lord Cecil's death last year I have not breathed a word of the story to anyone. With my expressed assurance, he went on talking.

"By now the possibility of my being some sort of a crank has occurred to you, I suppose?"

As a matter of fact, it had not. But why not? One brother a suicide—the other disappearing off the face of the earth——

"I see it had not until I mentioned it. That was kind of you. At best, Mr. Riker, sanity is only relative. I believe I am in my right mind at the moment even if I have had reason not to be——"

He was watching the smoke curl up from his cigarette, lost in thought. With a visible start he brought his attention back to me.

"However, you will have to take my word for that. Now if you are comfortable, I will begin at the very beginning and give you all the facts surrounding this new venture of yours. First, about my family—unless you already know some of our history?"

This was an embarrassing question to answer, and I stammered out the fact that I had glanced at the Register.

"I rather imagine the Register was silent on the present generation, and—I am sorry to say—rightfully so. Suppose I introduce you to the Burnleighs? My father had three sons, in the order of our ages, Edward, myself —and Robert. Father was rather an odd type and he had two great passions in life—my Mother, and Egypt. His early manhood was spent there in the diplomatic service and he knew that great country as few Englishmen have ever succeeded in knowing it. My Mother died when Edward was twenty-three and my father two years later, from grief."

As if to punctuate his sentence, the ash dropped from his cigarette to the floor unheeded.

"As the eldest, Edward became the head of the house. He inherited two things from my Father—the finest collection of things Egyptian privately owned in the World —and his love for Egypt itself. To the former Edward added all his life, spending at least half of his time in the country of sphinxes and pyramids. Returning from one of these long stays, he surprised us by bringing back a wife. She, too, was Egyptian—in fact she could trace her descent far back into that charming past of a vanished race. Mr. Riker, she was unquestionably the most beautiful woman I have even seen. The entrancing mystery of the East was about her like an invisible veil and it made of her something that defies——"

He shifted uneasily in his chair and his eyes avoided mine.

"Words are inadequate and it would not help us with our story. One thing that is probably incomprehensible to you is the question of younger brothers in my country. At my father's death, all of his property and influence went to the eldest son, Edward. For myself and for Robert, the youngest, there was a mere pittance. This did not bother me in the least. I expected it and was happy in my work, but it always irked Robert. He was a handsome chap—lovable, talented, and popular. Although given to sulking on occasion, he was always welcome at Edward's home and spent much of his time there. I was by nature and occupation a wanderer and saw little of them. There was one time each year that we all gathered under one roof—that of Burnleigh Manor—and that was Christmas. We never failed to get there Christmas Eve and for a few days we would be together. Lady Burnleigh was the most charming hostess that ever lived, and that sample of her hospitality and sweetness remained with me for the rest of the year. Then something happened to Edward."

His voice died away and he sat looking back into the past he was describing. As we sat there in silence it seemed as if something crept into our cabin. Something cold. Something oppressive. Something black and bitter tasting. Burnleigh leaned forward abruptly and took another cigarette. When the first puff of smoke was on its way ceilingward, he picked up his story again.

"I reproach myself for not knowing more about this part. I should have remained in England and tried to —to help. As I look back now I think the first warning I had of the way things were going was a letter from Robert in which he stated that practically the entire collection of Egyptian pieces had disappeared. The fact that he carefully avoided mentioning Edward's name in this connection convinced me that he felt our heritage had been sold and the funds diverted to the personal use of our older brother. Rumors reached me that Edward was changing from an hospitable, generous and brilliant man, to a morose, silent—almost vindictive caricature of his former self. Naturally it was with some trepidation that I approached the Manor on that last Christmas Eve that we ever spent together. From the very first moment my visit was unpleasant. I entered the doors of Burnleigh Manor and found my brothers in a violent quarrel that ended abruptly on my entrance. Neither one would discuss it with me or explain its cause, so I was helpless to smooth it out. During my short visit I felt a terrific tension existing in the household. Edward was taciturn and moody. Robert was unnaturally gay, reckless and charming. Underneath Lady Burnleigh's evident effort to carry things along smoothly, I sensed a desire to tell me something—warn me of something that was threatening—but Edward never allowed her out of his sight. A day later I left in pique, feeling I was no longer welcome under my brother's roof. I know now that my egotism closed my eyes to the truth. The next evening the papers were full of my brother's disappearance. Robert had vanished from Burnleigh Manor the night of the day I had left. No one saw him go, nor have I ever found anyone who had seen him since. For five long years I did nothing but search for him and in all that time, or in the time since then, I have never found a trace."

An ugly suspicion flashed across my mind and I interrupted him for the first time.

"Did Edward aid you in the search? You spoke of a—a quarrel."

"He did not. You see, Mr. Riker, his wife disappeared at the same time—the same night."

He bowed his head for a second. I could understand what it meant to share this with an outsider and I began to get a glimpse of the reasons for the deep lines in his face and the white hair that seemed somehow premature.

"It seems quite clear at this point, does it not? But the Yard thought of that, too, and no stone was left unturned that might yield evidence against Edward. It is not easy to fool the Yard, Mr. Riker. He refused to help the police, but he in no way hindered them, and in the end they gave it up. It left him a crushed man. He rarely spoke to anyone and went about like a man in a dream. So you see we really do not know what did——"

He checked himself and continued quickly.

"There is not much more to tell, so be patient. You must be frightfully bored."

Boredom was far from me at the moment!

"During my search for Robert, or in the years that followed it, I never saw my older brother. Then one winter that I happened to be spending in my London quarters I received a telegram from him summoning me to spend Christmas with him. It was a bit of a shock, for I had had no replies to my letters to him and it was quite common gossip that no one was welcome at the Manor. However, I left at once for what had once been our home—Burnleigh Manor."

He stopped and I noticed his face was slowly paling. From this point on I do not believe he was conscious of my presence in the cabin. He was feeling the relief of unburdening in speech a horrible memory that had been pent up within too long.

"It had been snowing for two days, but when I stepped down from the train at King's Lynn it was a clear, cold, starry night. The station was deserted. There was no sign of a waiting car, and believing that my telegram in reply had not reached the Manor I stepped over to the Inn to secure a conveyance. I will pass over that if you do not mind, by simply saying that there was no one in the town who would drive me to Burnleigh Manor and no one who would tell me why they would not. So I walked those long, cold miles through the snow."

The howl of the wind at the porthole and the creak of the ship as it rolled made a fitting accompaniment.

"I could never describe to you my feelings as I came toward my brother's gates. They hung open on dilapidated hinges, but not a track showed in the snow. The Lodge was dark and empty—most of its windows broken —its door standing ajar. The shrubbery had grown up in wild disarray as if nature were making an effort to hide its shame. I started up the long, winding drive. I could now hear the pounding of the sea on the cliffs beyond and below. Above the bare trees with their crooked arms the two towers of the Manor lifted themselves into the sky like two sentinels guarding the nothing that was left. Below them was the black dismal bulk of the house with not a light showing. So far there had not been a single indication that would lead me to believe that a living soul was within miles of the place. I began to wonder if the telegram had not been a hoax or a trap to lure me to this lonesome end of the World. The drive ended at the terrace steps and not a footmark marred the snow even here. As I approached the big front doors I saw that there *was* a dim light somewhere in the hall. Weary and cold, with a heart torn by grief and evil foreboding, I knocked. Nothing but hollow echoes that reverberated across the great hall and went rambling through the gallery and the rooms above answered my rapping. Again I knocked and again only the echo answered me. Reluctantly my cold hands turned the handles and I pushed the doors open before me. There, facing me, seated at an old table piled high with indiscriminate looking refuse and with a dingy oil lamp at his side, sat my brother. His shaking hand held a revolver leveled in my direction. He was emaciated—shrunken beyond belief and sat huddled down in a pile of rugs and blankets that looked filthy. At sight of me he dropped the gun to his lap and burst out in a gale of cackling laughter.

" 'So it is you, brother dear? Come in—come in—and welcome to Burnleigh Manor! What a sorry welcome I did give you but'—he held his finger cautiously to his lips and whispered—'but I should have known that ghosts do not have to *open* doors!'

"And he gave another of those horrible cackling laughs. I realized that I was dealing with a man who was stark, raving mad—a physical derelict with an insane pilot— my brother. I shuddered and those darting eyes of his detected it.

" 'Keep your coat on—it is cold in here—cold as the —grave!'

"It was not the cold that kept me shivering. All that had in the previous years been so bright and cheery was now cold—bitter cold and damp and evil smelling. The great fireplace that had held the blazing Yule log each year was dark and full of trash. So far I had not been able to bring myself to speak. I stood there staring stupidly at the heart-rending sight before me, conscious of the stare of his eyes that looked like the peep holes of a furnace, so glittering was the fire within him that was consuming his brain.

" 'I suppose you think I am crazy? Well, I'm not. Not yet. Perhaps I will be if they do not get me first.'

"Here was something more tangible to work on and for the first since I entered, I spoke.

" 'If *who* does not—get you—Edward?'

" 'The ghosts. Laugh, if you wish, but you will hear them.'

"His hands that had been lying quietly over the revolver in his lap began to twitch, and he moved his head from side to side with an odd jerky motion. Stepping quickly to his side I patted his shoulder reassuringly.

" 'Do not speak of such things! There are no ghosts except those we make for ourselves. The real truth of the matter is that you are too much alone here. Where are the servants?'

"Again he gave that laugh that was weirdly devoid of mirth.

" 'They couldn't stand it. I am the only one with nerve enough to stay in this ghastly place. So there are no ghosts, eh, Cecil?'

More Books Are on Their Way to You!

SINCE THE ANNOUNCEMENT OF THE MYSTERY LEAGUE PLAN WHICH BRINGS MYSTERY AND DETECTION READERS BRAND-NEW BOOKS SUCH AS THE ONE YOU ARE NOW HOLDING, IT HAS BEEN NECESSARY BECAUSE OF THE ENTHUSIASM WITH WHICH EACH SUCCEEDING TITLE WAS GREETED FOR OUR PRINTING ORDERS TO BE ALMOST DOUBLE THE ONE PLACED ON OUR FIRST SELECTION. THUS FAR THE MYSTERY LEAGUE SERIES HAS INCLUDED:

> *THE HAND OF POWER by Edgar Wallace*
> *THE CURSE OF DOONE by Sydney Horler*
> *THE HOUSE OF SUDDEN SLEEP by John Hawk*
> *JACK O'LANTERN by George Goodchild*

WITH THOUSANDS OF NEW READERS ENTHUSIASTICALLY AWAITING EACH NEW SELECTION, YOUR EDITORS ARE BECOMING MORE AND MORE DEMANDING IN THE REQUIREMENTS FOR EACH BOOK.

AUTHORS WHOSE NAMES ARE KNOWN THE WORLD OVER HAVE INDORSED THE PLAN WHICH BRINGS THROUGH THE UNITED CIGAR STORES, WHELAN AND NÈVE DRUG STORES THESE STANDARD $2.00 BOOKS FOR 50 CENTS, MADE POSSIBLE ONLY BY THE TREMENDOUS DISTRIBUTING POWER OF THESE THREE ORGANIZATIONS.

THE EDITORS OF THE MYSTERY LEAGUE TRUST THAT THEIR READERS HAVE ENJOYED THE SELECTIONS ALREADY PUBLISHED AND HEREWITH PROMISE TO MAINTAIN EACH MONTH THE HIGH STANDARD OF EXCELLENCE THAT HAS BEEN THE PRIME FACTOR IN THE PLAN'S SUCCESS.

THEY BELIEVE EACH MONTH'S ANNOUNCEMENT OF A NEW MYSTERY LEAGUE BOOK WILL BE A PLEASANT SURPRISE TO THEIR READERS AND ASSURE THEM THAT NO EFFORTS ARE BEING SPARED TO PROVIDE EACH MONTH A TITLE THAT IN QUALITY, BINDING, TYPOGRAPHY, AND PRINTING WOULD, THROUGH ANY OTHER CHANNEL, BE A DISTINCT SUCCESS AT THE REGULAR $2.00 BOOK PRICE.